Adam Berlin (signature)

HEADLOCK

30 July 2000

For Jackie and Steve,
    It's always great to see
you. Thanks for coming out to
The reading and I hope you
enjoy the book.
                    Fondly,
                    Adam

1

THE ONE IN FRONT of me was looking at me like I was the stupid one. He was the one walking through the bar, he was the one with the full drink, he was the one in my way and he hadn't moved his shoulder just like he thought I hadn't moved mine. I had moved mine. I had moved my shoulder into his shoulder to send the alcohol over the edge of the glass to make him stop walking and he'd stopped. He'd turned around. He looked at me like I was the stupid one but he was the stupid one. He didn't know what I did best.

He told me to watch where I was going. I was watching. I had watched his head turn when I bumped him and I had watched his eyes focus on mine. I was watching his mouth talking, one of those losers who talked first. I had been talking to myself in the bathroom mirror but that was to myself. I had to do something. He was still holding the glass and some of the spilled alcohol made his hand wet and that was the hand I took. I held his wrist with my one hand, held his hand around the glass with my other hand and pressed his palm hard and harder into the glass until the glass broke. He screamed and I pressed harder until a triangle of glass came out the back of his hand. All his focus went to his hand and away from me. He couldn't take his eyes off his hand that was squirting blood on the sleeve of his shirt. The crowded bar had made space and I could hear other people screaming but no one came near me. It was a smaller circle than the one I had wrestled in but it was a circle and I went to work. I turned him around and pulled him to me, put a half nelson on him, forced his neck down. The circle opened up. There was a free space at the bar and I drove him forward, drove his face into the side of the bar. I moved my hand down his back and between his legs, picked him up and held him there, feeling his weight above my head, feeling the power in my muscles and I threw him to the floor. His head bounced once and his body relaxed. The hand with the glass sticking out of it was leaking blood onto the floor. I wiped my shoe across the blood, lifted my foot and brought it down and brought it down, triumphant, foot on the back of a fallen opponent like a classical statue, like in the pictures my college wrestling coach showed the team at the beginning of each new season. White marble figures graceful in victory. I pictured my grandfather like that, standing over some long-ago Russian opponent, his mouth set firm like I remembered, like in the old photographs from a time when people posed without smiling. Strong and beautiful the way it was supposed to be on the mat when it was done right.

I ran out of the bar. I ran through the streets. My breath was heavy in my chest from all the drinking but I needed to run to get the other rush out of me and I ran past the meat-packing warehouses with the smell of dead blood and past the cut-rate garages closed for the night. I was at the West Side Highway and I ran across the highway with the headlights coming too fast and the feeling was almost out of me and I ran to the promenade that bordered the Hudson and I stopped running. I walked downtown along the river. The Statue of Liberty was in the distance, the torch lit up. A car slowed and I could feel eyes looking over my body but it was almost all out of me so I didn't do anything. The car drove off and I kept walking and I walked until it was out of me.

2

I WAS A ROSE. A good name my dad told us when we were kids. Be proud of your name. Beautiful. Vibrant. Red. The color of love which Derek and I didn't really care about. The color of bravery which we did. My grandfather had come up with my name. Odessa. After the Russian city. Dess for short. As we grew older, my dad told us other connections to Rose. A symbol of a dying Jesus, thorns cutting into his head, a wound at his side. Giving roses to Mary, the rosary, a penance for sins. Juliet's line about a rose by any other name would smell as sweet. The thing about a name was that we couldn't escape it. That's what my dad told us, always trying to make us think, always trying to teach. He tried to make me look outside of myself, outside of my body, but finally he stopped trying.

I parked cars. Good cars. That was how I made money. The suit and ties drove up, grabbed briefcases, left keys in the ignition and I did my job, sliding into bucket seats like the cars belonged to me, driving forward looking for the end of the line. Squeezed Mercedes, Jaguars, BMWs, sometimes even a Rolls into the allotted room. Room was always a premium there, everywhere in the city. Even the guy with the Rolls didn't have the space he wanted in Manhattan, I was pretty sure of that. I certainly didn't. I lived in an illegal sublet in the Village with the background noise of Seventh Avenue traffic moving downtown. I parked cars for tips that kept me in rent, food and beers from the bodega. A buck a car or sometimes two. Around Christmas time they'd throw each of us a twenty or a fifty if they were feeling like good sports and for a fifty they expected us to be extra pleasant all year round. I'd been parking cars one full year round. Christmas was coming. The big tips hadn't started but the commercials were already constant. I killed a lot of time watching TV. Going out. I killed a lot of time.

Two other guys were penned in, Magic Markered really, on the white board inside the booth where Mr. Caparello collected the money. There was Lou, about my age, slicked-back hair, gold chain around his neck, a real hustler. His dream was to make enough money to open his own garage. Not to park cars but to fix them. On weekends he did tune-ups and oil changes off the sidewalks of his Bay Ridge neighborhood where he lived with his mother, a view of the Verrazano and Staten Island beyond. I'd visited him one Saturday afternoon, drank bottles of Budweiser, ate veal scallopine, homemade cannolis for dessert, actually watched his mother point the cloth pouch into the pastry shells and squeeze the cream. Lou loved cars. He gunned engines as soon as the owners were out of sight, not to make look-at-me noise but to hear the power. He made tires squeal to feel their grip and tested brakes on the cement ramp going down. That was his way to make the day move. His mother stitched his name into his garage suit, LOU on the pocket in cursive.

"There's a beauty," he'd say when the rush slowed and one car came in at a time while we stood around outside, the minutes clicking off audibly on the punch clock. Lou liked fast cars best. Porsches. The occasional Lamborghini.

"I'll take that one," he'd say when a Corvette rolled in.

There was Berger, high man on the totem pole in age and years on the job. Red faced in the morning, every morning, hung over, the lines around his old eyes defined by drunken nights. He smoked Marlboros tucked between his thumb and middle finger when he wasn't parking. The suit and ties didn't want their cars getting stunk up. He cursed them all, stinking rich motherfucking bastards need to be separated from their money. He was a communist. He quoted from Marx whenever he could and Lou would laugh at his constant anger. Berger lost his index finger, all three fucking knuckles of it he'd say, in a machine shop pressing dominoes. Working workingman's work while the boss got fat on profits, Berger would say. The suit and ties always thanked Berger when he took their cars, more than they ever thanked us, silently leaving their cars in our hands, just kids in their eyes, but Berger could have been their father, their fucking grandfather Berger would say. Berger never said a word back when they thanked him and he just stuck his hand out when he took their tips. He didn't care what kind of car came in. He stood away from the punch clock so he didn't have to hear the minute by minute clicking. As soon as the shift was over he changed out of his uniform. Underneath he wore a white button-down and a thin black tie. When the days were cold he added an overcoat and hat. After work he drank at a bar on Church Street. I'd seen him stumble out of there one night with his head down and his tie pointing off to the side. Weaving and talking. He came to work the next day and drove the cars straight, steering wheels poised between thumb and middle finger.

I wore my uniform to work and kept it on for the walk home. I'd cut the sleeves off practically at the shoulders to make me feel free. Work boots all year round. A grease smudge across my temple or forehead always there when I washed up in front of the broken mirror before lunch like it was part of the look. I went through the motions, parked cars, pocketed tips. I was living in the city. That was something. I worked from before rush hour to after rush hour when most cars were parked. I ate lunch at the diner every day to keep me going through the shift. The waitresses let me sleep in the back booth when it was slow and I had a few more minutes until my break was over. Then they'd touch my leg, whisper, Dess, Dess, wake up, Dess, and I'd go back to work.

I had stamina. It was a necessary part of wrestling. The most important part, my high school coach told us, the coach who had taught me how to wrestle, to perfect the moves that seemed to be in my blood. To build our stamina he had us run around the high school after practice, the whole team in a line, lightest to heaviest, the sound of sneakers on polished linoleum floors echoing off the lockers on each side of the corridor, the senior corridor blue lockers and the junior corridor green lockers and the sophomore corridor beige and back to the senior corridor, around and around, sweating off the excess weight, stripping us down to muscle, expanding our lungs until a breath could keep us going a long time.

After work at the garage it felt good to strip off my clothes and take a shower, scrub all the grease and the exhaust smoke off me. I felt I'd done a day's work. If I didn't have to think, it didn't matter right then. The hot shower and clean smelling soap and the feel of my skin, squeaky clean when I rubbed the excess water off before I grabbed the towel, a trick my dad taught me and I guessed my grandfather taught him, it felt earned somehow. Like outdoor work. Raking our yard or shoveling the driveway as a kid. Painting the house every third summer. Like some indoor work, I assumed, since the suit and ties seemed a little high on Fridays when the work week was done and not just from a couple of beers with the guys. Like wrestling. The showers always felt good after practice, better after a match, best after a match I'd won and I'd won most matches. It was in my blood. The balance. The strength. The speed. The instinct to find weaknesses in another man's body.

3

THE DAYS WENT BY, the Christmas commercials increased, the sky above the Hudson turned pink then gray then dark before the rush hour home began. I turned on the headlights at the end of the day before I got out of their cars, leaving two even beams like bright skid marks along the cement and out to the street where they dimmed against the curb. It didn't change the amount I palmed, stuffed into my front pocket, money to be unraveled and separated into neat piles, singles and singles, sometimes a five, all turned in at the end of the shift for bigger, crisper bills. I folded those in two and walked the streets home, kept a free single for a beer at the bodega.

I stayed in shape running late at night through the streets, took Greenwich Street past the UPS warehouses down to the World Trade Center, around the courthouses, back across town on Houston. I did push-ups and sit-ups and bar-dips on park benches and pull-ups on the metal supports set up under construction sites. I didn't wrestle. I didn't practice the cradle, the switch, the high crotch, the classic half nelson. I'd lost my wrestling scholarship when I was a second semester senior. I still owed the university the last semester's tuition. When I was kicked off the team my scholarship went with it. I was in no rush to pay the money back and threw the loan service's envelopes away as soon as they came in the mail. Interest was accruing but not enough to think about.

My grandfather had been a wrestler. A real wrestler. For money and not the WWF bullshit on TV beating out Saturday morning cartoons in the ratings and no more believable. Stone Cold Steve Austin. Hulk Hogan. Macho Man Savage. The Million Dollar Man Ted DiBiase. Slam dunks. Sleeper holds. I doubted any of them knew what a real wrestling mat looked like.

My dad was not a wrestler. He was an economics professor. He believed a sound mind was more important than a sound body. Instead of the physical exercises my grandfather had forced him to do as a kid, I had to do math problems and compose essays. My mom taught Latin at the high school and she'd work my language skills and vocabulary. I had to keep my grades up if I wanted to wrestle. Mind over muscle. My parents wondered what I was doing with myself in New York and their voices on the phone were quizzical, listening for clues when I responded to their questions about how life was treating me. I said it was treating me fine. My dad gave me lectures about having to establish a future. He told me about wasting my potential parking cars. He asked if I planned to work in a garage the rest of my life. I made the mistake of bringing my uniform home to Massachusetts one visit and dropping it into the washing machine without doing the laundry myself. My mom washed it and folded it beautifully but the look she gave me when she handed over the uniform made the perfect creases practically cut my hands. My kid brother had graduated valedictorian and was making the dean's list every semester at Harvard. Whenever we were home together he would run to the end of the driveway, open the garage door with a flourish and ask me if everything looked okay and I'd think about taking him down.

My grandfather took people down. He came to New York from Russia and while he was walking to work, a job where he stuffed mattresses with goose feathers, a man tried to pickpocket him. A bright summer morning on one of his first days in America and my grandfather felt another man's hand in his pocket. My grandfather could not call out for help. He didn't know the language. So he grabbed the pickpocket's hand while it was still in his pocket and walked the guy to the police station. Inside the precinct my grandfather pointed to the hand he held in his pocket and that was all the evidence the cops needed. My grandfather's hands were mighty. This was the story I told about my grandfather when the discussion turned to histories, ancestors, bloodlines, which of course wasn't often. I didn't tell the other stories. How as a kid my dad had to stop my grandfather from stuffing their landlord down the incinerator, his ten-year-old frame clinging to my grandfather's back. How my grandfather threw the local butcher through the butcher shop window because he didn't help my grandmother when it was her turn. How my grandfather broke a man's arm when he gave my grandfather the finger.

Growing up we would drive down to Florida in the summers to visit him. My grandfather would always be standing at the curb in front of his building keeping a parking space open for us and there was always a space. There was no way he could have known when we were going to arrive and there was no telling how long he'd been standing there, stopping other cars from pulling in. Even at eighty he could keep a space free. We'd get out of the car and I'd watch him hug my dad and my mom and then it was my turn. He'd kiss me on the cheek and I'd kiss him and his skin was soft from age and smelled sweet from the cologne he used and only his hands gave him away.

4

"I'LL TAKE THAT JAGUAR," Lou said.

I watched the Jaguar pull in and the lights hit my eyes and I waited to give the guy a ticket. It was my turn. The Jaguar was yellow with a black roof, a sports car model and not one of the sedans. The shift was almost over. I was looking forward to my beer, my walk home, my shower. The automatic window went down and there he was. Cousin Gary. The smile just for me.

"Your folks said you were still working here," he said.

"I am. What are you doing?"

"Taking a drive. When's your break?"

I looked at the punch clock.

"I'm out in eighteen minutes."

"Great."

A new Lexus pulled up behind Gary. The guy stayed inside his car. They hardly ever got out until they reached that line where the garage wall began, thinking once the car was there it was safely in our hands. Berger was next and he dropped his cigarette butt to the ground, didn't bother to crush it with his foot.

"You work all five days?" Gary said.

"Monday through Friday."

The clock punched off another minute. The guy behind Gary hit the horn. Gary ducked his head back inside the car to look in the rearview mirror. It was easier for him that way than to lean out the window.

"Everyone's in a rush," he said. "Do I trust this place?"

"I don't think this guy will let you back out."

"You want to bet?"

"I'll keep an eye on your car. I'll park it in the best space in the house."

The car horn went off again. I looked past the windshield and found the guy's eyes.

"Forget it," Gary said. "You dent this thing I'm telling your folks."

Gary got out of the car. One leg, then another and then he stood. That's when Berger took full notice and even Lou took time out from admiring the Jaguar's sleek lines to check out Gary's body. He was my height but he'd packed four hundred pounds onto his frame. His back was as wide as two men. That was the most impressive feature about him. He stepped away from the car door and waited for me to get in. Other parts of his body were also impressive. His giant thighs. His stomach stretched with red zebra marks that my brother and I would talk about after Gary visited when we were kids, the crazy cousin from Long Island always our favorite. His fat neck. His small hands that were quick for a big man. And his smile that could be so disarming it took the focus away from his body. Gary's smile. Like he got a kick out of the whole world. I got into the Jaguar and drove it forward, nice and easy for my cousin's benefit to show him that I could park a car like nobody's business, which was a joke in the large scheme of things but it was my joke.

When I walked up the ramp Gary was talking and Lou was laughing. They were arguing about which was a better car for the city, a Jaguar or a Porsche. Gary was insisting a Jaguar since it was made in England and the English were experts on traffic congestion. He waited for Lou to ask him how come. He used to do that to my brother and me, direct us to wherever he wanted us to go. Lou said How come on cue. Gary explained it was because the Brit car manufacturers had stick shifts shoved so far up their assholes that they knew about congestion first hand. Gary asked if Lou had ever seen a relaxed Englishman and Lou said he didn't know whether he'd seen any kind of Englishman. Lou started reciting statistics about horsepower and zero to sixty accelerations and Gary kept shaking his head no and saying Jaguar.

It was cold and Gary's breath came fast and smoky. He always breathed hard but I usually heard it and didn't see it. No other cars came in. There was always a lull right after six-thirty and then later there was supposedly a small rush of people coming out from dinner but by that time I was off and the night crew was on. A man walked over with his ticket at the ready. It was Lou's turn.

"I'll prove it to you in a minute."

"You can't prove anything," Gary said.

"Jaguars break down all the time, man."

"No they don't," Gary said.

"They're legendary for breaking down."

"No they're not."

"I've seen the numbers."

"No you haven't. The numbers say Jaguars ride faster and smoother and quieter. And they're definitely better looking."

Gary smiled victorious.

Lou took the man's ticket and went jogging down the ramp. Berger walked up the ramp and moved off to the side to light another cigarette. Caparello was inside the booth protecting all his money. He was staring at Gary and he didn't like it that I was talking on his time but he didn't say anything. Caparello could be a prick, especially in bad weather when people took public transportation to work and his money drawer was a little lighter.

"When did you speak to my parents?" I said.

"I called them yesterday to see how everyone was doing and they said you were still at the garage. They sounded real proud."

"Their dreams for me have come true."

"By the way, congratulations on your graduation."

"Thanks. How are you doing?"

"Great."

He was ten years older than me. His father was my father's older brother. Growing up, my brother Derek and I had always been in awe of Cousin Gary. He didn't take anything seriously and we thought that was a fine trait in an adult. We were entranced by his larger-than-life frame and his larger-than-life stories. He was a fuckup according to all the adults I knew who knew him. He'd dropped out of college with three credits needed to graduate. He'd been arrested for passing bad checks, cuffed in front of his house, the most embarrassing time in my uncle's life, my uncle said. He'd spent a month in jail for tax evasion, an experience he described enthusiastically since everyone inside played cards.

Gary was a professional gambler. My brother and I begged to stay up past our bedtimes so we could listen to his stories of easy money. Tales of good days at the racetrack, well placed bets on the World Series, running football pools with entry fees of a thousand bucks a head, casino nights in Atlantic City, junket trips to Las Vegas where he put up all his friends in first class hotels with names like Caesars, Circus Circus, the MGM Grand. His success was measured by the meals he treated me and Derek to when he visited our house. Gary would sneak out in the afternoons with us in tow, my brother and I making sure to run out the side door and not the front, keep our heads low in his car until we were out of the driveway. He would buy feasts of food. Five different kinds of pizzas ordered at a time. Family sized buckets of fried chicken at Kentucky Fried. Banana splits at Friendly's for dessert. Bags of potato chips and popcorn for the five-minute drive home. My brother would squeeze his head between the two front seats, Gary driving and me in the passenger seat. Derek would look at me, puff out his cheeks, and say I'm stuffed. We'd laugh painfully, our guts bursting from all the food we'd eaten, and the good thing about Gary was that he'd laugh too.

By the time I started to wrestle in high school I had to watch what I ate but by then, as he got older and we got older, Gary visited less and less. I told my brother it was because he grew tired of my dad asking him questions that his own parents did not ask him. After each of Gary's visits my parents would deflate all the myths of gambling while we sat around the dinner table. They told us how Gary's stories about winning were only the tip of the iceberg, that there were far more stories of losing, we could be sure of that, and just because Gary talked big and drove expensive cars, cars that were being leased and not owned outright by the way, didn't mean a thing. They told us how Gary's father, our uncle, had lost half his savings to pay off Gary's debts. My dad would then ask us why we weren't eating and my mom would say Gary had taken us out.

Lou got out of the car, pocketed the tip and came over.

"I still say the Porsche is a better city car."

"Jaguar," Gary said.

"They have more muscle."

"Less muscle," Gary said, shaking his head for my benefit. They were like two kids.

"I'll tell you the best city car I ever had," Gary said. "When I was in high school I had this beat up Chevy Celebrity that I bought for eighty bucks. I remember because the guy wanted two hundred for it and I bargained him down so well that the guy was convinced he was the one making out. The back windows were smashed in and the locks were busted. All the upholstery was cracked and there was more rust than paint on the thing. But it was my first car and it drove great and I never had to worry about smashing into anybody. I used to drive into the city with my friends all the time. If someone parked too close to me on the street, I'd smash my car into theirs before I left the space. If someone cut me off, I'd hit them at the next stoplight and drive away. Sometimes I'd find guys sleeping in the backseat when the car was parked for a while."

"What did you do?" Lou said.

"I woke them up. I didn't care. I wanted to get the full eighty bucks worth of use out of it. Forget Jaguars and Porsches, that was the best city car. It was so beat up it didn't matter what happened."

"My first car was a Valiant," Lou said.

"What year?"

"Seventy-one."

"The seventy-one Valiant. I just read about those in *Consumer Reports*. They said the seventy-one Valiant sucked."

Lou started laughing. Time was up. The two guys for the night shift punched in and I punched out. I cashed in my money for bigger bills, told Mr. Caparello he was my cousin when he asked who the fat guy was, walked down the ramp, washed my hands and face in the bathroom, looked at myself in the broken mirror to make sure there were no grease marks streaking my cheek or forehead, got Gary's Jaguar, drove it up the ramp. Mr. Caparello let me through without having to pay but he ruined it when he kept his eyes on mine lest I forget his momentous gesture.

I left the keys in the ignition and got out of the car. Lou handed Gary his business card and told him if he ever needed a good mechanic to swing by Bay Ridge, that he'd cut him a deal even if it was a Jaguar. People always wanted to connect with Gary. Lou made sure to shake hands. Berger walked past in his white shirt, thin tie, overcoat and hat, didn't say good night, never said good night, glanced at Gary, crossed the street in the direction of the bar. Gary tried giving me twenty bucks for getting his car but I told him I didn't want it. He worked himself into the driver's seat, no small task, and I got into the passenger's seat just like old times and we drove uptown through the downtown streets.

"We'll go to Katz's," Gary said. "I'm in the mood for delicatessen."

He weaved through the traffic, pulled up short of the car in front of him at the red light, broke loose when the light turned green and caught all the lights all the way to Canal. I sat back and enjoyed the drive, enjoyed the way New York looked from a car window, passing by fast, like the whole city was there for the taking. Gary was a great driver. He didn't move his head at all, just used the mirrors to full advantage. The car still smelled new. There was a crumpled bag of potato chips and some Snickers and PayDay wrappers on the floor and some Hershey's Kisses foils with the white line of plastic that said HERSHEY'S.

We found a space a block from Houston and I waited on the sidewalk while Gary worked himself out of the car. He was breathing heavy and the smoke from his breath was exaggerated by the streetlight above. We walked into Katz's, took the price tickets the guy handed us that looked like movie theater stubs. I followed Gary to the hot dog section.

"Pick me up a pastrami sandwich and a corned beef sandwich and get whatever you want. I'll get some hot dogs. You want hot dogs or knockwursts?"

"A hot dog's good," I said.

"You want two?"

"One's good."

"Get the sandwiches and meet me at that table."

The sandwich line was smaller than the hot dog line and the old man carved me off a slice of pastrami to try. I gave him the buck in my pocket I always kept separate for my afterwork beer. I asked for two pastrami sandwiches and one corned beef. I watched the old man spear the meat with a fork and slice it with quick knife strokes. He put the plates on the counter and circled the price on the ticket. A sign above him read SEND A SALAMI TO YOUR BOY IN THE ARMY. When I got back to the table Gary was already eating, a full plate of hot dogs and another plate with two knockwursts placed between his fat arms.

"Great," Gary said. "Pick up a couple orders of fries and some sodas. I'll have a Coke."

The man circled the price on my ticket, handed over the tray with fries, two glasses of ice, a can of Coke and a can of black cherry soda.

"Best hot dogs in the city," Gary said.

He finished one in three bites and went to work on a knockwurst.

"You like ketchup on your fries?"

"I do."

"Put some on."

He was too busy eating. I put ketchup on the fries and finished my hot dog. People walking by with their plates looking for a table stopped to look at Gary, the fat guy with all that food. I felt invisible next to him until I caught the eye of a girl sitting two tables over and she smiled and I smiled back. She looked familiar but I wasn't sure which bar I'd seen her in. Maybe Max Fish down the street or the Verkhovyna Tavern or the Holiday Cocktail Lounge or at 2A, the bars I started at on Friday nights to finish the cleansing process of a full week's work, after the shower, after the usual pasta with garlic and oil I made for myself, after a nap, rest important to keep me strong for the night.

Gary reached for one of the pastrami sandwiches, spread mustard on it, took a bite.

"So how's it going?"

"It's going fine," I said.

"Your dad didn't sound too happy with you parking cars for a living."

"He's not too happy with a lot that I do."

"I told him not to worry. I told him you'd grow out of it."

"Thanks."

"How's your brother doing?"

"He's doing the way he always does. He's at Harvard getting straight A's."

"At least your folks have him."

Gary smiled, just joking, but I wasn't in the mood. Every time I spoke to my parents I heard about my brother's successes at school. My dad would force himself to ask me about work at the garage and then he'd tell me about Derek at Harvard like that would make me rethink my own life. When I called home, I called before I worked out. It was better than stretching. After the phone call, my muscles were filled with blood.

"We're a lot alike, me and you," Gary said. "I've always felt that way."

"Why is that?"

"We do what we want. We're free spirits. I respect you for not taking the first good job offer that came your way right out of college."

"I didn't have any job offers."

There had been sign-up sheets at the Career Development Office during my senior year. I went to some interviews but I saw the faces change when they looked over my résumé and asked about my academic achievements. At first I tried to explain how time-consuming the wrestling season was. Then I stopped bothering. Then I showed up at an interview wearing my wrestling uniform so the recruiter would see where my effort had gone. My shoulders were more square, my arms were more defined, my stomach was flatter and my hands were stronger than the soft body asking me questions. That was my last interview.

"There's nothing wrong with taking time off," Gary said. "Don't worry what anybody else says. Fuck them. You see me worrying?"

"I don't see enough of you to know."

"I'm not worried what people think. They look at me like I'm a fat pig. I don't care. Some people look at me like I'm not stable, like I'm doing something wrong, leading the wrong kind of life. I don't care about that either. I don't worry about it. That's real strength."

Gary took time out from his sandwich to wash the big statements down with his Coke.

"Look at me," he said. "Everyone I know loves to hear about what I do for a living even if they don't approve. They love all my stories and try to match me with their own low stakes escapades. It's baby shit, but it's their way of bucking the system. They all want to sound like they're rebels, but they're full of shit. They'd never trade their lives for mine. Never. They don't have the balls to take a big chance and see what comes along."

"I don't gamble either."

There had been sports betting all over campus but the coach warned us against gambling. He didn't so much care that it was against school policy but that it cut into the integrity of sports. Sports were pure. Wrestling was the purest.

"I'm not just saying money gambling," Gary said. "You're taking your own chances, I'm taking mine. How long have you been at your job?"

"A little over a year."

"Are you sick of it yet?"

"I'll give myself to the summer and see what I'm feeling then."

"How does your boss treat you?"

"He pays me."

"He looked like he really values your work. You want some of this sandwich?"

"No thanks. I'm full."

Gary opened the corned beef sandwich, spread mustard on it.

"They have great corned beef here. Not as good as the Carnegie, but I was in the mood for hot dogs."

I drank some black cherry soda. I didn't have to puff out my cheeks and pretend. I was stuffed. Gary's eating slowed. He finished the sandwich, ate the other knockwurst, asked if I was done with my side of fries and finished those. He looked at the table and I followed his eyes to see what he saw and it was like surveying the damage at a car wreck, plates all over the place, drops of mustard and ketchup, a stray sliver of french fry, crisped beyond gold. There was no room for Gary to lean back in the small chair but if there had been he would have. He looked content.

"You want anything else?"

He meant it too. From my aunt, I'd heard about the meals he bought his friends, how there would be three delivery trucks at a time running food to the house while the guys sat around the living room and watched sports.

"No thanks."

"You sure? Another hot dog?"

"I can hardly walk," I said.

"You don't need to. I've got a car."

Gary smiled. He found the piece of french fry on the table, mostly grease really, picked it up in his small fingers and ate it.

"What would you say to quitting your job?" Gary said.

"What for?"

"What would you say to it?"

"Did my dad put you up to that question?"

"No. I'm on your side."

"Why should I quit?"

"I can give you a couple of reasons. Exhaust fumes are very bad for your health. Your boss sits in a glass booth like some war criminal. You have to deal with annoying customers the whole day. I'm sure you want to punch them. Or pin them. You still working out? You look in shape."

"I work out."

"I'm sorry I never saw you wrestle."

"Not many people did."

"You should have gone to college in Russia. Then you would have had crowds."

"I wish I had seen Grandpa wrestle. He must have been good."

"I bet he was," Gary said. "Good enough where your dad had to jump on his back to keep him from throwing the landlord down the incinerator."

"I know that story. My dad was still a kid."

"Grandpa was always looking out for the family."

"He was."

I could hear my grandfather's voice. For the family. Family is first. I had to work for the family. I did it for the family. My grandfather's clipped sentences as firm as his beliefs.

"He would have loved watching you wrestle."

Gary spun the empty soda can around on the table. He was always doing something with his hands if he wasn't eating. I remembered he used to bring a ball with him when he visited us, a pink rubber ball, and he'd toss it in the air and catch it between his middle and index fingers. As soon as he left, Derek and I practiced until we could do it too. The Coke logo spun and came to a standstill, the red side facing me.

"I'm taking a trip to Vegas," Gary said. "Why don't you join me?"

"What am I going to do in Las Vegas?"

"I'll give you some spending money."

"I have spending money."

"It's great there. Great food. Beautiful women. There's no place like it."

He didn't mention the craps tables, the blackjack tables, the roulette tables, the baccarat tables.

"What do you say?"

"When are you going?"

"Tonight."

"Thanks for the notice."

"That's what your boss is going to say when you tell him you're coming with me."

"I can't do that."

"Sure you can. Tell him you want to take off a few days. A week."

"This is a bad time. The holidays are coming up."

"I'll get you home before they start. We'll have a great time."

Gary started spinning the can again.

"Why do you need me to come along? You've made it to Las Vegas before."

"I won't bullshit you. I'm driving. I thought it would be fun."

"You need another driver."

"I'm sick of flying there. I've always wanted to drive."

"What about your friends?"

"They're all too busy."

"I went to Atlantic City once and lost a hundred bucks in fifteen minutes."

"I've seen worse than that," he said.

"It took me three hours by bus to get there, fifteen minutes to stay there, three hours to get back."

"I bet the bus ride was nice too."

"Beautiful. If you like looking at a bunch of old people sleeping with their mouths hanging open and dribbling on their shirts."

"I took one bus ride home in college," Gary said. "I brought a ton of food, most of it the kind that smells after a while like tuna and egg salad sandwiches. Every time the bus stopped and people came on, I cracked open my giant bucket of Kentucky Fried. I was the fat guy with the greasy chicken. I had two seats to myself the whole ride. After that I got a car."

"Good thinking."

"Vegas isn't anything like A.C. You've got to see it to believe it. And we'll be driving across country. We'll be free."

"You just said I was free."

"You'll be freer. You know you want to."

Gary smiled his the-world-is-there-for-me smile. It was contagious, always had been. Even my parents admitted Gary had a great smile.

"You know you're bored," he said. "How much time can you spend hanging around Lou and that old guy?"

"Berger."

"He looks like a lot of fun."

"He was a communist. A card-carrying member."

"I'll teach you how to play blackjack on the way. To tell you

the truth, I need a good partner to count cards for me. Someone I can trust. You know, family. What do you say? We could
make some money."

Gary was directing me but unlike Lou I knew some of
Gary's tricks.

"I say I'll think about it."

"I'm leaving tonight."

"Why do you have to leave tonight?"

"Spur of the moment."

"It feels good to say that, doesn't it?"

"I'm not just saying it. Come on. How free are you?"

"Obviously not as free as you are."

Gary didn't say anything to that. He didn't look worried.
He never looked worried or at least I'd never seen him look
anything but happy, his smile, his laugh, his fat face that was almost angelic, curly hair, light brown and tight, a handsome
face really if there wasn't so much weight under it. Gary. Always smiling. Always entertaining. Always a surprise. We had
the big family dinners with Uncle Jack and Aunt Laura but my
first memory of Gary alone was when he just showed up one
day. That was how he came. No calls. No plans. He'd show up.
Later I sometimes wondered what he would do if we weren't
home. Would he drive around for a few hours hoping we'd be
back soon? Would he stay in a motel for the night and try again
the next day? Would he grab a meal at a fast-food place and
drive home? Would he even care? Would he be lonely? Would
he visit someone else? Was there even anyone else to visit? I
didn't think he was close to his mother's side of the family.

Gary drove into town with style even then, honking the
horn of whatever car he was driving until we came running
out. His cars always had that new car smell, salted and sugared

with the snacks he'd been eating on the drive up. He was in his first year of college. I remembered that because he said he was a freshman and that was a word my dad used a lot when he talked to my mom about his classes. Gary walked up the steps to our front door with Derek holding one hand, me holding the other, smiling his smile, telling my dad how the courses were going great except for the ones where he had to read books. My dad had wondered what college courses didn't require books and Gary said he didn't mind reading texts, books about things, like math texts or statistics texts or economics texts, but books, regular books were a different story. Books were boring. Gary said one of his frat brothers was an English major. I didn't really know what an English major was back then, guessed it was someone who could read books in English very quickly. Gary said he was paying his frat brother to write papers for him and that he was doing great on the papers. He'd even been nominated for an academic prize. He'd started a betting pool in the frat, giving four to one odds that he'd win.

"I'm very proud of you," my dad said. "Really very proud."

My dad couldn't help smiling sometimes with Gary and that made me smile too and Derek laughed out loud.

"I'm very proud of you too, Cousin Gary," Derek said.

"I'm proud myself," Gary said.

He picked Derek up which made Derek laugh even more and set him on his wide shoulders. I remember thinking I was too old to be picked up like that. Grandpa didn't pick me up anymore because he said I was too old to be held so I knew it was true. He was a wrestler so he knew.

"What if I win?" Gary said. "Wouldn't that be great?"

"Then you'll have fooled everyone," my dad said.

"I know. All those distinguished men of letters will think I'm the next great writer."

"You'd like that?"

"Why not? If my bets keep winning, I'll be the most scholarly student on campus."

"That's a big if," my dad said.

"Not really. Not if you know what you're doing."

Derek and I listened to Gary's every word. I was already calculating what I'd saved in my top desk drawer, thinking how I'd be homework-free if I held on to my weekly allowance.

"Why don't you write the papers yourself?" my dad said. "Maybe you'll learn something."

"I already know what I need to know."

I remembered that line. My dad stopped me from using it a day later. I know everything I need to know. I don't need to do my homework because I know everything I need to know. I don't need to go to school because I know everything I need to know. My dad told me to remember how to walk down to my room and do my homework.

My mom would make Gary special sandwiches, grilled cheese sandwiches with olives in them. He loved the way my mom made them with the cheese melted all the way through, the bread buttery and golden, never burned. Derek asked Cousin Gary if his mom made grilled cheeses for him and Gary said no one made them as good as our mom, that we were lucky kids to have a mom who made such great grilled cheeses. Gary said my mom was the only one who made them special with olives and not just any olives but olives with red pimentos.

I asked my mom to make me two grilled cheeses like Gary's. She said I wouldn't be able to finish two sandwiches.

We'd just eaten lunch and she knew I was full. I said I would be able to eat them. I'd been thinking how I could do what Gary did. Gary was a man in my eyes but he was like me in a lot of ways too. He didn't like school. He liked to do whatever he wanted. His grandfather was my grandfather. I could eat two sandwiches and I asked my mom to make them. My dad called me a glutton. I asked him what a glutton was and he told me. Gary said he was a good example of a glutton. I said I didn't care if I was a glutton, that I wanted two sandwiches. Derek said he wanted two also. He looked up to me back then. We insisted until my mom got sick of hearing us and started buttering the bread, separating the cheese slices, cutting the olives.

As she made the sandwiches she told us that we were not to leave the table until the sandwiches were completely finished. Gary was smiling. That spurred me on. I said I was starving. My mom took out a big skillet and started melting butter. Derek was laughing, saying he was starving too. My mom said we'd get our grilled cheeses but we had better finish them. My mom slid the sandwiches onto plates with a spatula, cut them in half, put the plates in front of us. Four perfect halves, slightly parted to show off the buttery bread, melted cheese, green olives with red centers.

Gary went through the first half in one bite and I tried to do the same but my teeth marks fell short. My bite was not as big as Gary's. We were full from lunch. The perfectly melted cheese started to congeal. The olives were becoming cold. I couldn't finish the third half and Derek was still on the second half. I asked my mom if I could leave the table and she said No. Derek asked if he could leave the table and my mom said No. I said I had to go to the bathroom and my mom said I could go as soon as I finished my sandwiches. Gary was laughing and that made me laugh and Derek laugh and my mom and dad were smiling but they weren't going to let us get up. My dad said this was a good lesson in gluttony. Derek tried to take a bite of his cold grilled cheese but it was too cold and he took it out of his mouth and put it on the plate. I told Gary he could eat the rest of my sandwich if he wanted but my mom said Gary was done eating grilled cheeses for the day.

After a while, my dad asked Gary if he wanted to get out of the kitchen and Gary said Sure and he winked at us and they left. My mom put Gary's empty plate in the sink, warned us not to get up from the table or we would be grounded for a week, and left too. I called to my mom that I had to go to the bathroom and she said that was too bad. We could hear my dad and Gary talking up in my dad's study, my dad's low, patient voice and Gary's slightly nasal one. Gary was no longer laughing.

Derek and I picked at our sandwiches. I tried hiding pieces of it in my napkin but it was too obvious. It was funny for a while and then it wasn't so funny. My dad and Gary came down. Gary whispered that we should piss in our pants if we wanted to get away from the table. It sounded like a good idea. We waited until my mom and dad came into the kitchen. I told them I had to go the bathroom and they said I could go as soon as my plate was clean. I told them I'd piss in my pants and my mom said I could do whatever I wanted to do as long as the grilled cheese sandwiches were finished. When they left the kitchen I looked at Derek and told him I was going to do it. Derek thought that was hysterical. I could have held it but Gary was in the house and Derek was laughing and it would be funny if I pissed in my pants like a baby and it was Gary's idea and he'd laugh. So I just did it and Derek followed my lead.

It was warm at first and then it too went cold. Cold piss. Sticky pants. Cold cheese. We sat there laughing and Gary was laughing but my mom wouldn't let us leave the table.

Gary sat with us for a while. He eased us through eating the sandwiches. He told us to pretend they were something else besides grilled cheeses. He told us to close our eyes and he asked us what our favorite food was, what we would still have room to eat if it was in front of us, even if we were full. We decided on hot fudge sundaes. We kept our eyes closed and chewed the sandwiches and thought of hot fudge sundaes the whole time, thought of sundaes hardest when we had to swallow. It worked.

Gary had convinced two disgusted kids that cold grilled cheeses were sundaes. He'd convinced us to piss in our pants. He was trying to convince me to go to Las Vegas, using my life, my job, my supposed freedom to sell me the trip. It wasn't a hard sell. Not with the way I was feeling lately. Not with Gary making it sound like the thing to do.

"If I get it in the glass, you go."

"If you get what in the glass?" I said.

Gary opened his small hand. Inside was a crumpled napkin yellowed with mustard.

"Which glass?" I said.

"Your glass. My hand can't cross the line of the table."

"I'm not making this bet."

"Are you that sure you'll lose?"

"When I lose I like to know it's my fault."

"You want to take the shot?"

"I'm not playing this game. Why do you need me to go to Las Vegas with you?"

I already knew Gary wouldn't give me the whole answer, at least not until he was ready.

"I told you. You're family. Remember how Grandpa used to raise his hand and say, I had to work for the family. He'd keep his hand up like that was the end of the discussion. That's all. I had to work. For the family."

"For the family," I said. "I can hear him now. All those years flipping mattresses."

"What a life," Gary said.

"It was honest work."

"Parking cars is honest work too."

"Exactly. There's nothing wrong with it."

"I'm not sure your dad would agree. Look, I'm asking you to come along as my cousin. My first cousin. I know your brother wouldn't. And it's not dishonest work. There's no cheating the casinos."

"You're right. My brother wouldn't go along. He has better things to do."

Derek didn't play a sport but he would have done well in school even if he had. He didn't fight with my parents, didn't mind doing his homework, didn't have a problem getting into the best university. I already saw the recruiters lining up to give him interviews, their faces glowing as they looked over his academic record. He belonged in school. I belonged on the mat, using my muscles, easing out the rush in my blood.

"I'm taking the shot," Gary said and I knew he meant more than a napkin in a glass.

I finished the rest of the black cherry soda inside, took one of the two remaining ice cubes in my mouth and moved the glass to my edge of the table. It was a tough shot. The diameter of the glass couldn't have been more than three inches.

I should have known. He probably practiced this like practicing rolling a can of soda, like practicing catching a pink ball between his fingers, like practicing his blackjack or whatever else he played. My dad used to criticize Gary for perfecting those stunts, said that if Gary spent as much time in the library as he did with his hand tricks he would have graduated Phi Beta Kappa.

I still remembered certain moments from Professor Gilmore's Introduction to Humanities class, certain pieces of information stayed in my mind more than supply and demand curves, more than Machiavelli's theories about power, more than the sociology courses I took to make it easier on my wrestling career, the easiest major at the university. In my senior seminar alone, a class of eight people, wrestlers filled half the seats. The 141-pounder, the 157-pounder, the 285-pounder who was heavy in a completely different way from Gary, and my perfect 165 pounds.

Sometimes I thought Gilmore was talking about humanities to himself and if someone in the class understood what he was saying, that was fine, and if no one did, that was fine also. I respected that. He didn't change his way for anyone. He had us read *Antigone,* the new one by Anouilh. Gilmore went over the part where the Chorus talks about the coil that sets everything in motion. He described the coil, the spring ready for action as soon as it was touched, how it took on an energy of its own once it was put into play and Gilmore told us that was how all classical tragedies began. Once the spring was set into motion there was no going back. That was fate. That was life. That was why Antigone never made it out of her play.

Gary was smiling his smile, saying we would have a great time driving to Vegas together, saying we'd made a bet and he'd won, I'd lost. Behind him was the old-time delicatessen. The salamis hanging. The workers working. I could practically hear my grandfather's voice, see him raising his hand. For the family. I looked at the balled-up napkin in the glass. The paper was already pulling water from the melting ice.

5

GARY DROVE ME BY the garage. He let me off in front and said he'd be at the corner. There was a newsstand there and he wanted some candy bars for the road. I said hello to the night crew and they said, What's up, Dess. What's up. They joked about the car I was getting out of, asked what kind of side business I had going, laughed out loud in the cold air. I went to the glass booth to talk to Mr. Caparello. He sat there the way he always sat there, hunched over the register, his hands at the ready to make change. Caparello prided himself on never having been robbed. The rumor was that he had a gun taped under his chair but no one was allowed into the glass booth so no one knew for sure and on weekends his son worked the booth, a younger version of the father.

Caparello leaned out the window to ask what I wanted. He knew I wanted something before I even spoke. Why else would I be bothering him after my shift was over. I told Caparello there was a family emergency and that I needed an extra week off from work and that I'd be back just after New Year's. He asked if I was asking him or telling him. I left that alone. I took a breath. I said the garage was closed for Christmas anyway and that I just needed the extra week off. Caparello asked what the emergency was. I told him it was private. He said the fat guy hadn't seemed too broken up about anything when he was standing around an hour ago. I told him my cousin had a strange way of expressing himself and that I needed the week.

I had worked a full year plus at the garage. I had taken a few days off in that year, never showed up late, never went after a customer, never showed any disrespect to Caparello or asked for a raise or made any demands about anything, never even bumped a car or scratched a fender. I had also seen the number of men coming by looking for work. That was all the reminder we needed that the job was easy come, easy go, like a New York City parking space where demand beat supply. Mr. Caparello told me not to bother coming back.

I put my hand through the small window and grabbed his throat. He had an older throat than throats I was used to, soft and fleshy and my fingers went into his flesh. I pulled him to me to get his head out the window. His mouth was open like he was trying to scream but not much was coming out. I took his ear in my other hand and lowered my head. I pulled his face into my forehead. I looked at him. His nose was off to the side. I pulled his face forward again and then again and I looked at him. He was cut above his eye and there was blood all over his face, the most blood on the side where his nose was. I tried ripping his ear off. I felt someone holding my arm and I turned into my arm, went low, got hold of a leg, took the body down. I lifted the leg up and up and I could hear him screaming and other screaming too, screaming from the booth. The one screaming closest to me was struggling with his other leg. I turned him around, got on his back, pressed my chin into his back. He was breathing hard. It was one of the night crew. He was still struggling. He got a hand in my hair and started to pull my head. His leg was kicking back at me and I got hold of his foot and turned it. He pulled harder at my head and I turned his foot some more until I heard the ankle bone break. He screamed louder and my head was free and he wasn't struggling anymore. I got up and spread my legs for balance. There was a man standing outside a BMW looking at me but he didn't move. Caparello's bloody head was resting where his hand usually rested waiting for the money.

I forced myself to walk away from the garage, to walk to the Jaguar on the corner, to get in. Gary looked at me but left it alone. I could feel blood on my forehead and in my hair. He stepped on the gas to get us away quickly and it wasn't all out of me and I stretched my shoulders and tried to breathe it out. Gary got to the avenue and turned uptown. I breathed some more of it out. I told Gary how to get to my apartment so I could grab some clothes for the trip. We heard a siren. Gary got off the avenue and shut his lights but when it passed it was just an ambulance. Gary took a right and a right and speeded on Sixth Avenue and smiled like isn't this great, us being here together in the Jaguar driving New York City's streets and I breathed it out.

"Greenwich Village," Gary said. "It's always on around here. I bet the boys love you."

"Turn here," I said.

"You have a girlfriend you have to call? Let her know you're going on a little road trip?"

"Nothing steady."

"Good man. Don't tie yourself down. The best-looking women in the world are in New York City."

I knew for a fact that Gary hadn't been in many places besides New York. He never traveled except to Atlantic City or Las Vegas but he was right. They were the most beautiful. Actresses and models and young executives in perfectly cut dress suits rushing past the library steps and older rich women in furs and gold clicking their Gucci heels against Fifth Avenue sidewalks and the struggling artist types hanging out at Lower East Side bars, dressed down, beautiful bodies in jeans and T's in the summer, work boots and leather jackets in the winter. I got along with them the best. They weren't quite sure what they were doing and I wasn't quite sure what I was doing. I worked in a garage, that was cool, had wrestled for a while, that was cool, hung out in New York, that was cool. I didn't tell them I sometimes beat people away from the mat.

"Right here," I said.

Gary pulled over.

"You want to come up?"

"Not really. I'm sure it's spectacular."

It was a five-floor walk-up and Gary wasn't interested anyway. I was just being polite, cousin to cousin. I knew he could picture what my place looked like and he'd be pretty much right. A basic studio. A piece of shit anywhere but in Manhattan. Gary's parents lived on Long Island in a nice house in Valley Stream. Uncle Jack had worked his way up in a factory, sweeping floors to owner, a regular Horatio Alger. Derek and I always looked forward to the dish of miniature chocolates Aunt Laura kept in the living room, Goodbars and semisweet Hershey's and Krackles which I'd never seen except in bite-size miniatures.

"Bring some summer clothes. It can get hot as hell in Vegas."

"What about the trip there?"

"We'll be in the car. And pack light. There's no real trunk space and two of my super extra large T-shirts, folded in half, take about three-quarters of it."

I walked up the stairs. It smelled of gas, slow leak, like it always did. There was a smear of dog shit on the third floor left by the resident Doberman. Its owner was a prostitute who let the guys come in and out, doing business sporadically from five to midnight and sometimes weekend mornings. Sundays men stood by the buzzer waiting to get in while the church bells called people for mass. The Doberman's name was Sweetie. Sweetie could pin most lightweights.

I washed the blood from my hair and face. I took my gym bag from the closet and packed. Two pairs of jeans. Underwear. Socks. T-shirts. Running sneakers. A pair of shorts. Sweat pants to sleep in. A dress shirt in case we took in one of the shows. Don Rickles. Engelbert Humperdinck. Someone like that. Tom Jones. I packed my toothbrush. It all fit in the bag with room to spare.

I unplugged my clock and TV.

I watered the one plant I had.

I checked that the window on the fire escape was locked.

I checked my wallet for my bankcard.

I changed the message on the answering machine. Recited my number, didn't add the usual I'll get right back to you.

I shut the light and locked the door behind me. If the cops came looking and smashed in the door, they'd find everything in place.

Sweetie barked when I hit the third floor and didn't stop

when my footsteps were on the second and first and out the door.

Gary popped the trunk and I squeezed my bag next to his. He wasn't kidding about the trunk space. I got into the car. I realized I still had my garage suit on. It was a look.

"You got everything?"

"What exactly do I need?"

Gary started the car. Twelve Jaguar cylinders sprung into action.

"Viva Las Vegas," Gary said and he made a whooping sound as he drove down the street, took a right and another right, looking over the beautiful women slow walking the sidewalks, the smell of the Christmas trees imported from the north making the air smell almost fresh. Gary sped on Seventh Avenue toward the Holland Tunnel that went right under the Hudson, right out of the city.

6

GARY USED THE TWELVE cylinders to weave and weave through Interstate 78. The Jaguar gripped the road, smoothed the nicks and bumps, sounded airtight quiet. It was a beautiful way to travel. I sat back in the bucket seat with my legs kicked out in front of me and watched the backs of the cars coming like a video game. We were going that fast, moving around them when we saw the shadowy outlines of the drivers' heads and then the cars were gone and there were new cars ahead moving in relative slow motion, minor obstacles to get around.

It was dark. There wasn't much to see. There were the cars with their taillights on. There were patches of highway between overhead lights where the stars were visible. There were houses lit up in the distance, people sitting down to dinner, lounging around some den, going on with their lives, probably secure in some routine so not thinking about what they were supposed to do. They were doing it. They had a house, a family, a TV, a *TV Guide*. They'd done it. We kept moving. Gary drove fast. There were the signs to look at. Speed limit. Deer crossing. Exits. Rest stops. Weigh stations. There were the other cars and the trucks carrying goods across America, speeding eighteen-wheelers with lettered sides advertising who they were, telephone numbers printed on the back to call if the vehicle was not being operated in a safe manner.

One eighteen-wheeler kept pace with us for a full mile and the truck driver tried to bully us, stayed close to the white lines and even a little over. It was a big Mayflower moving truck painted yellow and green with a full-sailed ship on the side. It must have been empty, going to a job and not weighed down in the middle of one. Gary kept pace with the truck.

"King of the road," Gary said.

"Him or us?"

"Us. Power thrills. Speed kills. Whenever I put money on a prize fight I put it on the guy with quick hands."

"What if the guy doesn't have a chin?"

"Then he'd look kind of funny."

Gary made a face trying to get rid of his chin. He looked more like an old man in need of dentures.

"You have quick hands?" Gary said.

"Bet on me."

Gary turned. His eyes narrowed a little. He nodded his head.

"I know you have strong hands."

The eighteen-wheeler sped up on a dip in the road and cut right in front of us. Gary had to brake. The truck moved back to the center lane. Gary didn't say anything. His face didn't change. I thought of the game my grandfather taught us as kids. The Hand Game. He would take one of our hands in his and squeeze it hard. The object of the game was to show no pain. My grandfather was a man of few words and fewer expressions but he did explain to me that in a fight it was important to show the opponent nothing. To show was weak. To conceal was strong. My grandfather would squeeze my hand, looking for signs of pain, looking for signs of weakness, and I always kept my upper lip stiff to make him proud. The more it hurt the more I felt my blood rush but I was able to control it for him. I guessed Gary had learned the same lesson, played the same game. I couldn't read him the way my opponents couldn't read me. His small hands looked calm on the steering wheel.

The highway lifted with a slight upgrade. There wasn't a cop in sight. Gary stepped on the gas, put all twelve cylinders to work and we started to pass the truck. The vacuum of wind pulled us to the right and the Mayflower sail practically fluttered. Gary kept looking straight ahead, not even glancing in the rearview mirror. I looked up into the truck's cabin to see the truck driver looking down on me. He had a beard and wore a baseball cap high on his head and I guessed that inside the cabin country music was blaring, some ode to the lonely life of a trucker, eating sunny-side ups and grits while the truck stop waitress poured a refill of coffee and they both fell in love for an instant. Gary sped forward, then pulled right in front of the truck and started to slow down. The truck was honking away and I could hear the power of brakes applied, all eighteen wheels starting to seize up. Gary slowed and slowed until he came to a complete stop. I watched in the side mirror as the cabin door opened and the trucker jumped down just above the mirror lettering that warned OBJECTS IN THE MIRROR ARE CLOSER THAN THEY APPEAR. The trucker started walking toward us. I could hear how fast the moving cars were going past, sixty-five miles per hour suddenly an impressive speed. The trucker was almost on us or at least he appeared to be in the mirror. I could see the I'm-going-to-kick-your-ass-all-over-the-highway-with-my-cowboy-boots expression. I readied myself to open the door so fast it would knock the wind out of him and then those shitkickers he was wearing would slip all over the hardtop while I took him down. I turned to see Gary watching my eyes. Like a test to see if there was grace under the pressure or something else. I turned back to the side mirror. The trucker's denims filled the view. Gary took off. The squealing tires spit gravel at the man.

"All those gears," Gary said.

In the side mirror I saw the truck grow small. It would take the driver awhile to shift up to highway speed.

"You were ready," Gary said.

"Could you tell?"

"Don't worry. Grandpa would have been proud. You know these truck drivers want to come after me, rear-end me and do some damage, but their job depends on a good driving record. So I win."

"You play this game a lot?"

"If they start, I try to finish. You ever drive a Jaguar before?"

"Just up and down a ramp."

"No need for a car in the city unless you can afford it. You'll like the feel of this one. It's a very responsive car, especially when you're going fast. You hardly have to move your hands on the wheel. What do you do, take the subways?"

"All the time."

"Too rough for me."

"Right."

"Too rough."

"It's all hype. Three in the morning and they're still packed. Out of towners come here scared shit to ride them."

"They don't have your wrestling skills."

"Wrestling can only get you so far."

It had gotten me through seven semesters on scholarship. As a sociology major I was supposed to be interested in how society worked and what I'd learned was that it rewarded someone who could pin another man to the mat before he got pinned. All those intelligent students walking around the university but the athletes were known. The football and basketball players and even the baseball players, not a big college sport, were treated with respect but the wrestlers were respected and feared. *Those are the wrestlers. Look at the size of some of them. Don't be fooled. They'd take you down. They'd tie your ass in knots. You wouldn't stand a chance.* We could beat most men and because of that we were admired as I had admired my grandfather. So the smart kids went about their business quietly and often suffered socially while the jocks strutted around with the best-looking coeds on their arms. Now those quiet students were all forging ahead in their professional careers where physical strength didn't mean much, meant less and less as we moved on, grew up. A couple of guys from the team had called me in the past six months. Both were getting married. Both had low-level jobs that sounded as if little advancement was possible. They didn't judge me for working in a garage. It wasn't that far from their own experiences and the experiences they knew. Their parents were not teachers. There was no pressure to do certain things, to be certain people because their families had different expectations. Sometimes I thought that was the way to live. In college I had not done much thinking about my future. When I was kicked off the wrestling team for good I started to think but I had needed time. It had been easy being a jock. I had enjoyed the admiration from students and especially teachers. Professors looked at me differently when they heard I wrestled, assumed I was not too smart but still looked at me with a quiet awe. It was a look that said I was somehow blessed with strength and more, plugged in to something primal, the stuff they sometimes talked about, lectured about, glorified, all those battles in literature and all those dark desires potential catalysts for creativity and success and how far one could go if one harnessed certain energies.

I was pinned once in my life. The fight had started over wrestling but it was before I became a wrestler. I was in fourth grade. Some older kids had been pretending they were professional wrestlers, the WWF kind. Even at my young age I'd heard enough stories to know that what my grandfather had done was real and that what these kids were doing was show. My grandfather was visiting that week and we had been playing the Hand Game and maybe that was why real wrestling was on my mind. I was excited to tell these older kids about real wrestling. I went up to the biggest kid because he seemed to be the oldest and the leader and I explained to him that the wrestling he was doing was fake and that the wrestling my grandfather did was real. He laughed at me. He told his friends and they laughed at me. They asked where my grandfather was and I said at home. The biggest kid picked me up and threw me down. I was on my back, I noticed the blue sky and then the kids came into my view. The biggest kid yelled Body slam, only he didn't pull up short when he jumped on me and then his friends joined in. I could take the pain, I could take it when my grandfather squeezed my hand, but I panicked with these three kids on top of me. My back was pinned to the ground. I tried to squeeze out from under them but I couldn't. I tried to move but I couldn't. I tried to control myself and I felt the rush of blood but there was nothing I could do. I couldn't move. I was screaming. Not words but a long sound.

I was screaming when I saw the blue sky again. They were already standing, laughing, asking where my grandfather was now. I rolled over, off of my back, stood up. The recess bell rang. I stretched my shoulders to assure myself that I was free and I felt my blood rush. I found the biggest kid that afternoon and while he was running down the stairs I tripped him. He broke his leg in three places and cried like the bully he was. One of the teachers saw me, grabbed me, walked me to the principal's office. My dad was called in and I was suspended for a week. That night at the dinner table my dad lost his temper. He couldn't help himself, his blood was rushing too, and he yelled questions at me, how could I have grown up in his house, what was I thinking, how could his own son trip a kid down the stairs on purpose. The questions didn't seem fair. I had told my dad the whole story about how the three kids ganged up on me after I tried to explain about real wrestling. I only left out my scream. My grandfather was with us and I didn't want my grandfather to know I had screamed. When my father finished yelling I left the dinner table and sat on my bed. I wanted to cry but I didn't. From downstairs in my room I heard my grandfather yelling at my father. He was a man of few words and my father didn't yell back at his own father. That was the order of things. My father showed respect even though he didn't agree, showed respect because that is what a son was supposed to do. One generation rebelled against the last so that it all came back and my father understood that and kept quiet. It was a circle, like the circle on the wrestling mat where I had spent my days. All three generations of the Rose family, a tight circle united by blood. My father hated the Hand Game. My son would probably hate the Hand Game too.

In Gilmore's humanities class I had written on the midterm exam that in many ways Oedipus was like a wrestler. He had been warned of his own possible weaknesses and so he worked to compensate for his weaknesses just as I had worked to perfect my balance, my strength, my speed. As a roadside warrior Oedipus was unable to escape his fate and ended up killing his father, fucking his mother. In my third college match I was in the heat of my own battle and I found my opponent's thumb and pulled, heard my opponent's painful cry, understood his Achilles' thumb which was how I described it on the midterm looking for the good grade, looking to impress Gilmore. The referee warned me to let go but it was a close match and I needed to finish what I started. I broke my opponent's thumb. When Oedipus learned what he had done, how he had gone against the rules of humanity in a big way, he tore out his own eyes. I was disqualified from the match. Loss by injury default. Flagrant violation of the rules. Unsportsmanlike conduct. My coach sat me out for two weeks. I didn't do it to myself but I wasn't a classical hero either. Gilmore wrote in the margin that it was a pretty forced analogy but an interesting one. He gave me an A minus. When he handed back the midterms he smiled awkwardly at me and then went on calling names in his monotone voice.

"If I lived in the city I'd get a garage space," Gary said.

"That's where I come in."

"That's where you came in."

Gary laughed and then stopped himself.

"Fuck it," he said. "I used to lose jobs all the time."

"I kept that job for over a year. I just asked for some days off."

"And he should have given them to you. Fuck him."

When Caparello returned to work, both his eyes would be black and his nose would be bent.

"I had this job delivering pizzas," Gary said. "I was the fastest guy there and I cleaned up on tips. My boss was this Greek guy. Busy nights on the weekend he'd ask me to work late, two, three in the morning late, and I always helped him out. At the end of the shift I'd bring home a couple of large pies. The boss didn't know about it, but I figured it was one of the benefits of working for a pizza place. They had great pizza too with this thick crust and great red sauce and the cheese melted over it. Really delicious pizza. One of the cooks was his son. An ugly looking guy with zits all over his face named Acropolis or something. We got in an argument one night about some bullshit and so he goes and tells his father that I'm taking home a couple of pizzas every night. The next day his father confronts me and I tell him that yes I do take home a couple of pies at the end of my shift since I'm not getting health insurance or any other benefits and he's not even paying for the gas I use to deliver his pizzas at three in the morning. His father wants no part of it. He won't budge. Two pizzas and I'm cutting into his profit margin. You know what the mark up in a pizza place is?"

"No."

"A ton. Believe me, you can get rich selling slices."

"I'll remember that."

"So I tell the guy to fuck off and he fires me. You know what I did?"

"You killed him."

"I had a key to the place just in case. In the back of my mind I always think I might have to get back at someone so I play the angles. I snuck in after closing time with a bucket of blacktop, the stuff you use to redo your driveway. You know how sticky that shit gets when it's hot and how much it stinks? I filled up both pizza ovens with blacktop and turned the ovens on to five hundred degrees. The next day I drove by and there was soot all over the windows and a sign in front that said CLOSED FOR RENOVATIONS. There was so much melted tar in those ovens that that Greek bastard would have had better luck parking his car in them than making pizzas."

"They never busted you?"

"They tried. I denied everything and there was no way they could put it on me. I hear their pizza pies still smell like a new driveway when you first open the box."

Gary moved up on a car in the left lane, cut to the right, passed the car and went back to the left lane. He didn't bother using his blinkers.

"My dad told me a story about a job he quit in the Catskills," I said.

"Teaching in the Catskills?"

"No. He worked as a busboy there in the summers."

"Do you remind him of that when he questions your garage duties?"

"No. He was fourteen. I'm not. One summer he was working in a new resort. It was his first night on the job and the boss was riding him, telling him to hurry up, said he wasn't clearing the tables quickly enough, all of that. My dad was hustling, but the boss was a nervous guy and for some reason he had it in for my dad. At the end of the night my dad was walking through the dining hall with a stack of dishes, a giant stack, and the boss came over and told my dad he was going to let him go at the end of the night. My dad strained his head over the pile of dishes and asked the boss if that meant he was fired. The boss said that's what it meant. So my dad nodded his head, said Fair enough and removed his hands from the dishes. The dishes smashed to the floor, the whole dining room went silent and my dad walked quietly away. The other busboys loved his gesture so much they passed a hat around at the end of the night and gave my dad a few bucks."

"That's the best way to do it," Gary said. "Go out with a bang."

Gary stepped on the gas a little.

"Sometimes that's the way to do it," he said.

I watched the rpm gauge jump, then settle.

"How much money did your dad get?"

"I don't know. Enough to get him out of the Catskills. Grandpa would have dropped the dishes on the boss's head and then gone to work on the guy."

"I've got to get some gas," Gary said.

The next service station was in thirty miles. Gary asked if I was hungry. I said I wasn't. He said he could go for a snack. Gary put on the radio to check the scores. He seemed happy with most of the college basketball results. I asked him if he bet big on basketball and he said he hadn't bet on these games but if he had he would have won big. I didn't ask him how big. I didn't ask him what kind of money he was talking about. It wasn't my business. I punched the knob to change the radio to FM. "Brick House" started playing. Gary said it reminded him of his college days and he started singing along and so did I. By the time the refrain came on the second time we were screaming out the words. *Mighty mighty. Just letting it all hang out.*

7

IT WAS TOO BRIGHT in the McDonald's. We were inside the Pennsylvania border, our third state of the night, past the signs for Bethlehem and just past Allentown with the steel factories working overtime a short distance from the highway, orange flames and blue smoke in the night.

The rest stop was packed. We pissed side by side in the urinals that flushed automatically as soon as we walked away, washed up in sinks that came on when hands went under the faucet, shut off when hands were removed. Water magic tricks to make life easier for Americans on the go, no time to lose, no time to waste flushing toilets, turning faucets. Gary's back was too wide for the allotted standing room and his thick shoulder touched mine while we pissed. It took him a long time to get started. I was zipping up when he finally got going and he stayed there for a long time with his eyes closed, an effort to piss, his mouth open, breathing heavy. I washed my face in cold water to wake up. An old black man mopped out the back stalls. He looked tired and broken and didn't look at any of the faces coming in and out, only at the tile floor that he pushed the mop over back and forth. The gray mop braids were like dead, emaciated tentacles. It had to be up there with the worst jobs like cleaning out the stalls in a porno shop at the end of a night or selling cow shit for fertilizer. We had that discussion at the garage sometimes. Listing off worst jobs while we did ours. Berger said that any job where a worker was exploited was a bad job and I told Berger I'd rather be a worker in a brewery tasting stouts and ales than be the boss of a manure stand. Berger said he'd rather be a dead dog than a living lion if it came to that. I really didn't know what I wanted. The garage had been a place to pass time until something came to me and I believed something would come, some opening. The match would be even, hold for hold, point for point, and then suddenly there was an arm, a leg, a moment of imbalance and I'd make the moment mine. I knew what I didn't want. I didn't want to work where they thought I was stupid. I didn't want to have to breathe easy every morning before I opened whatever door I was paid to open.

The road had been empty as soon as traffic for Allentown got off on the appropriate ramps but the McDonald's was crowded. The uniformed kids behind the counter worked slowly with the whole night shift in front of them. Not a good job at all. Only two registers were open. A girl worked the fry machine, waiting for the automatic timer to go off, giant salt shaker in hand. Behind the grill I could see two capped heads waiting for their own timers to start flipping burgers. The corporation had it down to the second and I thought of the old days that I'd never known but only imagined where roadside diners were mom-and-pop establishments and the grill man smoked a cigarette balanced off his lower lip while he decided the right moment to flip the burger, place the cheese slice, toast the bun.

Gary ordered two Big Macs, two regular cheeseburgers, fries and a vanilla shake. I just wanted a medium Coke to keep me up, not much ice.

"The ice is automatic," the cashier said.

"I just want two cubes."

"I can't do that. When I put the cup under the ice dispenser it dispenses an automatic amount of ice."

"You can't do that manually?" I said.

"You're welcome to fish out the ice with a spoon, but I can't fill it up with soda."

"Get two sodas if you want," Gary said.

"Do you want two sodas?" the cashier said.

"No. Give me one with extra ice."

The cashier took the cup and put it under the ice dispenser. The sound of ice hitting plastic went on for the programmed time and then the cashier filled the rest of our order, pulling out burgers from the appropriate shoots, putting a large cup under the vanilla milkshake spout. Gary paid and we found a table. I saw the black man with the mop bucket move past.

Gary concentrated on his food and I looked around, sipped my soda, wondered what a passerby would think of us. Gary in fat-man's polyester pants and a big untucked shirt. Me in my blue garage uniform cut off near the shoulders. No one was really looking. Dead eyes focused on dead burgers, faces whitewashed by fluorescent light. I tilted my head down hoping for some shadow to distinguish me. Gary finished his Big Macs and unwrapped his first cheeseburger.

"I get hungry at night and then I usually crash. You up for driving?"

"I'm ready."

"You ever fall asleep at the wheel?"

"Not yet."

"I did one time, but all I lost was a front fender before I woke up. I was dreaming about a place with palm trees. I still remember that."

"A near-death experience. Maybe heaven is tropical."

"Not that near," he said.

Gary finished off the cheeseburger in four bites, unwrapped the second one and stood up. He was too fat to maneuver in the McDonald's seat bolted to the floor. I'd read that all fast-food places specifically designed their chairs to be uncomfortable after twenty minutes to keep the crowd moving. I could picture some guy in a lab coat holding a stopwatch and a clipboard watching for signs of sore asses. Gary reached into his front pant pocket, pulled out a thick stack of cards held together by a rubber band, put them on the table and squeezed himself back into the chair. The cards were from the Trump Casino, Atlantic City, blue backed with gold lettering. They were a little beat up.

"You know how to play blackjack?" Gary said.

"Twenty-one."

"Right. It's the only game where you can beat the house. It's all math. If you watch what the dealer's up card is and if you know how to play each hand perfectly, you can make a bundle. If you're counting cards and you get on a streak, then you can monopolize on it."

"This sounds like economics."

"Just money," Gary said.

He took the pile of cards, separated them into four equal piles and shuffled them in his small hands. He worked expertly. I wondered how much he practiced, like I had practiced the Hand Game. Before I visited my grandfather I'd have my brother squeeze my hand with both of his so I'd be ready. I always had to threaten him before he really tried to hurt me. Gary folded the four piles into each other.

"You should be a dealer," I said.

"Dealers can't play. At least not in their casinos. I've got two decks of cards here. In Vegas they use six decks. With one deck it's easy to count. With two decks it's harder. With six decks it's very hard, but if you're quick you can do it. It evens out the fluctuations, but there are still times when the count gets very high and then you up the ante. When you bet big you win big."

"If you're lucky."

"That's why they call it gambling. Cut the cards."

I cut the double deck in half. Gary moved the bottom pile to the top and flipped the first card. It was a jack of diamonds. The jack was winking up at me and held a sword.

"Listen closely."

I didn't like to be told. Listen. Study. Be like your brother. I breathed easy.

"I am listening," I said.

"This is basic counting. When low cards are removed from the deck, the player has the advantage. When high cards are removed from the deck, the casino has the advantage. The way to count is simple. Every time a two, three, four, five or six is removed from the deck you count plus one. Every time a ten, jack, queen, king or ace is removed from the deck you count minus one."

"Low cards are plus one. High cards are minus one."

"Great. The ace can be one or eleven, but for counting purposes it's considered a high card so it gets a minus one. Seven through nine counts as nothing. When a seven, eight or nine comes up, the count stays the same. When a lot of low cards are removed from the deck then the remaining deck is considered ten rich. When the deck is ten rich, full of tens and picture cards, the player has a better chance of winning."

"A better chance."

"A good chance. A ten-rich deck can make you rich. You can always use tens. You double down looking for tens. That means the casino will let you double your bet in exchange for one card. Let's say you have an eleven and the dealer has a nine. You double down and receive one card. If the count is positive, chances are you'll pull a ten and have a perfect twenty-one. So you'll win twice as much money."

"What if the dealer pulls to twenty-one?"

"Then it's a tie. No one wins. But chances are that won't happen."

"Just checking."

"You also split looking for tens. If you have a pair, you can split it in two. You just put down another chip and the dealer separates the cards. So let's say you have a pair of sevens. That adds up to fourteen and if the deck is ten rich, you'll bust if you pull a ten. You'll go over twenty-one. But if you split the sevens and start fresh and pull a ten on each one, you'll have a couple of seventeens. That's not a bad hand. And if the deck is ten rich, the dealer has a better chance of busting when he pulls. So any way you look at it, tens are good for the player. Low cards are bad for the player. When the deck is ten poor, all those low cards can kill you. Got it?"

"I'll get it."

"With six decks you have to wait until the count is high, until the remainder of the deck to be dealt is ten rich. Then you start betting big. So what's that? Start the count."

I looked at the one-eyed jack.

"Minus one."

"Great. Picture cards count as tens so it's a minus one. The remaining deck is ten poor."

Gary flipped another card. It was a three.

"Plus one," I said.

"Plus one and minus one. What's the count?"

"Zero."

"You don't have to be a rocket scientist to do this. You don't even have to be an economics professor."

"I guess I'm up to the task then."

"Just kidding," Gary said.

He flipped two cards at a time. A seven and a four. I did the math in my head.

"Plus one."

Gary flipped two more cards and two more and I spoke out the count. He speeded up and I stuck with him through the deck.

"The cards come out fast, especially at the higher stakes tables. You need to concentrate on the cards and count perfectly."

"A perfect count."

In wrestling the perfect count was one. When I pinned my opponent, the referee slapped the mat once. Match over.

"Those are the basics," Gary said. "When you have the counting down, when you can do it perfectly, I'll show you more. I'll be the one playing. You'll be the one counting and together we'll be the ones winning."

"It's that easy."

"If we get on a lucky streak it could be. Here. I'm sick of carrying these around."

Gary handed me the decks. I opened the chest pocket of my garage uniform and put the decks in. They fit snugly. Gary finished his cheeseburger and worked himself out of the seat.

"I'm hitting the men's room," he said.

There was a small shop with tacky gift items near the exit. The shelves were crammed with souvenirs. Paperweights. Pen knives. Dolls. Glass bubbles with famous sights like the Statue of Liberty, the Liberty Bell, a bad replica of Mount Rushmore, the marines putting up the American flag in Iwo Jima. I shook Lady Liberty and the snow started to fall. There were racks of postcards, three for a dollar. I looked them over but there were none of Las Vegas. It was a long drive away and then we'd just show up, a surprise visit like Gary had surprised us when we were kids. This time I'd be the unexpected one. There was a special on disposable cameras. I bought a camera with twenty-four exposures and a built-in flash.

I waited for Gary outside. It was too light in the parking lot and all I could see was a big piece of moon and a few stars. On the highway some cars sped by but mostly trucks. It felt very late. It felt very far away from New York. My hands were cold and I tucked the bag with the disposable camera under my arm and rubbed my hands together. Gary came out and threw me the car keys.

"Stay on this until you get to the end of Pennsylvania. Then look for Route 70."

"You have a map?"

"I looked at the map. That's how you do it. Straight across the country going west."

A man was walking to the rest stop. I asked him if he'd mind taking a picture of us and handed him the camera. I stood in front of the Jaguar with Gary, arms around each other's shoulders, looked into the lens. The man said Smile and the flash went off. He asked where we were headed and I said Las Vegas and he wished us good luck.

"You going to make a photo album when you get back?" Gary said. "Show your folks where we've been?"

"I figured we'd see some things."

I unlocked the car, put the camera on the dash and adjusted the seat. Gary reached for his ski jacket in the back, a giant blue one.

"If you get tired, wake me up. If I don't wake up, find a rest stop and pull in. If you wake up first, start driving."

"What's the rush?"

"I want to get there by Sunday."

He was already leaning his head against the door using the jacket as a pillow but he was looking straight ahead. I didn't ask him why Sunday. I started the car, put it into drive and got on the highway. The car gripped the road even more powerfully from the driver's seat than the passenger's. I sped up to nine miles over the speed limit and weaved through a small pocket of traffic. By the time I reached the next exit Gary was snoring. I turned on the radio, kept the sound low, drove on, just me and the trucks and the exit signs passing by, just the road, feeling kind of lonely but kind of good too, disconnected in the right way and thinking maybe this was what I needed.

8

I DROVE THROUGH THE NIGHT. Heavy skies made heavier by the lights along the highway. The color of the night sky beyond the overhead lights reminded me of the ocean when a storm is coming and the crests have rolled slightly, turned white, made the gray behind grayer. With the darkness all around I could imagine it was ocean upside down. Water to pass under to get to the final destination. Land to move through to Las Vegas. Different elements, same idea, but the element mattered to Gary. No air. He wanted to drive instead of fly but driving at night made no sense, no sights seen, nothing new, just hours on the road. Whatever time we made was nothing compared to a jet. I needed time to study the game, to perfect the count, to get to know my cousin all over again or for my cousin to get to know me. Maybe that was some of it but it couldn't be all of it. He had looked at me like sizing me up before a fight. Seeing what I had. He had to know that I could tie up his fat frame and hurt him once I got a grip on his flesh.

With the signs I counted off the miles to Pittsburgh. I listened to the DJ's banter between songs, one radio station fading into the next as if the airwaves were formally divided by terrain. I pictured the map of the United States, multicolored, with the Jaguar a yellow dot moving along, making time, covering distance. It was a big country, a good place to get lost for a while. Pennsylvania seemed to go on forever but it would be dwarfed next to the western states, chunks of primary colors, swatches that led to the Pacific painted blue.

The Jaguar drove more smoothly the faster it went. Gary still slept with his head against his jacket. He was snoring lower now and more rhythmically. He had hardly shifted at all, the fat on his back and sides a comfortable cushion for muscle and bone. His lids flickered, maybe a bad dream. I went over the cards in my head and practiced the count. Plus one. Minus one. A deck started at zero and ended at zero. Like life. Ashes to ashes, dust to dust, but with the right shuffle the fluctuations could be great like blips in a flat line. That's when the moment had to be seized, the diem carped, the big bet made, the vulnerable limb grabbed and pulled.

There was a detour in Ohio and suddenly there was traffic under the dark skies. We were on a small two-lane road, one lane east and one lane west. It was stop and go, stop and go, orange detour signs pointing the way, blinking lights on top warning cars to slow as if they had a choice. I forced my eyes to concentrate on the braking taillights of a huge truck in front of me. The plates were from Louisiana. We weren't playing the license plate game like we did as a family in the backseat of our Volvo, searching for all the states, trying to make all fifty by the time the trip ended, Hawaii and Alaska the rarest of finds, my mom making the official list in her flowing cursive. My mom always said they'd planned our days of sightseeing around us and how that was good, how they'd seen things they wouldn't have normally seen. Each night, before we went to bed, my parents had us write about the day's events in a diary. I filled the pages writing down the opposite of what my brother wrote. If Derek liked the blacksmith shop in Colonial Williamsburg, I'd write that the blacksmith was just a fake wearing a costume. If Derek described the thrill of the roller coaster at Six Flags Over Georgia, I'd write that the ride was too slow. My parents said it was nice to see how much I was enjoying the trip. I told them I'd enjoy the trip if I got to just enjoy it and not write about it, how I was surprised they weren't collecting our diaries and giving us grades. My dad would look at me, disappointed. Then he'd take our soda orders, go into the hotel hallway, return with the cans and the bucket of ice. We'd drink our sodas and go to bed, Derek and I in one double bed, my mom and dad in the other, the sound of the late news putting me to sleep.

I felt a little dizzy from the hours of speeding. I turned the radio up.

The detour lasted for miles. The light started to come out. Dawn in Ohio. It was a freeing feeling with the sun not yet visible but the light illuminating new land for me. For a moment I forgot about where I was going and where I had come from and it was just the car and the road and the land and sky around me and no thoughts about what I was doing or supposed to do, thoughts that were with me all the time, echoes of conversations with my parents that I tried to squelch but could not or doubts about where I was headed that were my own. For a moment I could see clearly. There were no garages, no fights, no family, just me, speeding, and I felt pure like the Jaguar moving fast.

We were in farm country. Expanses of land with gradual rises and falls and barns and silos that looked movie-set fake, too peaceful for belief. There were streaks of purple on the horizon and I caught myself looking too long, the taillights of the truck too close to the windshield. I had to brake hard. I forced myself to concentrate on the stops and starts. There was no place to pull over and sleep. I glanced at Gary. His curly hair was matted down like a kid's, a big kid, cheeks full of baby fat in the dim light. My parents said it was hard to believe but he'd been gorgeous as a child. He'd been a troublemaker, always, but as a kid it was cute, not evil, irresponsible, not criminal. Gary's father told the gambling stories to my father, his brother, criticizing Gary's abuse of money but proud also, his son the big shot, his son the high roller, his son who could take a group of friends to Vegas all expenses paid, forgetting for a moment that the potential money dropped at the casino tables more than made up for comped rooms, all-you-can-eat buffets, free plane tickets first class. My parents didn't let us forget. They reminded me and my brother what was behind the romance. They didn't want us getting the wrong ideas.

When he was five Gary filled a neighbor's car with water from a backyard hose. At six he put Krazy Glue in the locks of every house on his street. At seven he broke into a Hostess truck and walked away with crates of cupcakes. At eight he stole an aquarium teeming with pet alligators, tiny babies, and put them in the pools and sewers of the neighborhood. Swimming kids were bitten. The other alligators grew full-size feeding on sewage, an urban legend made real by Gary.

Uncle Jack was constantly shelling out money to cover his son. It was a routine that lasted into adulthood. He paid Gary's entire college tuition right up to the last credit before Gary dropped out just one class shy of graduation. That story was repeated at our dinner table, my dad furious because he'd been persuaded to pull academic strings to get Gary admitted. All Gary learned in college was how to gamble. The only connections he made were bookies. My uncle paid the rent when Gary was short on money but not too short to act the big spender with his friends. There had been other stories. Payments my uncle made to people who visited late at night. My uncle would shake his head and his eyes would go far away and he'd say When will he grow up? I don't know what to do. When will he ever grow up?

It was stop and go for miles with the same truck in front of me. I hit the button to open the window to get some cold air in my face. It smelled fresh. I could hear birds calling out excitedly like Ohio was new for them too, a new day, and maybe it was. I'd heard that a fish's memory lasted two seconds and if fish had two seconds of memory then I figured birds might have no more than a day's worth. And what about gamblers? How long did it take them to forget their losses before they returned to the casino or the racetrack or the phone where the bookie waited knowing the calls would come in? Gary shifted his weight. I looked at his sleeping face and his fat body. We didn't look anything alike but he was my blood, my family, my name. Rose. Gary Rose.

It was beautiful the way the light started to take over the sky and the tip of the sun actually moved up from the horizon, not giving birth to a new day but looking like it was being born anew. I could make out where the crops had been planted and pulled, color variations in the burnt brown like the variations in state colors on a map only less varied, less bright, less dramatic, more real. It was what I expected America to look like. The detour ended and I sped up.

When Gary got older things that were once cute weren't cute anymore. He went wrong and he stayed wrong my dad would say and he was still wrong now sleeping next to me as I drove and the odometer ticked off the miles behind us, from there, from wherever we were, had been, to Las Vegas. I had gone wrong too in my father's eyes, the word he used to sum up how I lost my scholarship and how I decided to work in a parking garage and how, had he known, I dropped everything to drive with Gary.

I had been going wrong. Since I'd moved to New York I had been in fourteen fights, close to one a month. On the weekends I usually went to a bar, picked up a woman, drank with her, talked with her, went home with her or at least her number to meet up another time. Some nights I drank too much. I went to the bathroom, looked at myself in the mirror, saw my eyes, too far gone to go back out and talk, flirt, whatever I did. My eyes were not the eyes someone would want to look into. I would stay in front of the mirror and look at my eyes and talk to myself and tell my family to go fuck themselves. I was a disappointment to them. I was the firstborn and I had never lived up. I hated school, probably no more than a lot of kids but their parents weren't teachers. My dad sat upstairs in his office reading, writing, preparing classes, correcting papers, always telling me about my potential and how I was wasting it, and later he wanted me to get into a good college, and later he wanted me to do well in college, get a good job, a job that fulfilled my potential whatever that was. It made me crazy. It felt like a pin, started to feel that way after I'd been put on my back in the playground, after my dad went against me and my grandfather went against him, my grandfather yelling at him. But he was my father and my grandfather went back to Florida. He'd tell me about my potential and I'd get mad and I couldn't do anything about it, couldn't defend myself, couldn't move away from the feeling.

It was a little bit like being crazy. It was being crazy. In my head I put my dad on his back and kept him there, pressed him down harder and harder until he was hurt and the craziness was in his eyes and there was nothing he could do, on his back, pinned. The picture came back to me when I was drunk. I would tell my father to go fuck himself and I would tell myself to go fuck myself, in the mirror, me in front of me. It wasn't easy to say Fuck me in the mirror and call it a night. I'd feel the mat near my shoulders like I was about to be pinned. I'd feel the blood rush. I'd leave the bar and run to someplace where I had never been before. Another bar. Sometimes a club if that was the first place I saw, a line of people behind a velvet rope. I'd go in and get a drink. I'd stretch out my back from the week of work, sitting and standing, turning ignitions, driving down and up the ramp, working for tips. It wasn't that easy. I would wait until someone was unlucky enough to cross me. *Excuse me, can I get in here to order a drink. Excuse me, if you're not using this seat can my friend sit down. Excuse me, do you know the time.* Anything. Sometimes just a look that I didn't like. It was in my blood. The balance. The strength. The speed. The instinct to find weaknesses in another man's body. I would take them down. Beat them until my hands were stained with blood. Until they were out. Then I'd run.

A chill of December air went through me. I hit the button to close the window all the way.

9

MY NECK WAS STIFF when I woke. My mouth was dry. I didn't feel rested at all. Gary stayed in the left lane and pushed the cars in front of him by riding their bumpers until they moved aside. Traffic was heavy so it wasn't worth weaving. He seemed in a driving groove of his own.

"Where are we?"

"About twenty miles from Indianapolis. You sleep well?"

"Perfect."

I looked at the clock on the dashboard. It was a little past ten. I'd been asleep less than two hours. I sat up, rubbed my eyes again.

"You ever been to Indianapolis?"

"No. You?"

"Never," Gary said. "You want to check it out? I could go for something to eat besides the roadside usual. What's Indianapolis famous for?"

"The Indy 500."

"Thanks. Foodwise I can't think of anything. There's New York cheesecake. Philly cheese steaks. Boston beans. New Orleans gumbo."

"Florida orange juice."

"Hawaiian luau pork."

"San Francisco sourdough."

"Las Vegas buffets."

"They're a food group."

Gary went after the next car in lane line, pushing, pushing.

"Wait until you see the spreads they put out at the casino hotels. Prime rib. Shrimp. Lobster. All you can eat for practically nothing. Pastas. Desserts. Ice cream. You can make your own sundaes. The Bally's buffet is the best. They have a Chinese food station that has great spareribs, sweet and sour chicken, great egg rolls and fried dumplings."

"I could go for a piece of fruit," I said.

The overhead signs pointed to Indianapolis. On the side of the highway it was all the same. Fast-food places. Gas stations. A small shopping complex with a supermarket, a drug store, a video store.

"King," Gary said.

"Let me wake up."

"You should be able to count in your sleep."

"Minus one," I said.

"Jack, three, two, nine."

"Plus one."

"Ace, ten, ace, two, king, seven, five, eight."

"Minus two."

"Four, nine, eight, queen of hearts."

"Zero. The hearts is the key."

"The count is the key. Queen, two, six, king, five, five, two, jack, two."

"Plus three. Start betting big."

"Not bad."

"You should see me when I'm rested."

"You have to be rested. You have to keep the count perfectly. If you see me making mistakes, stupid tired mistakes, make sure I get up from the table."

"How will I know?"

"I'll teach you while we drive."

"I assume we're getting a hotel room when we get there. I could use a horizontal sleep."

"Don't worry. I'll hook us up with two king-size beds and a view of the strip."

Gary came up fast on the car in front of him. Indiana plates. The numbers added up to a plus four count. Gary rode the guy until the guy pulled over a lane. I looked out the side window to catch the driver's dirty look.

"The way you play each hand depends on the count, but if you know the basic strategy you have a fifty-fifty chance of winning even without counting cards. Let's say you have a ten and a six and the dealer's up card is a seven, what would you do?"

"I'd probably stick."

"Never stick. You always hit when you have a sixteen and the dealer has a seven showing. That's the biggest mistake you'll see at the table. It separates the men from the boys."

"Chances are you'll pull a card bigger than a five."

"So?"

"So then you'll go over twenty-one and lose."

"Chances are you're going to lose anyway. If the dealer has a seventeen you're going to lose with a sixteen so it pays to take a chance. I've got computer printouts based on tens of thousands of dealt hands. If you pull a card on sixteen you'll cut your losses. Anyone who doesn't hit on sixteen doesn't know the game."

"They're playing it safe."

"There's a difference between playing safe and playing stupid. That's stupid. Pulling on a sixteen may seem risky, but it's smart."

I wondered if this was Gary's basic strategy for all his gambling. To attack instead of retreat. Like a wrestling strategy that said a good offense was the best defense. The only problem was that cards were cards. Cards didn't care. They didn't fear. I assumed Gary knew this too. I assumed he knew cards better than most. I pictured Gary sitting in an oversize lounger shuffling and reshuffling the deck, turning card after card after card over, studying computer printouts until he saw through the cards or saw them in a different way, had an intrinsic understanding of them like I understood the moves I practiced on the mat.

"Remember, you make your money doubling down and splitting," Gary said. "You always double down on eleven. Unless the dealer has an ace showing, you double your bet. Chances are you'll pull a ten, jack, queen or king and win twice as much money."

"Unless you don't."

"Odds are you do. And always split aces and eights. You have two aces, they're worthless. But if you split the aces and draw a ten on each one you've got two twenty-ones, two winning hands. The same thing with eights. Sixteen sucks. But once you split them you open yourself to all sorts of winning possibilities. You can even double down on a split and really rack up the money."

"Guaranteed," I said.

"I'm telling you. Winning is a matter of understanding the odds and I understand the odds. Check the glove compartment."

I opened the glove. There was a reserve of loose candy bars, a small bag of Cheetos, a snack pack of Oreos. Nothing half eaten. Once Gary started, he finished.

"Take out that book."

I took the book out from the bottom. The title was *The Business of Blackjack*. Cards were stuck into the pages at various spots for bookmarks and I opened to the place where the first card stuck out. Under the heading of "Chart 11: Advanced Count Strategy for Six Decks" was a colorful grid of boxes. Yellow H's to Hit and red S's to Stand, green D's to Double Down and blue P's to Split. In each box was a different minus or plus count. The page was smudged with food stains.

"Turn to page forty-eight," Gary said.

I did. There was a card in the page. It was a statistical analysis of why it was always mandatory that aces and eights be split.

"Aces and eights," Gary repeated like a mantra. "It's all there. You study this book and you practice counting cards and you can make some serious money."

"If it's that easy, how come everyone doesn't just memorize these charts?"

"I didn't say it was easy. People are lazy."

I stretched my shoulders and breathed. I'd heard that word too often growing up.

"Anyone who says I don't work hard doesn't know me," Gary said. "I put in the time, serious time. I study baseball in baseball season, basketball in basketball season. I spend all Saturday getting ready for football Sundays. I crunch numbers like an accountant during tax season. I out bookie the fucking bookies."

Gary's hand was clenched on the steering wheel.

"Most people gamble for fun so they don't understand the work. They're mostly recreational gamblers in the casinos. Instead of traveling to Europe they go to Vegas, check out the sights and the entertainment and blow their money. How do you think they build all those new casinos?"

"Not in a day."

"If I wanted to sightsee, I'd sightsee. I'm not interested in sightseeing. We're going there to win."

"How come you don't live in Las Vegas then?"

"I never needed to make money at cards before."

I knew Gary wasn't telling me everything.

"I've made money at cards before," Gary said. "But I've never had to make money at cards."

In Gilmore's class we had read *King Lear*. Gilmore spent a lot of time discussing the line *Reason not the need*, Lear's response when his evil daughters decided to strip him of all his men. The gist of the moment was that the daughters had no business questioning the king's desire to keep a few soldiers around even if he was old and even if he had abdicated the throne. He'd been the king and that gave him the right. I didn't question Gary's need. I didn't ask him why he stepped on the gas a little harder and started to weave through the traffic.

I put my feet back inside my unlaced work boots and kicked my legs out as far as they would go. I moved my tongue around my mouth to get rid of the dryness. My armpits felt sweaty but I was cold. Traffic became congested. People were driving into the city to begin their workday. I remembered it was Friday. I had lost track of time.

"We'll try to find some indigenous Indianapolis food," Gary said. "See what they've got besides race cars."

The Indianapolis skyline was nothing compared to New York's. It could fit handily into a downtown section of Manhattan, a part that didn't even make the postcards like the part where I had worked.

Gary took the second exit into Indianapolis. I asked him why and he said we were parallel to the tallest building and the tallest building was usually the center of town. He said look at New York. The World Trade Center didn't count but the Empire State did, it was still the big building, topped by its famous spire which the original King Kong had climbed before saving the girl, smashing some fighter planes, beating his chest, saying in his ape way the equivalent of what Jimmy Cagney had screamed out. Top of the world.

"Top of the world," I said.

Sometimes walking the streets I felt that way, even when my body was ground level, felt top of the world, full of New York City energy. I would feel my potential, not my father's, mine, strong enough to do whatever I wanted. It was a strange high, a sober high, sometimes too full of my potential. I could take the world if provoked which is why I kept walking, looking straight ahead and not at the eyes of the passing people and eventually I would walk it off and if I hadn't walked it off by the time I got to my apartment I would get down on the wood floor and do sets of push-ups until my arms were pumped full of blood but the blood itself was no longer rushing so hard. I could picture my grandfather flipping mattresses at such moments, picking up the pace to ease the rush, really throwing the heavy mattresses high into the air to keep away the anger from working too hard for too little money, day after day after day to pay rent to some landlord who if he didn't check his greed would get thrown down the incinerator. My grandfather could do whatever he wanted. He was that strong.

Indianapolis and its relatively puny buildings that didn't scrape the sky let alone the low-lying clouds was not a city that could inspire top-of-the-world highs but maybe it didn't matter. The city streets were surprisingly empty and some of the buildings appeared abandoned. One store with a large window sold custom-made frames. The neighborhood must have been the equivalent of Soho. Gary pulled over to the curb. Two blond women looked over the Jaguar and the fat man inside.

"Excuse me," he said. "We're from New York. If you were going to eat in one restaurant in Indianapolis and it was your last meal, which one would it be?"

The two women just stood there. They weren't sure if Gary was dying or if he just wanted some decent food.

"You drove here just to eat?" the prettier of the two said.

"Look at me. What's your fast paced city famous for? New York has its cheesecake. Boston has its baked beans. What does Indianapolis have?"

"I don't know. There's a Steak and Shake down the road."

"Great. They don't have Steak and Shakes in New York. This is my cousin, Dess. He's sick of eating meat."

"Nice to meet you," I said.

I wasn't sure if they could see much of me behind Gary's body.

"Can you tell we're cousins?" Gary said.

The prettier woman bent to get a better look.

"Are you first cousins?" she said.

"We're kissing cousins," Gary said.

"Is the racetrack worth checking out?" I said.

"Yes it is. You should definitely visit our Speedway. It's only a short drive from here."

"Vanilla or chocolate?" Gary said. "Which is the more authentic Steak and Shake shake?'

"I like chocolate," the woman said

"Chocolate it is. Thanks for your help."

Gary drove off.

"I could really go for a glass of orange juice," I said.

"No chance. We're not in Florida. We're going to the Steak and Shake and we're ordering chocolate shakes. That one was kind of cute. I think she liked you."

"She loved me."

"Should I turn around?"

"Let's check out the racetrack."

"The Speedway," Gary said.

Gary drove through the streets like he'd been raised in Indianapolis. He found a sign to the Speedway and then he found a Steak and Shake. Gary pulled into the entrance but the restaurant was dark inside.

"They probably don't open until lunch," I said.

"We blew it. Like the line in *Easy Rider.* Did you ever see it?"

"The motorcycle movie."

"Right. Their pure on the road experience is corrupted by a drug deal and when their trip is almost over Peter Fonda says, *We blew it.*"

Gary pulled into a drive thru McDonald's, the fast-food places always stacked one after the other, clusters of easy choices. He called off his list of menu items like there were six hungry kids in the nonexistent backseat of his Jaguar.

I handed Gary one burger at a time while he drove. The

Speedway looked closed. The parking lots were empty except for a trash truck that moved slowly along. It was probably too cold for racing season in this part of the country. The track itself looked like it stretched for miles. Gary drove through a half-open mesh gate with a NO TRESPASSING sign attached to it and parked in the shadow of the Speedway.

"It's pretty impressive," I said.

"I never bet on the Indianapolis 500. We have a few minutes if you want to sneak in."

"We must be making good time."

"We are. I just want to get there by Sunday."

I took the disposable camera and we walked past more NO TRESPASSING signs and up some stairs to the bleachers. Wedged underneath one of the benches was an empty champagne bottle, the foil around the top ripped and jagged, the party long over. The track itself was wide and not as smooth looking as I expected it to be. A hundred feet down was a pole that must have been the pole of pole position, the place where the race started. Gary walked down the bleachers. For a fat man he moved surprisingly well and I watched him climb over the protective barrier and walk onto the Speedway. He would have taken the focus away from any race car next to him. I looked around but there was no one to see us. I heard the garbage truck's engine in the distance.

I walked down, jumped the barrier, and stood near Gary who was making engine noises and buzzing around the track with his arms out as if he were an airplane. We were both giddy from being in a place that we were not supposed to be. I took a picture of Gary striking a runner's pose, smiling up at me from a crouch with the pole behind him. He took a picture of me running, my head turned around, pretending to be chased by cars. I wanted the film to capture the illusion of speed as I ran from the camera.

"Look at this place," I said.

"The culmination of a parking attendant's dream."

"I was just killing time there."

"Not anymore."

"And what's your big dream?"

"I just need to make some money."

I took a breath. It had been a long night. My dad told us the story of how when he was a kid and his parents argued, Grandpa would take my dad out of the house and buy him an ice cream. My grandfather just wanted to get away before he did something he might regret and an ice cream for my dad was his excuse to leave. My dad joked that he still couldn't eat an ice cream cone without feeling tense.

Gary lifted his leg and let out a loud fart. Fucking around for me.

"Gentlemen, start your engines," he said.

"I hope these pictures come out."

"I'll buy you a photo album for your birthday."

"You don't even know when my birthday is."

Gary lifted his leg and farted again.

"False start," he said.

"Get one more of me running away," I said.

Gary looked into the lens, took a step to the right, looked into the lens again.

"Go."

I started to run until I heard the click of the camera.

Gary climbed back over the barrier and walked up the bleachers. I bent down and touched the racetrack. With my garage uniform on I could have been mistaken for Speed Racer testing the conditions before the big race and when he raced there was always something more at stake than just getting to the finish line. Go Speed Racer. Go.

I climbed over the barrier and walked up the bleachers. Nobody was going to make me write about my day at the Speedway in a diary. Gary was already inside the Jaguar, the engine idling.

10

THE JAGUAR WAS PARKED on the side of the road sandwiched between two eighteen-wheelers. I opened the door and went outside to wake up in the cold air. I leaned against the car with my arms on the black roof and watched the traffic moving on the highway. The speed looked deadly. It was easy to imagine how quickly a body could be sent hurtling a hundred feet through the air before skidding on the pavement, blood and guts and shattered bone.

I stood there until the speed didn't make me want to shudder. It was like looking at the approaching subway, head just over the imaginary line where the first car could clip me, holding it there until the conductor hit the horn and holding it some more. With practice it became easier. Before every match I jogged slowly around the wrestling circle outlined in black, then crawled around with my knees skimming the mat, my elbows taking most of the weight, an adult crawl where I forced myself to stay balanced at all times. I practiced falls, tucking my body under to break the force, pulling imaginary arms and legs toward me as I went down to create a small circle of my own, a circle around my opponent's body and onto his back so the referee would raise his hand and yell Two points.

I walked along the breakdown lane to loosen my legs. We were in Illinois. On my right the tall grasses moved, indentations forming and reforming, spreading out and closing, choreographed by eddies and jets created by the passing cars on my left. I rubbed my hands together, blew air into them, looked at them. My hands were strong like my grandfather's hands. In high school I had taken an old mattress into our basement and I would flip the mattress over and over until my hands ached. In college I had flipped my mattress every morning before I made the bed. Derek had made fun of me flipping mattresses, calling me the maid. He listed off chores for me to do. Did you do the hospital corners the way I like? Did you wash my linens with fabric softener? Did you squeeze my orange juice? Did you scrub the toilet? I took the pen he always kept in his pocket and broke it in two over his head, the ink running into his hair and his shirt. Derek said he assumed the maid would clean up the mess. He always knew how to get the last word. Sometimes Derek came to see me wrestle, sometimes without my dad. He'd sit in the high school bleachers and watch me on the mat and afterward he would shake my hand. He usually didn't say anything but one time he asked me what I could do with wrestling and he looked like he really wanted to know the answer. I looked at my brother and told him. Whatever I want.

I woke Gary by opening his door. It was the gentlest way I could think of. I could feel his weight against the car door as I opened it. Gary caught himself from falling, opened his eyes,

looked at me, worked himself out of the car, walked around
the front, worked himself into the passenger seat, pulling his
legs in one at a time. He adjusted the down jacket and the in-
dentation where my head had been disappeared. Gary started
breathing heavily, his mouth open, his head sunk into the
fleshy folds of his neck. I looked at his fat face with cheeks that
seemed puffed by a steady stream of helium and at his double
chin now tripled in repose gently rising and falling into his fat
neck. It was fascinating how fat he was. His small hands were
folded in front of his crotch, body language that said protection. It was the only sign that he might have had a worry on his
mind. I was already in the driver's seat. I watched the cars
speeding past in the side mirror and at the first opening I hit
the gas. It was Interstate 70 straight on through.

I looked at the signs. Counted down the miles to St. Louis.
Practiced the count in my head. Pushed traffic away from me
the way Gary did, tailgating cars until they moved. Watched for
cops waiting in the brush with their speed guns bouncing
radar off moving metal. Listened to one radio station fade into
the next. Counted the restaurants at each rest stop. McDonald's. Roy Rogers. Wendy's. Burger King. A real variety. The
farther west we drove, the less Gary stood out. There were
large bodies all around. Heavyweights. Super heavyweights.
Super fatweights. Fat people in Manhattan were scarce. Sometimes on the news there would be an item about someone so
fat that he had to be lifted out of his apartment by a crane. In-
variably the owner of a neighborhood restaurant would be in-
terviewed and he would list off obscene quantities of food, a
warning to the viewer in his moralizing words. You stuff your
face constantly you deserve to be humiliated, attached to a
crane and lifted like the fat fuck you let yourself become. The

stories were freak shows. I didn't let it get to me but I always noticed the eyes of the person being hoisted through the roof, saw the fear of falling, the embarrassment of being seen, the depression that must have led to that first extra piece of fried chicken, then the second, then the third, until gluttony became comfortable. I had starved myself to make weight before some matches. I had exerted total self-control. I had scorned anyone who had a round stomach, a flabby arm, a pectoral that was soft like a tit. I was driving with a fat man across country.

I mostly remembered Gary as fat and funny. He was strong too. I was fourteen, my first high school wrestling season over. I had won all but one match against a junior and in that match the junior had bled and I had not. It was almost summer, school was almost out and we were working in the yard. My mom was pulling up weeds. My brother was helping my dad turn over soil for some annuals. Marigolds, zinnias, pansies. I was cutting dead branches from the trees that lined the side of our house. We heard a loudspeaker up the street.

"The Rose residence is now going on sale. All offers will be considered."

I recognized the slightly nasal voice and walked out from under the trees. Gary pulled into the driveway in a new car. He spoke into a handheld microphone.

"The Rose family will stop doing yard work immediately."

Mr. Klokotka across the street opened his front door to see what was going on. Gary smiled at us over the microphone. He held it out to me and I spoke into it, my voice amplified.

"Now wrestling for the United States, Odessa Rose. Odessa Rose."

I repeated it twice like we were in a big Olympic stadium, echo effect. Gary took the microphone.

"Now batting for the Yankees who will kick the Red Sox butts, the ex–Boston player traded away in the stupidest move of all baseball history, the Sultan of Swat, George Herman Ruth."

He reached into his pockets, pulled out two baseballs, threw one to me and one to Derek.

"Catch. I caught these at the Yankees game," he said.

He'd driven from the Bronx to Massachusetts. When Gary had been a kid he used to skip school and go to Yankee Stadium with a butterfly net, roam the bleachers, even then his fat frame able to block out all kids and most men. He'd caught over a hundred major league balls. My family went to a few Red Sox games every year, in the summer, after school was out, but we'd never caught a single ball. My dad and Derek kept an official scorecard and my mom read the paper. I watched how the hitters balanced themselves when they swung.

Gary spent the night and the next day was my dad's economics department picnic. Gary sat with us on the worn blanket and plowed through the food. When it came time to pick sides for the softball game, Gary and I ended up on one team, my father and brother on the other. Gary played first base so he wouldn't have to move much. I was in the outfield.

When Gary came up to bat, he looked gigantic next to the other players. His arms were so thick it seemed almost impossible that he would be able to get around on the pitch, the bat tiny as he rested it on his fat shoulder. Then the pitch came and Gary moved into it. He smashed the ball so hard that the outfielder just stood there, looked up and then turned around to see how far the ball would travel. Gary walked the bases and touched home plate to cheers and handshakes. He did the same thing the next two times he came up to bat. No matter how far back the outfielder played him, Gary still hit the ball farther. He could have crawled the bases and made it home safely without getting tagged out. I remembered Gary owned an old Babe Ruth photograph with an autograph written across the bottom. Ruth too looked out of shape, certainly out of wrestling shape where every pound had to be stripped off or made into muscle, but he was still the home run king. Sometimes it was hard to tell where someone's strength came from.

Gary had already dropped out of college and was gambling full-time. He wasn't yet out of control but my dad gave him a lecture anyway when the softball game ended and we sat on our blanket for dessert, Gary's paper plate loaded up with brownies and cookies and pie. Three credits, my dad said. One literature class. Only three more credits to get your degree. Gary said every English class had a final exam and he wasn't going to take some bullshit final to prove himself, then apologized for saying bullshit in front of my mom and dad.

"I hate tests too," I told Gary.

"But you take them."

"Of course he takes them," my dad said. "He's in school."

"Most of my high school tests are ridiculous."

"And putting someone in a headlock isn't ridiculous?"

"Not to the guy in the headlock," I said.

"I'm not going back to college," Gary said. "It's not about the three credits anymore. I'm not going back."

"Don't you think you owe it to your parents?" my dad said. "They paid full tuition for five years and you still didn't finish. Even Odessa would finish."

Gary didn't say anything. I didn't either. Gary's parents, especially Uncle Jack, thought my parents had done something right when they brought us up and that we weren't troublemakers, that there was no tension at home, no conflicts, that we were good students and good kids compared to their son. I sometimes wanted to tell my uncle that it wasn't true, not with me anyway. I wanted to tell him that I had problems with my parents too, that I hated school, that I could never pull the grades that Derek pulled, that I wasn't unlike Gary that way and what did it matter anyway when you could pin a man or hit a long home run.

Gary picked up a brownie and ate it. My dad didn't let it go.

"It's no life," he said.

"It's my life," Gary said.

"Don't you ever feel that you should get a regular job? You must know plenty of gamblers who have lost everything."

"I'm not one of those."

"Not yet."

"So far so good."

"Living for the moment is a nice idea," my dad said. "But sometimes you have to think ahead."

"I do," Gary said. "I'm going to prepare some doggie bags so I can have more of these brownies for dinner."

"Good, Gary."

"You're lucky, you like your job."

"I am lucky. You could be too."

"I'm very lucky."

"He's a gambler," I said.

My mom gave me a look.

"You could have made more money," Gary said.

"Of course I could have. I chose to teach so I would have time off to do my own work and so I could spend time with my family. That was my choice."

"My choice is to live like I'm living."

Gary finished the last brownie on his plate.

"Money was never important to you?" Gary said, testing my father, looking for a reaction, listening.

"Money is fine, but it's far from everything."

"You're an economics professor," I said.

"I'm a professor, not a stockbroker."

"Don't you know what Dad does for a living?" Derek said.

"Shut up."

"Wrong. He teaches economics."

"I'll teach you how to be broken."

"I'll teach you how to be fixed," Derek said.

"Boys," my mom said.

I turned to Gary so he'd see that we weren't perfectly be-haved kids but Gary wasn't listening to us.

"Money was always important in my house," Gary said. "My dad always valued money. Big money."

Uncle Jack always talked money. He didn't want to live the same poor life my grandfather had lived so he'd worked him-self up the factory ladder, floor sweeper to foreman to owner. That he always talked money, that he judged people on their wealth and possessions, went against my father's values but my dad didn't touch this with Gary. Instead he told a story about a moneymaking scheme Uncle Jack had devised in high school and how he had persuaded my dad, still a kid at the time, to go in on it with him. It involved a camera contraption that took miniature photographs, which were then put in a viewfinder that magnified them big as life. My uncle and my dad would go around the parks in Brooklyn and take pictures of babies. When a mother would say that her kid was sick, Uncle Jack and my dad would tell her that sick babies photographed the best, with their glossy eyes coming out sparkling and their feverish cheeks looking rosy and cute. For a while they made some decent money. But they didn't have a license. Eventually a cop busted them, confiscated their camera and their stint as photographers came to an end. My dad said get-rich-quick schemes didn't always work. Uncle Jack had learned the lesson and had worked harder at his regular job and had supported a family and wanted the best for his son. Gary said it was a good story. Their talk was over.

Gary was not my father's son. My father came to some of my matches and complimented my wins but it wasn't enough for him. He'd tell me I'd done well or that I'd looked strong but I knew he was thinking that there was more to life than wrestling.

Altamont. St. Elmo. Bluff City. Vandalia. Traffic became heavy around St. Louis and I could see the small skyline, the famous arch smaller than I expected, once again not much, a bump on the New York City horizon, and we were on a bridge and the sign said MISSISSIPPI RIVER. Mark Twain. Deep water. Jim calling Huck honey to come onto the raft. I pulled into the right lane so I could get a better view. There were no rafts. There were plenty of freighters. A tugboat pushed a large barge in a straight line. Cargo cranes that could hoist a hundred fat men lined the far shore and it was not unlike the row of chairs I faced when I sat in my own row before the match began, when the warm-up was over and my muscles were loose and I'd put a sweatshirt on and a wool hat to keep my body warm and I'd look at my hands made mattress strong as I waited for my turn to be called to the mat.

The river itself was dirty gray. Thick looking and polluted. A clogged major artery moving through the States, falsely depicted as a bright blue line that cut the colorful map squares until it emptied into the Gulf. Still it was the Mississippi and I felt like I was somewhere. I kept looking out the side window to see how fast the current was moving but I couldn't tell. I would have to pull over, stop, stand at the bank that was once wild. I would take off my shoes and test the water and if I had time I would wait for night to block out everything except the river but I didn't have time or at least Gary didn't. The paved river of Interstate 70, cutting across instead of up and down, stretched ahead.

11

I HAD THE TWO decks out and was playing hands of blackjack, being both player and casino, the player's cards on one leg, both facing up, the casino's cards on the other leg, one down and the rest up. I was pretending to play ten dollars a hand. I'd dealt myself two blackjacks. I'd pulled a five on sixteen when the dealer had a seven showing and won just like Gary said. I'd won a lot of easy hands, a lot of twenties where all I had to do was flip over the dealer's down card to make the win official unless the dealer pulled to twenty-one, a lucky pull but not completely. The dealer was the casino and the casino didn't operate on luck. For the casinos every day was a good day. I was trying to keep the count and play by the rules of basic strategy. When I had to refer to the book, Gary made me recite the play out loud, testing me like a true teacher while his eyes scanned the highway.

We drove. Evening became night. Gary told me gambling stories to pass the time. He'd probably told the stories so often that he'd perfected them. I had been well trained by my parents not to believe everything he said but I played along, expressed disbelief at the right moments. He told of a time he'd won twenty-five thousand dollars at Aqueduct Raceway betting on a long shot he was sure had Mafia backing. The horse's name was Corleone, the jockey's name was Sal Salamino and the horse's colors were red and green like the Italian flag. Gary said he put all three things together. I knew he was stretching it when he said he actually jumped for joy.

He told of a roll on an Atlantic City craps table. He was just passing through the Showboat Casino, looking to win a couple of bucks for a meal, when the stick man handed him the dice. He described how he felt a heat in his hand like a sixth sense while his lunch money turned into eleven thousand dollars. He treated his buddies to a feast and he himself ate two New York sirloins and an eight-pound lobster served in a chafing dish it was so big. I could picture Gary with a giant bib on, cracking claws, forking out meat, dunking it in drawn butter and sucking it all down.

He told me about a collector named Blue who wore blue sunglasses all the time and was so expert at breaking people's kneecaps, legs and hands that the doctors kept X rays of his work as exemplary models of broken bone to be used in the medical textbooks they were writing. Gary told me of Blue's more creative ways to collect owed money. Blue sometimes branded people's asses with a dollar sign so that every time they sat down to read the sports section they'd remember the importance of paying debts. Gary told how Blue once held a guy by the foot over Yankee Stadium's roof and threatened to let go if the guy didn't hand over his bankcard. The guy literally shit his pants. When he had to visit the guy again, Blue made the guy wear a diaper before he executed the more conventional task of breaking a knee.

I asked Gary if he'd ever met Blue and Gary laughed it off, said he'd never had the good bad pleasure, he'd only heard the stories and seen a few limps.

"The guy's supposed to be a real character. If you were casting a movie and looking for a guy who broke kneecaps, he wouldn't be the typical guy. You usually picture some no-neck in a three piece suit. The blue sunglasses are a good hook, a good detail that works against type."

"He still breaks kneecaps."

"That's his job. The people who pay him don't care what he looks like as long as he collects the money or breaks the bones. What he looks like is his personal choice. What's the worst you ever did to someone?"

"When I wrestled?"

"When you danced ballet."

"I broke a guy's thumb once. I broke another guy's collarbone. I reversed him, lifted the guy up, expected his leg to wrap around me, but his leg never came and I took him down hard, heard a crack. Injury default is the official call. I took it. A win's a win. What about you?"

"I'm a lover, not a fighter. Me and the ladies, we get along great."

"Didn't you break some kid's nose in sixth grade and get suspended for a week?"

"Yes I did."

"I remember that story."

"So that's how you see me."

"I see you as the cousin my brother and I liked best."

"Keep it that way."

Gary flipped through the radio stations listening for sports scores. A commercial came on for a home appliance holiday sale replete with Christmas sounds, sleigh bells and Santa ho-ho-hoing.

"That's how I still see you," I said. "From the eyes of a little kid. Cousin Gary."

"I still see you as a little kid too. My little cousin. The only difference is that I don't remember you wearing a garage uniform back then."

Gary flashed his brights and the car in front moved over. The driver kept his right blinker on until he was squarely in the next lane, playing it extra safe.

"So what are your adult plans? Just curious. No pressure."

"No pressure," I said. "Did you used to feel pressure when my dad came down hard on you?"

"He still comes down hard on me," Gary said. "When I called to find out where you were working he asked what I was doing and then gave me one of his lectures. Your folks must use me as an example of how not to live your life."

"That's why we look up to you."

"Great. Your dad didn't sound too pleased with you either."

I looked in the side mirror. The headlights of the passed cars diminished. A thousand flicks of the eye. That's what my dad said when he taught me how to drive. Rear view. Side view. Straight ahead. A thousand flicks. He'd never been in an accident. I totaled our Volvo the day after I graduated from high school. It was my fault but that didn't stop me from throwing the driver of the other car against the Volvo's crumpled hood. He had been driving straight. I had made the turn. The insurance company said I was the one to blame but when it happened all I saw was the driver's eyes looking at me like I was stupid. With him facedown on the hood of the car, I didn't have to look at his eyes.

"I told him not to worry," Gary said. "I told him you were finding yourself."

"What did he say to that?"

"He asked if I'd found myself yet."

Gary flashed his brights. The car in front moved over. The Jaguar's rpm needle jumped.

"Do you ever take your dad's advice?" Gary said.

"I listen."

"He always says I should use my skill with numbers to advantage and get into accounting. He's still pissed at me for not getting my college diploma."

"He helped you get in."

"That's between me and your dad."

"You can always go back. You only needed three more credits."

"Fuck that. I don't exactly see you making your dad proud."

"My brother makes them proud."

"You're lucky. I don't have any brothers."

I tightened the rubber band around the two decks of cards and threw them on the dash next to the disposable camera.

"Then you have no one to look bad against."

"And no one to worship me," Gary said. "Derek always followed you around."

"Not always."

"When he was young he did."

"Once he started school, that stage of his development came to an end."

"He grew up. You don't want him to be a sheep his whole life. He's a good kid, your brother."

"I just don't want him held up as a model son."

"Don't worry. I'm sure your parents still love you. He's great at school. You're great at beating the shit out of people. Everyone has their own unique strengths. If your dad needed somebody's arm broken, he'd turn to you."

Gary was smiling. I turned and looked out the side window. The cars in the right lane were hardly moving.

"Every now and then I get an application in the mail for the CPA exam," Gary said. "I know it's your dad who sends the applications because I never wrote away for them and no one else would take the time to do that. He still has hope for me."

"Really."

"I open them up when they arrive, look them over, think about it for a while. Then I picture myself having to go to an office every day and I put the forms back in the envelope. For some reason I never throw them away. I have some applications that must be collector's items they're so outdated."

We saw some flashing lights ahead and Gary slowed. It turned out to be a tow truck picking up a broken-down car. Gary got back to speed.

"I've done all right," Gary said.

"My brother and I used to think you were a millionaire."

"Not yet."

"How come you're going to Las Vegas this time?"

"Something to do."

"Something to do for the holiday season."

"Don't worry. I'll get you home for the holidays."

"I'm not worried."

"I'll put you on a plane if I have to. My treat."

"We can drive."

"Maybe I'll cash my car in for chips."

"You're kidding."

Gary smiled his smile and didn't say a word. He flipped through the radio stations. Most of the AM stations were preaching Jesus, not sports. He switched to FM. Cheryl Crow was singing about leaving where we were going.

"Does your dad still sing that shaving cream song?"

"Not in a while."

My dad used to sing to us in the car when he drove the neighborhood kids to school on snowy days. I knew his songs so I never fully appreciated them like the other kids.

"I loved that song," Gary said.

He started to sing it. He had a nice voice, not nasal at all. It was as if singing made the fat behind his nose disappear and his words came out clearly.

A baby fell out of the window.
You'd think that his head would be split.
But good luck was with him that morning.
He fell in a barrel of

Gary held the note, then belted out the refrain.

Shaving cream.
Be nice and clean.
Shave every day and you'll always look clean.

My dad had a nice voice too. It filled the car and all the kids listened. It was hard for them to believe that a parent could fool around that way. They thought I had the best father on the street.

"He used to test me on things all the time," Gary said.

"Birds. Trees. Things I'd seen. Math problems. I always thought that if I ever had kids I'd treat them like your dad treated you two. I used to love visiting your folks when I was young. I even remember when they got married. I was the ring boy. I hid the ring in a stuffed mushroom until Grandpa gave me one of his looks."

"My mom always tells the story about how you came long for the ride when your dad drove them to the airport for their honeymoon. You were leaning over the front seat, looking at my parents, sweetness and light, and all of a sudden you punched my dad in the nose."

Gary smiled at that, pleased with his childhood antics.

"I was a sweet kid," Gary said. "About as sweet as you were. I remember you used to squeeze all your muscles and force yourself to stop breathing. Your face would turn red like you were angry at the world. You were hardly old enough to stand, but you could clench up your muscles like a madman."

"Supposedly Grandpa loved when I did that."

"I'm sure he did. Grandpa was from another time."

"In some ways."

"You used to turn bright red," Gary said, remembering the child with clenched hands, feet, teeth.

"I guess I did."

"At least you kept everything inside."

"I just didn't know who to take it out on. Or how. Sometimes I wish I could keep it all inside and let the other stuff out."

"Stuff," Gary said. "The other stuff."

Gary made a *shhh* sound, stretched it out like he was going to say *shit* but he didn't finish the sound, not shit, not shaving cream. We listened to the radio for a while. We watched the road.

"I didn't even bother telling your dad about my last plan."

"What was it?" I said.

"I wanted to act. I wanted to be an actor."

"It's a good thing you didn't tell him."

"It was just a quick dream. It came and went."

"Did you do anything about it?"

"Not really. I was always too busy gambling. Then last year I enrolled in an acting class over at HB Studio on Bank Street, not far from where you live. I always saw their advertisements in the paper so I said what the hell and took a class."

"I never knew you wanted to be an actor."

"Nobody does. I didn't want people asking me about acting. I talk about gambling all the time because everyone knows I'm a gambler."

"How was the class? If you don't mind me asking."

"I'm talking about it. The class was good. We did a lot of sense memory work. The good actors make method acting look easy, but if you don't have specific memories attached to each line then the acting comes off like crap. I could see it in the scenes people did for class. When they put in some time and did their homework and figured out what made their characters tick, then the scenes went well. When they just recited lines, trying to get through it, the scenes sucked. Most of the scenes sucked. I think you either have it or you don't with acting, but if you have it and you do some work then you're on to something."

"You sound like my dad."

"I was great."

"The next James Dean."

"I was. I could act. I'd put myself in the character's shoes and I'd do all my homework, attach a specific moment in my life to every moment the character was in or talking about and it all came naturally. I didn't get nervous either. Once I was up there doing the scene I became another person and didn't think about the people watching. The teacher took me aside after one class and told me to stick with it, that I had something. Maybe it's from telling stories about gambling or maybe it's from bullshitting people all the time, from being the life of the party when I have to be. The teacher wasn't just saying it like you'd think, trying to keep the enrollment up in his class. He's a working actor. Stage work, so you've never heard of him. He didn't really care if we came to his class or not. When people dropped out he'd cross their names off the roster, no skin off his ass."

The car in front of us didn't move. Gary flicked the brights on and off, on and off, drove up on the car's tail, hit the horn, hit the horn again and the car finally moved over. I didn't bother looking at the driver's face. I'd seen the gamut of expressions.

"It's when I started auditioning that things fell apart," Gary said. "I had a picture taken. I sent it out to some casting directors and got some calls. But when I showed up at their offices I realized that they had just called me in because I was some fat guy. A fat guy with a smile. That's what they always told me. You've got a great smile."

"You do."

"I wanted to do more than just smile for the camera like a happy-go-lucky pig and sell cheeseburgers. I wanted to be a real actor. I asked them if they would send me out for film work, a more serious part here and there, but all they did was smile back at me and say I was cut out for commercial work. They said commercial work was where I could make some money. I didn't need the money."

"You should have pushed them."

"It wouldn't have mattered. I thought about going to Hollywood. It all made sense. I knew about gambling and Hollywood was the big gamble. I knew I could act and I had all of these experiences that could be used to create serious characters, interesting characters. I've seen some crazy things. I've done some crazy things. I've lived through things that could layer a performance and make it real. There are so many movies about gambling and making money illegally and characters working on the fringe that I figured I'd be perfect. I had myself so fooled that I even checked out some local newspapers to see what rents were like out there until I finally accepted the fact that the casting directors in Hollywood would be no different from the casting directors in New York. I'd walk into their offices and they'd look at the size of me and the dollar signs would go off in their heads and they'd tell me I had a great smile. They'd see the same fat guy, the same flash-in-the-pan way to make a buck on a few commercials which was not why I wanted to go to Hollywood."

"That's stupid. There are fat people in movies."

"You go to many movies?"

"I go to some."

"Not fat like me. Jackie Gleason played Minnesota Fats in *The Hustler*, but he was about half my size. Orson Welles made it when he was young and in shape."

"What about John Candy? Chris Farley?"

"I'm bigger than both of them were. You never see a man my size in a serious movie. I had Hollywood in my eyes so I wasn't thinking. When I finally looked in the mirror and tried to see what the casting directors saw, I knew they were right for not taking a chance on me. I'm just a fat man. My eyes are embedded in a fat face and my fat face is stuck on a fat body. I took my acting pictures and threw them out."

I didn't say anything. I knew that once the pictures were thrown in the trash, it was over.

"That was my short-lived career in the acting business," Gary said.

I just looked at the highway.

"So what about you?"

"What about me what?"

"What's your dream?"

"I don't really have one," I said.

"There's nothing you would do if you could?"

"That's romantic shit."

"So what? What we're doing right now is romantic shit. Driving across country. Feeling free. Making the highway our home. We're two American guys going west looking for adventure."

"Is that what we're doing?"

"Sure."

"I hope we find it then."

"You must want something."

"I used to dream of winning a gold medal. Being the best in the world at my weight."

"What happened?"

"I wasn't good enough. I lost to a guy in the division semifinals my senior year. Then I got kicked off the team."

"Why?"

"I just did."

"What did you do? Throw the guy down the incinerator?"

"I just lost it."

"You showed your pain."

"Whatever. I guess Grandpa was that way too, but he did it for the family."

"For the family," Gary said and he raised his hand like grandpa had done.

"Sometimes I feel like I need to do something or else I'll go crazy."

"I know."

"But I'm crazy for doing it too. Out of control."

"The worst is when you can't even lose control. When you're not even that free. When other people have so much control that if you lose it you could lose forever. That kind of fear keeps you from losing it all the way."

It didn't really make sense. When I lost control I felt no fear. Maybe I was still too young or too stupid. I heard in Gary's voice and in his words something that hinted at something else and I knew he was starting to tell me the truth about our trip. I was still the kid cousin. He was still Cousin Gary. He would tell me why we were traveling to Las Vegas in time, when he was good and ready, when we had put in enough hours and miles together and could talk man to man, face to face, eye to eye with less of the past skewing our vision and more of the present making it clear.

"You hungry?" Gary said.

"Not really."

"I can wait too."

Gary started singing "Hooray for Hollywood" only he didn't know any of the words. The only word he knew was *Hollywood* and for the rest of the song he just sang *da da da*. He went through it a couple of times and I looked at the highway in front of us and how the beams lit up an ever changing section of road so that the lit portion was like its own small world with its own small horizon that we could get to if Gary slowed the car and parked it and left the lights on and we started walking but even then it wouldn't be exactly clear where the beam ended and the night began. I started to sing with Gary. I didn't know the words either but our Hollywoods came out loud and clear and overpowered the music on the radio and covered up everything else as well. We must have sung for a straight five minutes and I almost wished we could sing all the way to Las Vegas.

12

GARY GOT PULLED OVER for speeding right outside a town called Sweet Springs. It took almost a full minute for Gary to dig his wallet from his front pocket. Gary joked that if he kept his wallet in his back pocket we'd be here the rest of the night. The cop laughed, looked over Gary's license and registration and asked who Jack Rose was. Gary said it was his father. I registered that and suddenly, as if by not moving, by not blurring the edges with speed, everything was becoming more defined.

The cop returned the paperwork and Gary pulled gently out of the breakdown lane. Friday night traffic going into Kansas City became heavier. We could practically tap our shoes Dorothy style against the gas pedal and we'd be almost home if home was Kansas. There was a large billboard off to the side of the road advertising Harrah's Casino and then another large billboard for the Flamingo Hilton Casino.

"They have casinos in Kansas City?"

"A few," Gary said.

"Why don't we stop here?

"I don't want to."

"I thought you were in a rush."

"I don't play on boats."

"The signs didn't say anything about boats."

"They're on boats. The hotels can't build casinos on land so they're all on these floating barges. It's a legal loophole, something about water having a different jurisdiction. That's why there's gambling on cruise ships. I stay away from those too."

"You never taught me that water affected the cards."

"The last time I played on a boat I lost. In New Orleans they have the same setup. Every time I walked onto a boat I dropped money. And at least New Orleans had great restaurants."

We passed another large billboard. It was for Harrah's again. The advertisement read YOUR BIGGEST NIGHTS HAPPEN HERE!

"See," I said.

"Don't believe everything you read."

"I don't."

I looked at the signs. I looked at the small skyline. Gary pulled off at the second exit for the city just as he had in Indianapolis. I asked if he'd changed his mind. He said he just wanted a real meal.

"What's the famous food here?" I said.

"Filet of Toto with Wizard of Oz gravy."

We found a restaurant with a full lot in front which could have meant it was good or just the only place still open.

A host in a ridiculous green shirt with ruffles sat us at a back table, handed over two plastic coated menus, also green.

I went to the bathroom, washed my hands in hot water, my face in cold. I looked like I had been on the road for weeks. My hair looked flat and greasy. I needed a shave. There was no one in the bathroom. I unzipped my garage suit, pulled my arms out of the sleeves, squeezed some soap from the dispenser, lathered my underarms, bent over the sink, rinsed myself off. I flooded the bathroom floor but it wasn't my bathroom.

Gary closed his menu. He got up to go to the bathroom. I looked around the restaurant at the people celebrating Friday night, all locals, all having a good time. I felt like having a beer but I knew I might be driving soon. Gary got tired after he ate. It took work to digest the quantity of food he shoveled in and so the rest of his body functions slowed. I looked over the menu. It was mostly meat. Gary sat down.

"You take a shower in there?"

"I wish."

Gary signaled the waitress over. He ordered two steak dinners and two Cokes and gave her the menu. I ordered a Coke and the roast chicken. The waitress asked what kind of dressing we wanted on our house salads, saying housesalads, one word. Gary said blue cheese and I said I'd have the same. I was craving fresh vegetables.

When the waitress brought the salads I saw my mistake. There were globs of blue cheese dripping over my lettuce and tomato, large spoonfuls of bacon bits dumped over the blue cheese, dozens of greasy croutons topping everything off. I was surprised they didn't serve the salad in a bowl made of lard. I tried to find an unadulterated piece of lettuce but the blue cheese had touched everything. I pushed the bowl away.

Gary finished his salad, asked if I was done, ate my salad and started spinning his empty glass. He told me to pull out the cards so we could practice a few hands but I had left the decks in the car. Gary tested me on the count. I didn't make any mistakes. He said the count had to be perfect at all times, saying it more for himself now.

"We're going to win," Gary said.

"If we're lucky."

"That's part of it. Good luck, good cards and a good attitude."

"What does attitude have to do with it?"

He was spinning the glass and looking at me.

"You ever heard that expression 'taking a bath'? A guy goes into a casino, loses all his money and says he took a bath. That's a bad attitude. He was a loser before he even started playing because he didn't feel he deserved to win."

"How do you know?"

"Because I know. What does 'taking a bath' mean?"

"I forgot."

"No wonder the floor was so wet."

"They can soak it up with some of their blue cheese."

"We'll be there soon. Think how good that shower will feel in Vegas."

"I'm too filthy to think."

"A guy who says he took a bath feels like he's been cleansed somehow, that by losing money he's clean. Which means that if he won money he would see it as dirty money. That kind of attitude will kill you. It's your money. How you make it, whether working for it or gambling for it, it's still your money. It shouldn't matter whether a murderer tips you or a businessman. A buck's a buck. There's no morality attached to money and there's nothing dirty about a wallet full of bills."

"So how does that change the odds?"

Gary kept spinning the glass.

"It changes the way you play. Some moron who feels he doesn't deserve to win will make double-or-nothing bets, or he'll bet on hunches, stupid moves like that. He'll do everything he can to give his money back to the casino. He'll lie to himself, make himself believe he wants to win with his daring play, but all he's really doing is taking a bath. He'll walk out a loser and he'll feel clean. You'd be surprised how many people go into a casino expecting to lose and even wanting to lose."

"Do you always think you're going to win?"

"Always."

"You never have a doubt?"

"Not while I'm playing. It's my money and I hate to lose."

When Evan Kessler threw me around the mat I had felt doubt. I had gone into the semifinals thinking I could take anyone. I was in great shape. I had gone out every night after practice to the large parking lot between the gym and the theater and I'd run wind sprints by the dozen. I did hundreds of push-ups in my dorm room after breakfast, after lunch, before I went to bed. I flipped my mattress over and over. I was ready. When Evan Kessler almost had my shoulders pinned against the mat I had become panicky. It took all my strength to work myself around, to get off my back. I spread out flat on my stomach and stayed there. It was a completely defensive move. From that position there was not much I could do except not get pinned and as I pressed my body into the mat I already knew that I had lost. He was too strong and too fast for me. I just tried to ride out the time without getting pinned. That was my way to keep it clean. If I didn't get pinned I could at least say I hadn't been pinned. Never pinned on the mat, never pinned since I'd started wrestling. I should have believed I could win, I should have tried to win, I should have broken my fear and taken a chance and made my shoulders vulnerable. I didn't. All I cared about was not getting pinned, not getting put in a position of complete helplessness, not losing completely. I just stayed on my stomach and waited for the time to run out. The referee raised Evan Kessler's arm. I tried to control it. I was squeezing my hands together to feel the pain and not show it. We had to shake hands and he didn't look me in the eye, didn't feel I deserved to be acknowledged, and he was right. He had felt my body. He knew how I had wrestled. I walked back to the row of chairs where the rest of the team sat and I had to sit down and there was nowhere to walk it off and nowhere to run it off and straight ahead of me, across the mat where I had not done what I once believed I could do, where I had not even done what I should have done, was the one who had beaten me and so I had started to walk forward.

The waitress came with the food. I did all I could not to smash the plate off the table. The mashed potatoes were drowned in heavy gravy and the gravy had leaked under the chicken. The simple dinner I wanted was ruined. Everywhere we went, everything we ordered was loaded up with shit. Extra gravy. Extra cheese. Extra bacon bits. Extra deluxe. Extra large. Extra extra. Fast food. Tacky restaurants. The buffets Gary described would probably be more of the same only on a larger, glitzier scale. It was exhausting. A fat lifestyle. No way to live.

I watched Gary eat his steak dinners. When he was done he signaled the waitress for the check. She cleared his empty plates and asked if I was done with my meal. I said I was.

"You didn't like the chicken?" she said.

"It was delicious. Especially the gravy. Very subtle. Compliments to the chef."

"Sorry about that."

"It's not your fault."

"Unless she was the cook," Gary said. "Were you the cook? Please don't tell us you were the cook."

"No," she said and smiled. "I wasn't the cook. Can I get you guys some dessert on the house?"

"That depends. Are the desserts better than the main dishes?"

"Not really."

"Then we'll take that check."

The waitress wrote out the check, handed it to Gary. Gary left money on the table, a twenty under the saltshaker for the waitress. The host with the ruffled green shirt watched us walk out and Gary nodded his head at him like we'd had a great dinner.

Gary pulled away from the restaurant and stayed on the city streets. The exit back to the highway was behind us but I didn't ask where Gary was going. He always had a plan. Gary turned corners, stopped and started on narrow streets. It was a break from the monotony of the highway. The buildings became more run down, the streets darker. It was like he knew exactly where to go. He took a right and then another right and there were the girls, hanging out, hands on pushed out hips, watching the cars go by.

"Eureka."

"How did you know?"

"Every city has them."

Gary drove slowly so we could look the line over in all its glory. One of the hookers pulled her blouse down to reveal a huge tit with a wide pink nipple, the kind the guys called a pancake nipple when girls were the subject in the locker room, which they often were.

"See anything you like?" he said.

"I'm not in the mood."

"You ever do a prostitute?"

"Never did."

"Plenty of college girls for you, I bet."

"When I was in college."

"You never banged a hooker in the city?"

"No."

"Who was the best-looking girl you did in New York?"

"I don't know. I slept with a model. Not a big-time model. She was starting out. We went to her place and she showed me her portfolio and then I slept with her."

"You slept with her or you banged her?"

"I spent the night."

"One night?"

"That's it. I wasn't looking for a relationship."

"I love those skinny ones. Was she skinny?"

"Model thin."

"I love them when they have small asses and small tits. Like that one. She's not bad. What do you think?"

Gary slowed the car and moved it close to the curb. She came over, walking gingerly on six-inch heels. She bent over to look in.

"You guys want a date?"

"I'm not sure," Gary said. "What are you asking?"

"That depends if I'm doing one of you or both of you."

Gary turned to me and I shook my head.

"Just me," Gary said. "How much for a blow job?"

"Eighty bucks."

"I'll give you forty."

"I won't blow you for less than fifty."

"Fifty bucks. Hop in."

"There's no backseat."

"Go around the other way."

I opened the door and moved against Gary. The woman slid in, tried crossing her legs, realized there was no room and closed the door. She smiled at me.

"You squeezed in too tight, sweetheart?" she said.

"I'm fine," I said.

"You are a big one, aren't you?"

"Sure am," Gary said.

"Drive to the end of the street and take a left."

I could smell the woman's perfume, cheap and too sweet. Her leg was against mine, black fishnets against garage uniform blue. There was an unlit lot at the end of the street and Gary pulled in and parked.

"If you want me to lean over your buddy while I'm sucking you off it's going to cost you an extra twenty."

"You into that?" Gary said.

"No thanks," I said. "Maybe next time."

The woman opened the door, got out, I got out, and I waited for her to get back in before I closed the door like I had taken their ticket, picked up their car and driven it up the ramp. I almost put my hand out for a tip, just for kicks, just for me.

I walked away from the Jaguar and across the lot to the street. It was dark and dead looking. All the trash cans were filled. There were a few lights on in some of the windows but most of the windows were boarded up. I stood there waiting. A car drove by, slowed, looked me over. A man put his head out the window.

"You working?" he said.

"Not tonight."

The man looked my body over and drove off. I paced back and forth. I could feel the loneliness everywhere. All the fast food and all the fast driving couldn't take that away. All of Gary's talk about gambling made it sound like business as usual. Winning wasn't always possible, not even probable, not if Gary had to take this trip. Even if he won what he needed he'd still want more, always more.

I looked back at the lot. I could see the shadow of Gary's body in the driver's seat and for a moment I thought I saw the back of the woman's head bob up and then bob down.

13

INTERSTATE 70 OPENED UP. Gary drove faster. I shifted in my seat trying to work the cramps from my legs that came quicker and quicker after each rest stop. I was afraid to sleep. Gary didn't want to pull over. He kept looking at the speedometer and then the odometer, doing the division, calculating the hours and the miles, figuring the time of arrival, destination Las Vegas.

"What's the prediction?"

"No prediction," Gary said. "We're getting there by Sunday."

"Why Sunday?"

"I like Sunday."

"That's a good reason."

"That's why I gave it. Sit back and enjoy the ride."

The trip was getting to us. I remembered the family trips we'd taken to Florida when I was young, stopping at the border welcome station for free orange juice and to pick up the tourist-trap brochures for the Monkey Jungle, the Parrot Rain

Forest, the Alligator Swamp where a man in war paint wrestled real live alligators. The drives seemed to go on forever. While my parents talked in front, Derek and I soon grew tired of looking for license plates, playing rhyme games or twenty questions, identifying the sights on the highway and checking them off on game boards my mom bought us. A telegraph pole. A cow. A locomotive. A church steeple. Eventually it all deteriorated into Sides. There was an imaginary line that ran across the backseat which separated my side from my brother's. When one of us crossed that line even by a fraction of an inch the punishment could begin. We'd taunt each other, slide a finger over the seat cushion, stick a foot across the border that ran from roof to floor, the hump in the middle of the floorboard a favorite battleground for squashing feet and kicking shins. At first we'd try just to keep each other off our official sides. But as the game progressed it became more brutal. Smashed fingers. Bruised forearms. Black-and-blue thighs. It was a sign of weakness to cry out in pain. Once the game was underway, I'd pull my brother's whole body to my side and work him over. Sometimes I let Derek get me just to make him feel like he was in the game and sometimes he genuinely landed a good shot. We'd wrestle around until my parents told us to stop, warned us quietly, then repeated themselves until the warnings weren't so quiet and if we still didn't stop my mom would unbuckle her seat belt and turn around and with her beautiful nails, filed to points and made strong with polish, she would grab the offending party and dig in. My arm usually got the nail treatment. I was the big brother and should have known better. I was the one playing rough. I was often too rough with my brother but he never cried out or even complained. When I got the nail treatment, it sometimes took an hour for the marks on my arm to disappear, four half-moon indentations lined in a row. We joked about it now. When my mom wanted to lighten our dinner table discussions, discussions most recently about my life in New York, she would threaten me with her nails.

If we were playing Sides, Gary's wide body would have been over the line the whole trip. We were tired, exhausted really. The signs kept changing, destination upon destination, Las Vegas still miles away. I wondered if the signs ever stopped or if there was a sign that said this was the last destination, the last official sign in the U.S. before the Pacific, or if there was a sign that said U TURN ALLOWED and then the turn was made and the signs started over going back.

Gary told gambling stories to pass the miles that led to stories about his college fraternity. Gary said he missed those days. I didn't remind him that he could go back for at least three more credits worth of time.

"My frat brothers were a great bunch of guys," Gary said. "I've lost touch with most of them. Most of them got married."

"I don't miss my college days. Whenever people tell me college was the highlight of their lives, it always strikes me as being depressing."

"Not me. I had a great time."

"Then you're admitting it was all downhill from there."

"Maybe it is."

"That's sad."

"Why? Did you have more fun being the big man on campus, wrestling, doing college girls, hanging out with friends, or did you prefer parking cars for a living? If you want, I'll try to pull some strings and get you a garage job in Vegas."

"Maybe you should pull some strings for yourself."

"I don't need to pull any strings. I work for myself."

"So you ordered yourself to get to Las Vegas by Sunday."

"What's wrong? You can't take a few hours on the road? You miss not working for someone? I can pull over so you can practice parallel parking."

"Parking cars didn't bother me. I knew it was temporary."

"It was. You got fired."

"Thanks to you."

"Don't worry. I'll pay you for your time."

"I don't need your money."

"You probably do. I can't believe your tips added up to more than chump change."

"They added up to enough."

"Enough for you maybe," Gary said.

"I'm not the one speeding away like I'm desperate for money. I was never desperate for money."

"How do you know what I'm desperate for?"

"Just a lucky guess. Maybe it's because the whole fucking trip you've been talking about how to win money."

"You have a problem with winning money?"

"No. That would be your problem."

"I don't have a problem. I always win eventually. I always make my money."

"Money. Money. My parents made sure I didn't have to think about money. So did yours. Or at least they tried."

"Good for them."

"It was good for us. They had real pressure so they worked to make our lives easy."

"Whatever pressure I'm under, it's my own. I'm my own boss. I'm my own man."

Gary glanced at the speedometer, the odometer, did the quick math in his head. I leaned back in my seat.

I looked out the side window. I could feel the wide sweep of states and I pictured the squares on the map getting bigger. The squares we'd passed had been mostly brown. The fields had been harvested, plowed under, left to rest until spring, the flat land punctuated by farmhouses, silos, horses grazing on whatever weeds they could find, their bodies silhouetted in the evening. Kansas had taken forever. Colorado was just starting. Open spaces going west. Behind us the sun rose, streaks of pink layering streaks of dark purple layering the gray backdrop, striations filling my side mirror. For a moment, I forgot the trip.

"What makes you think our parents had it so hard?" Gary said.

"They did. They're the sandwich generation."

"The sandwich generation. What kind of sandwich? Liverwurst? Salami? What the fuck are you talking about?"

"They were supposed to become successful because their parents were immigrants. Look at our fathers. Grandpa slaved away in a mattress sweatshop so that his kids could have a better life. He devoted his whole life to that end and his kids knew it. When Grandma and Grandpa were old, our parents were ready to take care of them. It was love, but they knew Grandpa had worked hard all those years and it was their turn to reciprocate. Then there's us. We didn't grow up poor. We never saw our parents struggle. We're not first-generation Americans so we don't have any burdens like they had. Now it's completely turned around. Our parents are in the middle of the sandwich. They took care of their parents and they take care of us. They would have paid for my education if I didn't get a wrestling scholarship. They're paying for my brother's education. Your folks paid for your education. We had it easy."

"I'm their only son."

"So what? They took care of their parents and they take care of their kids. We don't take care of anyone."

"We take care of ourselves."

"Whose name is on your car registration? I can work in a garage and kill time because I know that if things get too hard I can always go home. Same with you. I doubt you would have started gambling if you thought your parents weren't going to be there to help you out."

"They're not always there."

"They always have been."

"Sometimes the help runs out. Believe me."

"Is that why you're going to Las Vegas?"

"I'm going there for the buffets."

Gary turned his eyes from the road and looked at me like he was going to tell me something.

"I'm the buffet generation," he said.

"All you can eat. Just you. It's like that joke my dad tells. A man calls up his father after he finally moves out of the house. He says to his father, Dad, you took care of me your whole life. Now I've got a good paying job. Take care of yourself."

"Grandpa had it hard," Gary said.

"Sure he had it hard, but in some ways I envy him. It must have been nice to have that one goal. It was like he had a plan already set up for him. Come to this country. Make a living. Work hard so that your kids have a better life. Sometimes I wish I had that direction so I'd know what I was supposed to do."

"So you could flip mattresses all day?"

"So I wouldn't have to think. And if anyone gave him shit along the way he could take it out on them. He was protecting his family. All the stories I know about him are that. Even the pickpocket story. That was food money. If he had to use his strength, he was using it for a reason. He could do whatever he wanted to do and he didn't have to feel bad about it after, didn't have to think about it after."

"Stop thinking. We're on the road. We're driving to Vegas. That's all you need to worry about."

"For now."

The lines of pink faded. The sky brightened. The flat land had been replaced by mountains, fir trees pointing in unbalanced angles off the slopes to get the most winter sun. A small river bordered the road and I saw a fisherman in thigh-high boots standing in the water, clear and hard rushing from melted snow, casting his pole at an angle that also picked up the sunlight.

"I used to flip my mattress to make my hands strong."

"I'm impressed."

"I'm not trying to impress you," I said. "I wanted to be like him. He was a physical man and I was a physical kid and in my eyes that had been all-important."

"For all his easy living, I bet you never beat Grandpa at the Hand Game."

"I didn't say his life was easy. And I was too young when he died. Did you?"

"He stopped playing with me. I would have beaten him."

"I don't know. Even when he was old he was strong. There was a lifetime of work in those hands."

On his deathbed he had broken an intern's hand. He was tired of being sick and he didn't want his family to put their own lives on hold any longer. When he said to my father, Someone's calling me, son, someone's calling me, my father said, Don't answer. My grandfather smiled and then his face changed to his usual stern expression. After visiting hours that evening, after my parents and Gary's parents had left, the intern tried to change my grandfather's IV because my grandfather wouldn't let the nurses do it. He moved his arm away but the intern persisted. My grandfather took the intern's hand, a young man who had never played the Hand Game, and squeezed.

"Grandpa would never make a sound."

"What does that mean?" Gary said.

"It means he had strong hands and he would never make a sound."

Gary was looking at me.

"You don't think I would have beaten him?"

"You didn't beat him."

"You think I'm weak because I'm fat?"

"I didn't say you were weak. Keep your eyes on the road."

"I'm taking you along because you're family."

"You just want to get close to me."

"I just want you to shut up."

"I forgot. I'm not here to talk."

"You're here to drive."

"My wrestling has nothing to do with it. Needing protection has nothing to do with it."

Gary swerved over two lanes and stopped hard on the side of the road. He shifted his body as much as he could to face me.

"Let's go, tough guy."

"I never said I was tough."

"You walk tough. You wear your precious garage uniform cut off at the sleeves to show off your arms. I bet I can beat you at the game."

"That's a bad bet."

"Let's go. Let's play."

He had his small hand out, ready to squeeze my hand first.

"No stakes?" I said. "No money on the line? That's something new for you."

"And what's new for you? A day without a shower? A night without a bed?"

"I told you we had it easy."

"Maybe you have it easy. Maybe all that easy living made your hands soft. It's been a while since you wrestled."

I felt the blood rush. I put out my hand.

Gary adjusted his small hand around my palm. He'd played the Hand Game enough to know where the bones were, where it would hurt the most. He started to squeeze. I kept my face calm and took it and took it and thought of Evan Kessler and how I should have fought harder, how I should have taken the chance even if it meant getting pinned, easy to think back on it, easy when the panic wasn't there, when my back was not against the mat. Gary's face turned red, his forehead beaded up with sweat, he breathed heavy. My grandfather had taught me well. Gary let go.

I watched him catch his breath.

"Let's go, tough guy," he said.

Tough guy. A tough guy who parked cars. A tough guy whose parents were disappointed, whose brother was making them proud. A tough guy who was kicked off the team, who beat men not ready to fight in bars, who beat his old boss. A tough guy driving to Las Vegas whose blood was always rushing. My grandfather's excuse was the family. I had no excuse. It was a headlock I couldn't get out of. I started to squeeze Gary's hand. Hard. Harder. Tough. Tougher. Like squeezing the mattress before I flipped it.

Gary cried out. It was a child's cry. I guessed it was the cry my grandfather heard and that was why my grandfather had stopped playing with Gary.

I let go of Gary's hand.

"You win," he said.

Gary put his hurt hand in his lap and his left hand on the steering wheel. He got back on the highway and drove.

The highway was no longer as straight. Not straight like the trip my grandfather had taken, not across country but across the ocean, a flat plane of blue with nothing to break the monotony, a piece-of-shit boat, everyone sick, eating fast, shoving the food down because a minute after one guy doled out the bowls of stew another guy came around to pick them up, that was the story, and then finally there was the Statue of Liberty, the torch probably looking like a waving welcoming hand from the distance, and then the cold-water apartment, the job stuffing mattresses, the two kids waiting for their father to come home from work, how tired he was, long day after long day, but he kept going for them, his sons, his boys. That's what my dad called me and my brother too, his boys.

"Do you know any other stories about Grandpa?" I said.

"The same ones you probably know."

Gary's voice was quiet. I could hear how he hated to lose.

"You knew Grandpa a lot longer. You must remember him as younger than I remember him."

"In those days people were never young," Gary said.

"It seems that way."

"I've seen photographs. I don't remember him like the old photographs."

"He was great looking. He looked like a movie star."

"He should have gone to Hollywood. He could have been my connection."

"Sometimes I wish the stories about Grandpa weren't so violent."

Gary slowed as the highway curved around a mountain. The slanted trees looked like they might rise with the sun.

"Supposedly your dad spent all his money on books when he was growing up. Whatever odd job he had, he spent his paycheck at the bookstore and Grandpa couldn't understand it. He said books were worthless, a waste of good money, all of that. So one time your dad brought home a copy of *Moby-Dick* and he showed it to Grandpa and asked him what he would give for *Moby-Dick*. Grandpa looked at the book and looked at your dad and said he wouldn't pay two cents for that junk. Your dad asked Grandpa if he was sure and Grandpa said he was absolutely sure. So your dad opened the book and stuck between the pages was a crisp ten-dollar bill your dad had planted there. Grandpa had one of his rare laughs and never complained about your dad's book purchases again. At least I inherited something from Grandpa. The only reading I do is *The Business of Blackjack* and *The Racing Form*."

"My dad never told me that one."

"He didn't want you to rebel and not read."

I had rebelled anyway. In the gym, on the mat, it felt natural. I didn't have to struggle like I struggled in school, hating my parents' expectations, ignoring homework, fighting about grades. I had to give my brother credit for not rebelling but he wasn't the oldest son. Derek studied, worked to be number one in high school, was getting straight A's in college. Of course Gary had chosen me for his driving partner. We were the keepers of the circle and on the wrestling mat the circle was painted in black, a thick mark around that would take generations of bodies sliding across it in grappling battles before it could be erased. Maybe one day we could step out of the circle. At the end of a hard fought match, hands were shaken. I had even seen wrestlers, other wrestlers, hug each other when the time ran out.

"Grandpa used to save us a parking space whenever we went to Florida to visit," I said.

"He did that for us too. He was always ready to kick some ass defending that space. I wonder what other people thought of him. There's old Mr. Rose spending the day saving parking spots."

"I know how that is."

Gary laughed. His hurt hand probably still throbbed but he seemed over it, at least on the outside.

The road curved. Saturday morning. A full day to Sunday. There was some construction on the highway and we were diverted onto a smaller route. We passed a town named Eagle. Welcome to. Population. Altitude. All I needed to feel at home. There were a lot of pickup trucks with full loads. Stacked near many of the houses were cords of wood, dried and ready to be split. We passed a town named Parachute, a good place to bail out but Gary was family.

"I'm beat," Gary said.

Gary pulled over and got out of the car. We both pissed on the side of the road. My piss steamed when it hit the snow and sunk in, created a clear line.

I walked around the hood. I got the camera, leaned over the top of the Jaguar, asked Gary to smile just as he was starting to work himself into the passenger seat. I steadied my arms and took a picture of the Jaguar's black roof, Gary's thick shoulders, his exhausted smiling face, the mountain in back of him, the slanted pine trees going all the way up. I got in and waited for Gary to settle himself. The car was idling. Gary pulled his coat from the back, adjusted it against the side of the car, leaned his fat body against it, relaxed his head, closed his eyes.

"Wake me when you get tired."

"I'll try."

"We're making good time," Gary said.

The highway went around a mountain, then another, then straightened out. I stepped hard on the gas.

"You ever think of going to Hollywood?" he said. His voice was tired. He was almost out.

"Not me."

"You got that look. That Grandpa look."

"I got the wrestling from him. Rose blood. That's enough."

14

I DROVE UNTIL I couldn't drive. I slowed, pulled into a rest area somewhere in Utah, parked, didn't care about the light, didn't care about the cold, didn't care about Gary's heavy breaths next to me, just needed sleep. I went out with images of the highway stretching before me, what I had looked at so long imprinted behind my eyes and then I went out all the way.

The car door slammed. I opened my eyes. Gary was walking across the lot to the bathroom, his untucked shirt flapping from the wind, his pants completely wrinkled. His hand went to his mouth. He was eating something. It was a clear day and cold looking and I was cold. I didn't know how long I'd been out. I got out of the car, stretched my legs, looked around. The country had opened up again.

Gary was leaving the bathroom as I was going in. I washed my face with cold water. I didn't care about my underarms anymore, how my crotch seemed stuck to my thighs, how my face felt filthy. There was no mirror so I didn't have to check my eyes.

Gary took the wheel. He weaved through the traffic. He tested me on the count. He told me the story about Bugsy Siegel's dream to build an oasis in the middle of the desert and how he never lived to see his dream come true. The radio played Courtney Love, Kurt Cobain, Tracy Chapman, Blues Traveler.

The highway was so straight that a steering wheel seemed unnecessary. I focused on a point in the distance and the car approached it and then I focused on another point. One radio station went into the next.

Gary turned off at Richfield and found a diner. He ordered a cheese omelet with hash browns and sausage and the meat-loaf special with mashed potatoes and two Cokes. I ordered a lettuce and tomato sandwich on whole wheat. The waitress asked if I wanted any bacon on the sandwich and I said No thanks. She asked about mayonnaise and I said No thanks to that too. I'd learned my lesson about heavy-handed condiments. Gary hardly fit in the lumpy booth. I would never get like that. Not even close. There were no more wrestling seasons but I stayed at my weight. At 165 pounds I was lean. My shoulders were square. My arms were defined. My stomach was flat. My waist was thin. The skin in my face was tight and my eyes were clear. In bars the women looked at my body and in bed I liked that they moved their hands over my muscles, felt my strength. Sometimes I thought they could feel all the fights I'd won. Gary took a napkin from the dispenser, crumpled it into a ball and shot it into my water glass.

"Double or nothing," Gary said.

"It feels like a month ago," I said.

Three guys were at the counter, swiveling back and forth on their stools, smoking cigarettes, drinking bottled beers. They swiveled around, looked us over. Next to them was a young kid sitting precariously on a stool. He kept asking when the pancakes were coming and the guy next to him told the kid to shut up and wait. The guy next to the kid was the biggest of the three. He called the waitress Honey.

The waitress brought the guys their food and put the plate of pancakes in front of the boy. I could see the back of the kid's head tilt, sizing up the stack of pancakes he'd been waiting for. He lifted his fork. His father grabbed the container of syrup and started pouring it over the pancakes and the kid started screaming, said he didn't want syrup on his pancakes, said he wanted regular pancakes and then he started sobbing while his father ate his own meal. The kid's body shook and it looked like he would fall off the stool at any moment. The sound of him trying to catch his breath filled the diner. I couldn't help feeling sorry for the kid.

Our food came out. The three guys kept swiveling to look at Gary. The biggest guy first. The other two guys followed him. He'd swivel, they'd swivel. He'd laugh, they'd laugh. My sandwich was dry, the edges of the lettuce turning brown and the tomato mealy. The leader swiveled again. The two other guys swiveled again. I heard the stools squeak, saw the position of their bodies change. The kid was still crying. Gary finished his omelet and started on the meatloaf special.

"You have quite an appetite there, big guy," the leader said.

I looked at Gary. He smiled at me and looked at them.

"Yes I do," Gary said.

"My friends and I just made a little wager on how much you ate during the day. I said six meals."

"You lost your bet."

"How many?"

"It depends."

"So some days you do eat six meals."

"Some days I eat five meals. Some days I eat seven meals. Some days I eat three squares, double portions like you see here. But I never eat six."

"We weren't betting for money anyway."

"Lucky you."

"I'm a lucky man," the guy said.

"Why don't you spread some of that luck and buy your son a new order of pancakes so we can eat in peace."

"Don't worry about my son. He's none of your business."

I chewed the dry wheat bread, brown lettuce, mealy tomato.

"You're right," Gary said. "Now why don't you let us enjoy our one meal."

"Am I bothering you? What is this shit? My son's bothering you. Now I'm bothering you. You have a problem?"

"I like to concentrate on my food. Have a nice day."

"He likes to concentrate on his food," the leader said to his two friends.

He laughed. Two laughs followed. If they'd been synchronized swimmers they would have taken home the gold.

"I can see that," he said. "I can see that's about all you concentrate on because you are one disgustingly fat motherfucker."

"You should know," Gary said.

"Me and anyone else who sees you. Anyone can see you're a fat pig."

"I mean about the motherfucker part," Gary said. "I didn't recognize you at first, but now I do. You're my stepson, aren't you? I stepped over you to fuck your mother."

"You fat fuck."

The big guy swiveled off his stool, bumping into his crying

son, and started coming. His arms were down. His head was too straight. He was already off balance trying to puff out his chest. I was out of the booth, shooting at his legs. He went down hard. I got his arm behind his back, pulled it over and up until it broke. I took his other arm, got a hand on his hand, broke his wrist. He was screaming and kicking his legs out on the floor. I felt a foot in my side and on my back. I covered my head, rolled, stood, turned, my hands in front of my face. The friend who had been kicking me picked up a beer bottle from the counter, emptied it on the floor, broke it on the counter. I looked at the broken bottle, backed away a step, crouched. The third friend just stood there looking at his leader on the floor screaming. The kid had stopped crying. I circled the guy with the bottle, touched his head with my hand. He thrust the bottle at me. I backed away. Gary had stood up. The guy looked at Gary and I touched the guy's head, pushed his head down. He thrust at me with the bottle. I backed away. I touched his head, pushed his head down, put off his equilibrium, put off his balance. The guy cocked his arm to take another swipe. He thrust at me hard, hesitated to see if he'd done some damage. I grabbed his arm, pulled it back, pulled him into me, the bottle fell. I put him in a half nelson, pressed his neck down. His other arm was free and I felt his elbow hit me above my eye. I put my head against his back and put my arm under his crotch, lifted, threw him down. His head bounced off the floor. I kicked him in the head with my work boot. Blood was coming from his face. I kicked him in the head. He was out. I kicked him again. I felt something against my leg. The big guy was trying to drag himself under our table. He was screaming that his arm was broken. His legs were kicking out in agony and I kicked his kneecaps, his thighs, his balls. He curled up with his broken arm hanging limply at his side. I lifted my leg and brought my boot down on his broken arm and he screamed and I brought my boot down and down until it was out of me.

The third friend was still standing there. I looked at him until he sat on the stool. Gary put money on the table to cover the bill, went over to the kid, gave him some money, told him to get a new order of pancakes, threw me the car keys, picked up his unfinished plate of meatloaf and we walked out. I opened the car door for Gary, went around, opened my door, drove forward, listened to Gary's directions like he'd grown up in town, ate at the diner everyday, worked in Richfield's chamber of commerce. I was out on the highway and Gary was licking meatloaf gravy from his fingers.

"You beat the fuck out of them."

"They're punks."

"They used to be punks. Now they're injured. You must have broken that fucker's arm in ten different places."

"Fuck him."

"That other guy was out cold. I didn't know you could use your feet like that in wrestling."

Gary told me to get in the right lane so he could throw the plate out. I waited for the smash but he must have thrown it past the breakdown lane and into the grass. I touched my head where it had been elbowed. I felt a knot just above my eye. A fight in a diner. The classic half nelson had been the only classic thing about it. It had been another ugly display and I was too far from the Hudson River to walk it off.

Gary started recounting the fight, glamorizing it, until it sounded like a movie scene. That was what nonfighters usually did. Guys would approach me on campus and after they complimented me on whatever match I'd won they'd tell me about their own big fight, probably their only fight in life, like that would connect us. They described their heightened moment in all its glory, the same story told over and over, like Gary's new story about the fight in the diner. I shouldn't have been surprised that he kept recounting the fight. My parents would not have been surprised. I never heightened my fight stories. I had been in too many fights, spent too many minutes on the mats, one fight blending into the next, one hold blending into another, one long wrestling match. I never built my stories into myth, making them technicolor, slow motion, exaggerated shit. Only one fight was like that for me. Only one. And after the fight was officially over there was more slow motion. I saw myself getting up from the chair. I saw myself taking off my headgear. I saw myself crossing the lines. Gym floor. Mat. Circle. Mat. Gym floor. I saw myself swinging my headgear at Evan Kessler's face. The technicolor red of blood. The perfectly white tooth flying in a choreographed trajectory. I saw myself grabbing his neck, lifting him out of his chair, picking him up, throwing him down. I saw myself holding a chair and hitting him, slow motion smashing his head in until the weight on my back and the hands on my arms were too much and Evan Kessler's teammates took me down.

The campus police were called and they took me out of the gym in handcuffs. My eye was half closed. My ribs hurt. I tasted blood from my nose. My father had jumped on my grandfather's back to keep him from killing the landlord. The landlord had unfairly raised the rent and my grandfather had gone after him. For the family. Evan Kessler had taken away my dream and I went after him. There was a connection there but it wasn't the same at all. There were no issues of justice or morality or family. I was in the wrong. I had beaten him but I had not beaten him on the mat. Evan Kessler was as far as I could go and I had felt my inferior balance, my inferior strength, my inferior speed. I had to go after him and when I thought about it later, I knew why I'd really done it. If I never wrestled again, I would never have to stay on my stomach for fear of being pinned, losing completely, losing, my dream done, Olympic gold gone, the other guy's hand raised, not mine.

I was kicked off the team immediately. Evan Kessler's coach filed criminal assault and battery charges against me. My parents had to pay a lawyer to get the charges dropped. The college held its own hearing. They let me graduate but didn't let me attend my own graduation. They would send me my diploma. They wanted me off campus as soon as my last final was done.

My dad drove in to pick me up. My things were already packed. We didn't look at each other when we passed, carrying boxes from dorm room to car. It was a long ride home and silent. We pulled into the driveway. He walked into the house. I started unloading the boxes from the trunk. I heard my mother scream. One long scream from the kitchen with no words attached. It was like my scream in the playground when I had been pinned. My parents had been looking forward to the ceremony, to watching their first son marching in the processional with cap and gown, to embracing their first son after the dean handed out the diplomas.

"You were great," Gary said.

"Stop talking about it."

"Why? That was a great fight."

"Just stop."

"What's wrong with you?"

"Time's running out," I said. "I thought you'd tell me when you were ready to tell me, but we'll be there by tonight. How much money do you owe?"

Gary turned his eyes to the road.

"I owe," Gary said.

"How much?"

"I owe a lot," Gary said and his voice was low. "I owe so much that no one wants to take my bets. You can only bet what you don't have for so long. They were going to come after me. They were calling up my dad's house, but he's all tapped out. I wasn't sure how far they'd go. If they'd break my knee or both my knees or worse. I thought if I got to Vegas and got on a streak I could make it all back. I could pay them off and I could pay my dad the money he's paid for me over the years and then I'd be free."

"How much?"

"About a hundred grand."

"About?"

"I owe one hundred thousand."

"Sometimes it's no fun to talk about things."

Gary kept his eyes on the road.

"Are you scared?"

"I am scared," he said.

I noticed again how small his hands were and how the fat started at the wrist and just kept going.

"I have to turn my luck around in Vegas. Monday is when I have to pay up. That's the deadline. That's why I have to get there on Sunday. In case they track me down."

"Do they know where you're going?"

"Not yet. That's why I didn't fly. Who drives to Vegas from New York?"

"Us."

"It's a small world, the gambling world. Everyone knows everyone. I guess you figured out why you're here."

"I guess I did."

"I wasn't wrong about you. I'd heard you were strong. Your dad used to tell me how strong you were. And we're family."

"And that."

"If you don't want to do this I can understand. I won't hold it against you. I'm going to win. I've been studying hard and I'm due for a streak. But if you want me to put you on a plane when we get there, I'll understand."

"I'm in," I said.

I touched the knot above my eye.

"What about you?"

"What?"

"What happened to you?" Gary said.

I looked at the sign. Interstate 70 was coming to an end in ten miles.

"Nothing," I said.

"Something happened. You changed."

"You haven't seen me in over two years."

"That's why I can see the change. Why did you get kicked off the team?"

"One event doesn't change a person."

"One thing leads to another thing leads to another thing. I wouldn't be driving to Vegas if it didn't. You must have done something."

I had told the story too many times to myself. I gave Gary the abridged version. Bold type. Simple pictures. I went after the wrestler who beat me in the semifinals. I picked up a chair and smashed his head in. I was kicked off the team. I lost my scholarship. I got my diploma in the mail. I needed some time to think. I moved to New York. I got a job parking cars.

"You never wrestled after that?"

"Never did."

"You looked in fine form today."

I touched the knot again. The pain was familiar. There was always some pain after a match, more pain after a good match. The knot above my eye didn't count. When Evan Kessler beat me nothing had hurt. I'd stayed on my stomach.

"I could have been a contender."

"Now put a little more feeling into it."

"It's just a bullshit movie line."

"So what? Attach a real experience to it and you'll make the line believable. If you use your own past and put it into the lines, the moment will be real. That's what good acting is all about."

"I could have been a contender," I said.

"Much better. I heard it coming through. Dess Rose. I can see your name in lights right now."

I sped forward. I looked at the signs. Interstate 70 became Interstate 15. Even numbers across. Odd numbers up and down. The highway was freshly paved to make the trip faster, to smooth out any hesitation, to keep the car speeding to Las Vegas.

"I hope the kid got new pancakes," Gary said.

"I hope so."

"His dad sure wasn't a sandwich guy."

I looked at Gary.

"No he wasn't."

15

IT WASN'T EXACTLY LIKE the movies but with the lack of sleep and the desire to get there and the darkness of desert miles it was close. The winter seemed to break as soon as we went over a hump of mountains. The air that had been cool coming in from Gary's window turned warm. And then it was in front of us. Las Vegas. All lit up and someplace to go, the place we were going, the getting there gone. One long strip of lights and from the center of that line the lights separated into the outskirts of town, then separated more into the desert. As we approached, the strip became more defined, colors more distinct, the outline of tall buildings with flashing lights a row of beacons calling us in from a far-off shore and like a couple of sailors we were pulling into port with big dreams or at least Gary was. It wasn't yet midnight. We'd made it by Sunday. Almost twenty-six hundred miles. I leaned back in the seat and watched the lights come closer and Gary started to point out the casinos, naming the names.

It was one of those moments and in feeling high I felt how low I'd been lately. The lights were beautiful. I already knew that the view would change up close like zooming in on a seemingly flawless face but while we drove closer I tried to just concentrate on the lights illuminating this piece of desert and it really did look like an oasis. Lights instead of palms. Casinos instead of water. A stewardess I met at a bar described to me what it was like flying into Las Vegas at night, jetting through miles of sky and then seeing the strip. I pretended we were flying. It wasn't that hard. It wasn't much different from what the stewardess had described before she took me to her hotel room.

My garage suit chafed my skin. I was overtired. I didn't want to stand on line at a buffet. I didn't want to stand behind Gary at a table. I wanted to stay in the passenger seat with Gary driving to the lights but never getting there. I wanted the lights to remain at a distance where they stayed beautiful.

Gary wanted to start playing right away. He'd seen these lights many times and to him they were just casino lights. I didn't know how many hours Gary could gamble but I guessed his stamina would be good. He was a Rose. For hours on end my grandfather had breathed in the mattress feathers that filled the room until his lungs were coated. I pictured his two lungs, covered with white feathers like a pair of angel's wings inside. My father had stamina in his own way. When I came home from school, he'd be upstairs in his study correcting tests, marking papers, working on his books about economic theory of which I knew nothing but saw in the hands of students as they walked across campus. They were reading my father's words. That was more than I had ever done. Whenever a new book came out, he'd inscribe one to each of us. I'd open the cover and see To Dess. With Love, Dad. Then I'd close the cover and put the book on the shelf. He knew it but he never said anything. It wouldn't have hurt me to read a chapter and tell him I'd enjoyed what he'd written even if I didn't understand it.

Gary drove. The lights became names. We were Roses. That was why I was here. The color of love. The color of bravery. The color of anger. The color of blood.

The road widened. Smooth like a runway. We were landing. A neon sign advertised the best slots in town. Yellow. Blue. Red. A lemon. A plum. Not a rose but a cherry.

16

WE HAD NEVER BEEN valets. Lou with his slicked-back hair, grease under the nails from fixing cars on weekends or Berger cursing the world, standing away from the time clock so he wouldn't hear the minutes punching out or me killing my own time. The guy who opened Gary's door was a valet. No one-piece uniform but nice slacks, a cotton sport shirt with a collar, embroidered B for Bally's. He politely held the door handle at attention like a military man awaiting at-ease orders while General Gary worked himself out of the car. I got out and shut my own door.

Gary handed the valet a twenty, out of tipping etiquette, money shown before instead of after when the car was picked up. The valet smiled.

"You guys drive in from New York?"

Maybe he checked off license plates to pass the time.

"All the way," Gary said.

"I was there last New Year's eve. We went up to see the ball drop. Talk about a crazy city."

"We used to go to Times Square with liquor," Gary said. "We'd buy small bottles of blackberry brandy, tequila, vodka and line our pockets with them. There's no place to go drinking when you're stuck in Times Square. We sold the bottles at a five hundred percent mark up and the drinkers would thank us for ripping them off. Supply and demand at its finest."

"So you were the guy."

"Listen, do me a favor and park my car close to the entrance. I'll be doing a lot of driving in and out."

"Whatever you want," the valet said, the money already talking in Las Vegas. "I'll put it on the first level, right near the exit."

"Good man," Gary said.

I watched the valet get into the Jaguar to see if his moves were any different. They weren't except that the ramp in New York went down and his ramp went up. Gary worked another set of keys out of his pocket and threw them to me.

"I believe you're quicker on your feet in case we need to make a speedy exit. You hungry?"

"Just tired."

"You'll wake up," Gary said. "They pump fresh oxygen through the casinos to keep the players playing. Your lungs won't know what hit them after breathing all that city smog. We'll win some dinner, eat and get to work."

"If you get tired we're calling it a night."

"Just keep the count and if I nod off then we'll find a place to stay. Maybe we'll get comped. You ready to start counting for real?"

"One, two, three."

"Great."

I knew how to count. I knew how to play each hand, at

least on the most basic level. We had decided that I would stand behind Gary with my hand on top of his chair. I would wedge my fingers between the chair and Gary's wide stretch of back to keep them hidden. When the count went to plus four, I would press my finger once into his back. When the count went to plus six, I'd press my finger twice. Plus eight, I'd press three times and he would start to bet heavy. On the minus counts, I'd rub my finger across his back like a minus sign. Once for minus four. Twice for minus six. Three times for minus eight. I was ready.

We went through the revolving doors and it was like being punched. A cartoon punch where the visual aftereffects, whistling birds or glittering stars, covered the pain. The casino right in the face. Cool air, bells going off, shouts, people playing, passing through, some dressed for a night on the town, some in sweats, cocktail waitresses in miniskirts and low-cut tops to show maximum cleavage, lights all over the place, too close. There were rows of slot machines, lights flashing, bells ringing, people sitting on stools feeding quarters to the one-armed bandits, pulling for the big jackpot that increased a dollar a second, digitally, lit up for all to see on a flashing sign while a brand-new Camaro rotated under it, part of the jackpot, thrown in for good measure to drive those bags of money home in luxury. Past the slots were the craps tables, players shouting for good rolls, stick men scooping dice. Past them were the blackjack tables, the players signaling with fingers against green felt whether they wanted a card or not, hit or stick.

Gary stopped at a ten-dollar-minimum table. The dealer finished the hand, removed the losers' chips, paid off the winners. Gary pulled out a wad of bills from his left front pocket and put a fifty-dollar bill flat on the table. The dealer called out Check change for the pit boss to come over and see the transaction but for fifty dollars the call was only a formality, check change for chump change. The dealer counted out ten five-dollar chips, slid them over to Gary, put the fifty-dollar bill into the slot. I pictured an elaborate tunnel system funneling all those bills to some underground vault built deep in the desert sand. Gary finished squeezing himself into the seat and put two chips in the circle in front of him. He turned to me, quietly told me not to bother counting this one, this was just for dinner, something he always did, something he'd done the first time he went to a casino, a little tradition. He said he'd never lost his meal ticket yet. I watched the dealer's manicured hands move clockwise around the table. He slid the cards into place, faceup for each player. The dealer put his own first card facedown and then he dealt around again and put his second card up, an eight. Gary had two pictures. Ten plus ten. A colorful gift of twenty. The dealer went around the table, didn't even bother asking Gary to signal whether he wanted a card or not. The dealer turned his bottom card over for all to see. A ten. He had to stick at seventeen or over. House rules. The dealer had eighteen. Gary had twenty.

"Easy money," Gary said.

The count for the table was plus two. I had done it automatically, two cards at a time. The dealer paid off the winners, gave Gary two new chips. He was up ten dollars. I did some quick math of my own. He only had to win ten dollars less than what he owed. Gary let the bet ride, stacked the two chips he'd won on his original two chips. The dealer dealt. Gary got a nine and a ten. Nineteen. The dealer busted after he had to pull on fifteen. The count was even. Gary let the bet ride again, added the chips to the pile. He won again. Gary was up seventy bucks. He picked up the chips, handed them to me, worked himself out of the seat and I followed him to the cashier's window. It was true what they said about chips. They felt great. It was the greatest single idea the casinos ever came up with to separate a man from his money. Colorful, smooth discs with a nice weight to them displayed in generous stacks at every table. It wasn't flimsy paper with serious green ink. The red chips, smooth against my palm, clicking against each other in a comforting way, promised a chance to win all night and all day and wasn't this better than working a real job for a living. I followed Gary past the craps tables which were packed and loud and past the bells and lights of the slot machines to the cashier's window, all winners here, all in a line. I gave Gary the chips and he put them on the marble counter. The cashier pulled the chips behind the protective glass. She unstacked the chips in stacks of five, stacked them back together, click, click, one short stack, announced seventy bucks and handed over the crispest fifty and twenty I'd ever seen. Gary kept the original chips he had bought in his shirt pocket. I guessed that was another little tradition.

"Food on the house," Gary said.

"It's your money now."

"Thanks. I'm glad you were listening. But we have to eat."

"Is this where you always gamble?"

"I've been here a couple of times. Usually I go to the MGM, but I'm not going there tonight. They don't know me here except at the buffet line."

"I see."

"I can't exactly go undercover. A false mustache or dark sunglasses won't hide me too well."

We took the escalator to the Bally's buffet. They were still serving. The hostess showed us our seats and I followed Gary to the buffet line. He picked up two plates. I picked up one. The slicing station was first. Roast beef with gravy. Roast turkey. Liver steaks wrapped in bacon. Barbecued chicken. Chafing dishes full of stuffing, mashed potatoes, boiled potatoes, potatoes au gratin, the cheese bubbling on top. The man slicing the roast beef lit up when he saw Gary, asked how everything was, asked how long he was in town for, didn't need to ask what Gary needed. The man sliced off a hunk of meat three inches thick, forked it onto Gary's plate, ladled on the au jus sauce. For the second plate, the carver sliced off a giant turkey drumstick and plenty of white meat, soaked it in turkey gravy with giblets. Gary followed the man to the chafing dishes, the blue flames from the sternos underneath gyrating as if they were magnetized. The carver spooned over a pile of stuffing and a pile of mashed. Gary tipped him twenty bucks. The carver said it was good to see Gary and wished him good luck. I asked for a piece of white turkey meat. When the slicer dipped the ladle into the gravy dish I told him No thanks. Gary was loading up his turkey plate with coleslaw, cranberry sauce, cold potato salad. He walked over to the seafood section and lined shrimp around the roast beef, doled horseradish sauce into the beef gravy, the biggest surf and turf ever created right before my eyes. I put some salad on my plate. There were dressing dispensers. Thousand Island. French. Italian. Spicy Italian. Diet Italian. Blue cheese. I swallowed and turned away. Gary's wide back was moving through the dining room to our table. He put the plates down, sat down, started separating the shrimp from their tails with his teeth. A waiter came over and Gary ordered two Cokes. I ordered one. I hoped the caffeine would wake me up.

"You don't like shrimp? The dipping sauce is great."

"I'm just not in the mood."

"You don't have to be in the mood. You just have to take as much as you want."

Gluttony Las Vegas style. I picked at the salad. I ate some of the too salty turkey. A drop of gravy spotted the edge of my plate, brown and pasty, already cooling and congealing. I remembered the cold grilled cheese sandwiches Gary had helped us eat. I remembered another time my brother and I went to an all-you-can-eat pizza place when he visited me in college. Everyone on line was talking about how much they were going to stuff their faces. The record was twenty-one slices. It was foolish competition but we couldn't help getting sucked in and by the time we were at the front of the line, ready to be seated, Derek and I had set up our own who-can-eat-most contest. The winner was allowed to puke. It was Derek's idea. It was almost summer and wrestling season was over. It had been a good freshman year. I had won all but two of my matches and the matches I lost I had lost to seniors, one by two points and one by disqualification. I was happy to compete with Derek in a physical contest I could win. The first slices tasted good. The fifth and sixth slices tasted less good. I had starved myself too long and my stomach was not ready to accept slice upon slice of pizza. On the eleventh slice, the food started coming up in my throat. Derek smiled. He asked me if I was done. I told him I didn't know yet. He waited a minute. He asked if I was done. I looked at my half eaten slice and told him I was done. It was just pizza. It wasn't the Hand Game. I thought about squeezing him until he puked. Derek finished his slice and raised his plate in victory. The group that had stood in back of us let out a cheer and Derek bowed for them. Derek was the expert eater like he had been the expert guesser when we were kids. My mom and dad would ask us to guess the time or the temperature or the number of miles we had driven and Derek almost always won and sometimes he guessed exactly right. He would say he was the expert guesser, the extra expert guesser, and I couldn't wait to start playing Sides so I could smash his head in.

Gary polished off both plates and headed for the Chinese food station. He returned with plates piled high with fried eggrolls and spring rolls and beef filled dumplings, sweet-and-sour spareribs, slices of pork that were so red around the edges they practically glowed, steaming fried rice, some kind of sesame looking chicken and another chicken dish smothered with cashew nuts. On the other plate he had lo mein, beef with broccoli, beef with peppers and onions, shrimp in lobster sauce. The waiter brought two more Cokes.

Gary finished everything and left a twenty-dollar tip. We took the escalator down to the casino.

I didn't know how long we had played until we walked away from the tables for the night, went to the registration desk and I saw the time. We'd been playing for four hours and Gary had played the hands perfectly. I had counted the cards perfectly. The count stayed high at the end of most shoes and Gary had upped his bets, placed stacks of green twenty-five-dollar chips in the circle, then stacks of black hundred-dollar chips, winning most double downs, winning most splits, getting blackjacks, perfect twenty-ones, ace and a ten or ace and a picture, any picture, the hand that paid off the bet plus a half, a buck fifty for every buck bet and Gary was betting more than a buck. At one point a man in a Bally's suit had come over to ask Gary where he was staying. Gary said the MGM but he didn't love the room there. The man said Bally's would be happy to accommodate him. Gary said he'd need a room with two king-size beds, preferably a high floor with a view since his friend had never been to Vegas before. The man asked Gary his name and Gary said Gary Dess, his first name first, my first name last. Just in case. The man told Mr. Dess to check in at the front desk whenever it was convenient and the room would be ready. Gary thanked the man and went back to playing until he'd won over ten thousand dollars. Then the trip hit us. Three days of almost constant driving pressed our eyelids down like a slow but mighty wrestler. I had helped Gary carry the black chips to the cashier's window. I looked at the money and the chips behind the bulletproof glass and saw there was no competition. The house had it all. Gary put the stack of crisp bills in his left pocket.

"You have enough room in there?"

"These are even bigger than fat-people pockets. I have a tailor at home sew them in special. They're my casino pants. My money is down so deep a pickpocket would need twelve-inch fingers to stand a chance."

At the front desk the woman's name tag read JANET and under that TOPEKA, KANSAS.

"We were just in Kansas," Gary said. "Great state."

Gary had slept through most of it but he was in a just-won mood. She handed over the card for the door and asked if I would need a separate key. Gary said I would.

"We were hoping to see a twister," Gary said.

"You don't want to see a twister. They look amazing from a distance, but when they get too close they're trouble."

"Kind of like this place," I said.

"You don't like Las Vegas?"

"He'll warm up to it," Gary said. "We've been on the road for days and once he gets a full night's sleep he'll be a new man with a new attitude."

"Enjoy your stay at Bally's," Janet said.

We walked outside to where the valets were standing around in the dry desert darkness. It would be morning soon and a new shift would come on. Gary showed his room card and parking ticket and said he wanted the bags in the trunk brought up.

We took the elevator to the twenty-fourth floor. It was a big room with two king-size beds as promised. I pulled back the curtains and looked out on the strip. I could see where we had come in, not the road but the direction. I stayed in front of the window, happy to just stand and look before I crashed, knowing I would be able to sleep soon. I blurred my eyes to make all the lights go out of focus. It had been a full day. A full three days.

I could hear him pressing the phone numbers behind me. He said Hey, Mike, and asked Mike if he'd heard anything. He asked him how the dogs were doing and told him not to forget to walk them like he was talking to a kid. He told Mike we were staying at Bally's under the name Gary Dess and that he should call if anything came up. He paused and said Whatever, tell them I went to get takeout. I knew he meant his parents. He said he'd had a great night, won almost eleven grand. I heard him hang up the phone.

"I didn't know you had a roommate."

"He pays half the rent. He's not a bad guy, just a little dim sometimes. We had a giant parrot. This big beautiful bird I taught to say Eat me. I went away for a week and Mike forgot to feed the thing and it died. You have to feed birds every day."

"You think your dogs will make it?"

"I've got two gigantic Great Danes. If they get hungry enough they'll go after Mike and eat him for dinner."

I dove onto the bed like Derek and I had done when we were kids, when my family was on the road. Hotel beds became trampolines until my parents told us to cut the roughhousing. I stretched out, closed my eyes, let all my weight settle onto the mattress. I hadn't been horizontal for days. Someone knocked on the door. I stood up, squared my feet, waited. Gary opened the door. It was the bellboy delivering our bags. I sat down on the bed. Gary tipped the bellboy and the bellboy asked if we needed anything and Gary said One hundred grand like he was joking. The bellboy laughed, wished us good luck, closed the door behind him. Gary took his clothes off and threw them on the floor. There were stretch marks on his shoulders, across his chest and stretch marks I had never seen before, wide red streaks like welts, on his hips and on the sides of his thighs. His underwear hardly covered his ass, the crack a canyon when he bent over to take off his socks. His feet were raw, his toes curved and blistered from carrying all that weight. A body like that could not last very long. I couldn't picture Gary smiling when he was naked. He went into the bathroom and I waited for the water to come on.

I called my parents. They asked how much snow we were getting and I said it wasn't bad, just a little slushy. They asked if anything was new and I said Not really. They asked if I'd done anything over the weekend. I told them I'd hung out, taken a couple of runs. My mom asked how I could run in this weather and I said it was easier running when it snowed. It was distracting and I didn't get as tired. They said Derek was almost done with finals and that he'd received an A on a term paper. I felt my muscles filling with blood. I told them I'd be home in about a week, right before the holidays, but that I hadn't checked the exact train schedules yet. They said I love you and I said I love you and we said good-bye.

I called Derek. He picked up on the fourth ring. I told him I didn't realize his dorm room was so big and he said Harvard only let their students live in palaces. He asked why I was calling so early on a Monday morning and I said it was earlier where I was. I told Derek I was in Las Vegas. I told him Gary owed some money and needed to make some money fast and needed someone along for the ride he could trust. I purposely didn't use the word protection. He was still my younger brother no matter how much older he sometimes seemed. He had probably guessed the truth anyway. Derek asked about my job at the garage. I told him I'd lost it. He said Mom and Dad would be very upset about that. I told him Mom and Dad didn't know where I was and to keep it that way. Derek said it made sense that Gary had put his trust in me. I didn't like the way he said it. I asked what he meant. He said Gary must be in real trouble. I told Derek to shut the fuck up and not worry about it, that he didn't know shit about anything except school. Derek said he'd given up worrying about me. He said he wished Mom and Dad would give up too, that every time they spoke they mentioned me and how concerned they were about my life. I told him I was sick of hearing about him, how he was a little pussy who could do no wrong, how Harvard wouldn't protect him when I beat the shit out of him one day. Derek didn't say anything to that. He just kept quiet so my words would stay there, so I could hear how stupid I sounded. I took a breath. I told Derek I was tired. I told him we'd driven across country in three days and I'd been thinking about Sides and how he used to say he was the extra expert guesser. Derek said Those were good days. I asked how his finals were going and he said he just had one more. Macroeconomics. He'd read Dad's book and it was excellent.

The water went off. I told Derek I'd see him soon. Derek's voice got serious and he told me to be careful. I said I would. He asked if there was anything he could do for me and I told him No, that I wasn't really sure what was going on, that I wasn't really sure what I was doing. I wished him luck on his final final. He told me to call if I needed anything. He told me to say hello to Gary and we said good-bye.

The towel wrapped around Gary's waist didn't fit. He had to hold it together in back. His breasts were red from the water or maybe it was all that orange shrimp, pork, and neon coming through. I unzipped my garage suit and left it on the floor, took off my socks and underwear that felt stuck to my skin. Gary looked me over to see what kind of shape I was in. I stood there to reassure him like I sometimes stood in front of the women I picked up to let them know they'd made the right choice. Like I stood, with only the slim covering of my wrestling suit, in front of my opponents to show them how confident I was, keeping my arms loose, keeping my shoulders relaxed while pushing them slightly forward to bring out the thickness in my neck, and all the time I kept my eyes hard, showing nothing. I was in good-looking shape. I needed to take a few runs to get all my wind back. I went into the bathroom and turned the shower on, stepped in. I made the water as hot as I could take it. I stood under the hot water and let all my muscles relax, soaped myself down once and twice to take the miles off me, washed my hair twice and then I stayed under the water until I almost fell asleep.

I dried myself off. I brushed my teeth. I smoothed away a clear space on the steamed mirror to see my face. There were circles under my eyes and my eyes were red and there was the knot above my eye. I stuck out my tongue. It was white and dehydrated. Gary was already snoring, his giant body under the sheet, the covers thrown to the floor, half covering his pants with the deep left pocket. I stepped over my garage suit. I shut the lights and got into bed. It felt good to be naked against the stiff sheets, the warm blanket over them, my head on a pillow instead of a jacket, still instead of moving.

17

PLUS ONE. PLUS TWO. Plus three. Plus four. Press. Plus five. Plus six. Press. Press. My hand on top of the seat, my fingers wedged under Gary's back. I kept the count. When the count went up I pressed my finger into Gary's back. When the count went down I rubbed my finger across in a minus sign. The pit bosses came and watched and went. There was the fat guy and the guy standing behind the fat guy. I knew there were cameras above us. I kept my finger movements slight and hidden and Gary's fat blocked the overhead view. My finger pressed into the fat and the fat covered it. The count went up, my finger pressed. The count went down, my finger rubbed. It was a rhythm against the same space on Gary's back over and over, breaking up the fat. It went on and on. A player's finger scratched on the felt table meant hit. Another card needed. A player's hand waved across the chips meant stick. No more cards. Gary's small hands played with the chips, separated them into piles. He was doing subtraction, how much owed minus how much won. The dealer shuffled the cards, the yellow cut card thrown out, picked up by a player, inserted, the cards cut, the cards fit into the shoe, the dealer's manicured hand sliding across the top edges to keep them even and firm, tight against each other. New shoes. New cards. New counts. Dealer after dealer after dealer. Players came. Players went. On the upswing it looked like a foolproof system. Gary's small hands caressed the chips, stacked them into a magical castle of different colored turrets. On the downswing the towers crumbled, hundred-dollar black chips traded into twenty-five-dollar greens, greens into five-dollar reds. Time passed but not like time on the outside where the sun rose and fell, where clocks told the time on church steeples, town hall facades, digital news ribbons, punch clocks outside garages. There wasn't a clock in the casino. The lights were on twenty-four hours a day. It was its own world. Always on. Always going. The play constant. A movie shot to show the passage of time wouldn't work in a casino, no fast-forwarding clock hands, no sun rising and setting in superspeed motion. The day went on and on and on. One long day. One long play. Outside time moved. Outside Sunday had passed. Outside Gary owed. Inside it felt like he could sit at the table forever and I forced myself to focus, forced myself to count. We played on, Gary's stamina good, great, his answer to almost every question, Great, I'm doing great, Things are great, Sure, Sure, Great, his wide back stretching into sameness, the material on his shirt going on. I had to look away, stay with the cards, focus on the cards, count the cards, count perfect, play perfect. Press. Press. Rub. Rub. When I closed my eyes to rest between shoes the cards kept coming like the road had kept coming, the curve of the highway across America now the curve of the table, a cut circle of green felt. Easy money. Hard money. Working. I had to work. Flipping mattresses with feathers flying blocking out the daylight or the evening light, New York City streets too bright even then for stars to come through and the feathers all around like a shake-up toy that starts the snow going, all those feathers, all those mattresses, all that weight, working and working, my grandfather working to pay food, pay rent, for the family, for his boys, my dad, Gary's dad, my dad keeping it going for his own boys. Plus, press. Minus, rub. Work. Why my grandfather had come over. Here's your documentation, here's where to sign your name, here's the ferry to the city, get out, make what you can, the hand of the Statue of Liberty not waving the way it looked from a distance but holding a torch, a beacon of light to come to, now there, too close, the torch can burn, the streets of gold just pavement, the land of milk and honey just the city, walking the streets, a hand in the pocket, going to work, strong hands, strong hands from wrestling, strong hands to pick up the landlord and throw him down the incinerator, for the family, strong hands to flip mattresses, stuff them, pull the long needle through heavy material until hands are pricked and punctured, skin healed harder than a mattress cover over muscle and bone, strong hands passed down and down again, my strong hands, fingers pressing into fat, cramping up, hours and hours wedged between chair and back, nothing compared to flipping mattresses years and years, nothing compared to that, staying on my stomach to keep from getting pinned, from losing that way, not man enough to lose completely and take that, keep it in, going after the one who beat me with a chair in my hands passed down from him. A new hand. A new shoe. The yellow cut card passed to Gary. He cut.

18

I WASN'T SURE WHAT time it was. It was Tuesday. I had stayed in
bed while Gary called the front desk, asked for a wake-up call
in half an hour, told me to meet him in front of the elevators.
He stuck his fist over his mouth and pretended to play the bu-
gle. I pulled my head under the covers to avoid the sound and
the spray. Gary walked over, put his mouth against the blanket
where my head was, told me to rise and shine, get my ass out of
bed when the wake-up call came or else he'd come up and wake
me less gently.

He was up twelve thousand dollars. We were at a hundred-
dollar-minimum table and Gary was playing two hands at a
time. There were no other players. Just Gary. Me behind him.
The pit boss watching the dealer. My finger was doing a lot of
pressing. He was past the Monday deadline but so far nothing
had happened. He wanted to make the money as soon as he
could, drive back to New York, pay what he owed. It was close
to the end of the shoe and the picture cards, the tens, had to

start coming out. Gary put down a thousand dollars on each hand. He drew a four and a six on one hand, a ten and an ace on the next. Blackjack. The dealer's up card was a five. The dealer paid off the blackjack, odds and a half, fifteen hundred dollars. Gary doubled down on the six and four, drew a king for a twenty. The dealer flipped his bottom card. A jack. Fifteen. House rules said he had to take a card. Another jack. Bust. The dealer slid two thousand dollars to Gary.

Gary clicked the chips against each other, then stacked them up. Their sound was pleasing. Their texture was pleasing. The count was plus seven. I pressed Gary twice. He pulled apart the stack and bet two thousand on each hand.

The dealer dealt. Gary got twenty on the first. Eighteen on the second. The dealer flipped his bottom card. He had nineteen. The dealer slid two thousand dollars to the twenty, pulled two thousand dollars from the eighteen. The count was plus three. Gary bet two thousand dollars. He got a blackjack on the first. Twenty on the second. Easy money. When the shoe ran out, Gary stood up and filled his left pocket with eight thousand dollars worth of chips. He was up over twenty thousand dollars.

"Finally," Gary said. "It's been a struggle since the first night. All we need is a streak, a real streak."

"That was a streak."

"You can feel a real streak. That was just a few good hands in a row. I was starting to fade. I was betting too much and I have to stay smart."

"Let's take a nap."

"No time. We'll eat something."

He looked tired standing there with his hand on the seat for support. The pit boss had moved two tables down.

"You have a quarter?" I said. "I want to try a slot machine."

"Don't do it."

"It's just a quarter."

"Famous last words. It's a sucker's game. They're rigged to pay off ninety percent, give or take a couple fractions. You put in a buck, you make back ninety cents. You put in ninety cents you make back eighty-one."

"What about a quarter?"

"Twenty-two and a half cents."

"Good job."

"I'm quick with the figures."

"Maybe you should pick up one of those CPA applications my dad sent you."

"Maybe I should. Maybe I should fast today. Only water and fried foods."

Gary gave me a quarter. I walked over to one of the slot machines polished silver to pick up the light. I looked at the list of payoffs on top. The maximum payoff for five quarters was five hundred dollars. The most I could win for one quarter was one hundred dollars. The least I could win was two quarters. I put the quarter in the slot, pulled the lever. It had a nice weight to it. The fruit spun and clicked into place. An orange. A lemon. A bar. The least I could win was nothing.

"Nothing for the bar?"

"You want another quarter?"

"I just wanted to see what it felt like."

'How did it feel?"

"It felt like I lost."

A machine behind me started paying off coins. There was always some ringing in the distance, a jingle-bell promise in the air. I followed Gary to the cashier's window. He was given crisp one-hundred-dollar bills. Eighty-three of them. I could have lived for six months on that, figured some things out maybe, or maybe I just would have killed more time.

The bathroom attendant was glad to see us. He was an old man with greased-back hair and a thin neck that didn't fill his collar. He smelled too sweet. I couldn't blame him for that. He asked how the day was treating us and Gary said Great. I took a piss. Gary worked to piss next to me. I washed my hands and looked at my face in the mirror. The knot above my eye had turned into a small bruise. The purple highlighted how pale and tired I looked. I was in the middle of the desert and my skin was not dark like it got in the sun, like waiting outside for the cars to come in, the construction workers not the only ones to get the first tans of the season. I told my dad that garage work couldn't be all bad if I looked good at the end of a day. The bathroom attendant held a paper towel in his manicured hand for my dripping hands. The attendant called me son, asked how I was doing today, son. I said I was fine. He asked if I wanted some cologne. I said No thanks. The attendant pulled a fresh towel from the dispenser and handed it to Gary with a flourish. He knew where the money came from. Gary let out a loud fart.

"Are we a little gassy today, sir?"

"We're always a little gassy," Gary said. "If it was helium I'd be a float in the Macy's Thanksgiving Parade."

"That's a good one, sir. That's one of the better ones I've heard."

"You must hear all kinds," Gary said.

"Yes we do. That's one of the benefits of the job. People come in here to freshen up and they start talking."

"Any celebrities?"

"I don't like to name names. An attendant has to learn to be confidential. For instance, you wouldn't want me telling your boss about that flatulence you just let go."

"I'm my own boss," Gary said. "I know exactly how much I fart."

"We've had plenty of celebrities visit us. Movie stars. Television stars. Politicians. Athletes."

"Any gangsters?"

"Confidentially speaking, yes we have, sir."

The attendant seemed proud. He passed the day keeping the bathroom clean, wiping up water spots, arranging colognes, replenishing mints and listening to the confidences of famous people while they pissed and shit between bets. I took a mint, unwrapped it, put the plastic wrapper in my pocket before the attendant stuck his outstretched hand in front of me.

"Any of the old-time gangsters? The guys they make movies about?" Gary said.

"My old man worked as an attendant right here in Vegas. One night he comes home and tells us we're not going to believe who came by. Bugsy Siegel. He had his own private washroom in the casino so my old man never saw him, but on this particular day he used the public washroom. He was a very good looker, Bugsy Siegel, and my old man spotted him right away. Mr. Siegel does his business and my old man takes care of him and Mr. Siegel drops a fifty spot in the basket, which in those days was a heck of a lot of money. They get to talking and it turns out Mr. Siegel's in a very good mood. A high roller had come in and won a lot of money at the craps table, but it so happens this same fellow was a big wine drinker. Mr. Siegel, he put two and two together. He tells the fellow the casino just received a shipment of fine wine and if he waits half an hour he'll have his workers in the dining room pack up a few bottles for the trip home to help him celebrate his good fortune. The fellow says that's a swell gesture and since he doesn't have anything else to do for the half hour, he goes back to the craps table and starts rolling. By the time the wine arrives, the fellow has given all his winnings back to the casino and then some and the only thing Bugsy Siegel lost was a couple of bottles of wine. Do you know what the kicker is? He told my old man that the wine wasn't even that good."

"I'm glad I don't drink," Gary said.

"Mr. Siegel was gunned down a couple months later. You meet all kinds in here."

Gary took a mint, put the wrapper in the attendant's open hand, took fifty dollars from the roll he kept in his shirt pocket, tip money for the cocktail waitresses and buffet workers, and put the bills in the attendant's tray. The attendant looked at the money, smiled.

"You're a class act, sir."

"Just like old times," Gary said.

The attendant wished us good luck and we went back to the casino floor.

"How's about a little walk?" I said. "A little exercise before we eat?"

"You feeling out of shape already?"

"Come on."

I spread my feet on the thick casino carpet, crouched, wrestling match ready.

"Don't let me get a hold of you," Gary said. "If I pin you, they'll have to scrape you off the floor."

Outside everything seemed muted. The door closed and

only then did I realize how bright the flashing lights were inside, how loud the gambling sounds. There was traffic on the strip but the car engines were quiet by comparison. The sun washed out the colors of the passing cars and the row of casinos.

We walked along the strip. Gary's fat body moved as much side to side as forward, his feet angled to support his weight, his thighs rubbing together, breathing heavy. I kept two feet between us as we walked so he wouldn't keep bumping into my arm. There weren't many people on the sidewalk and it felt good just to be outside. We walked past a row of shops selling tacky trinkets with racks of postcards in front. Pictures of half-naked women standing in front of slot machines, pulling at the one-armed bandits, legs poised midair in exaggerated excitement. Pictures of the different casinos lit up on the strip. Pictures of the surrounding sights. Grand Canyon. Hoover Dam. Death Valley. We walked by the New York, New York casino, a horrible imitation of the city, the Empire State Building looking out of proportion, the point of the Chrysler too short, the Statue of Liberty painted the wrong shade of green.

The lion head in front of the MGM casino was impressive. The symbol seen roaring live on the films they produced was painted gold and royal green, its eyes dead looking. It was where Gary usually played but was afraid to play now. A large poster by the entrance advertised an upcoming fight. Two boxers wearing championship belts with arms folded across muscular chests scowled at each other. Wrestlers never received the money or the publicity that boxers did, not real wrestlers. I had cut short an already short career. Gary said we had to get back to the tables soon. He said we needed to get on a real streak.

"It's hard work," I said.

"It's felt that way."

"How did you get into this hole?"

"I made some bad bets."

"When your dad used to bail you out, didn't he tell you to stop gambling?"

Gary's swinging arm touched my side.

"My dad was up at seven every morning for forty years. He ended up making a decent living, but if that was the American dream I wanted no part of it. One of my frat brothers introduced me to this and I was hooked. Look around you. It's growing every day. Casinos are shooting up like cactus."

"They're ugly in the daylight."

"I'd rather be here than working like a slave in some office."

"You're working like a slave here. You've got nothing to show for your work."

"Right now I have nothing to show, but I've had plenty. More than plenty. You used to love my stories of gambling."

"I was a kid. We were kids."

"I was practically a kid when I started. I had no responsibilities except to go to class and I didn't even do that. All I had to do was call up a bookie, place a bet and if I bet right the money came in. I was betting right most of the time then. I always loved sports anyway. I didn't mind studying the sports pages, crunching those numbers, watching the games on TV."

"My parents used to hate all those phone calls you made when you came over."

"I know," Gary said.

Gary breathed heavy. He wiped his sleeve against his forehead and it came away wet.

"It's all I can do," Gary said.

"That's not true."

"Sure it is. I'm not cut out for office work. I'm not going to sit in some cubicle talking small talk and kissing some boss's ass. They don't make suits big enough for me."

"Your boss won't break your legs if you fuck up."

"No one's breaking anybody's legs. I'll make the money back."

"What if you don't?"

"I will. I have to. That's motivation. That's my motivation. I have to win. It's a real need. Method acting at its finest. I need to keep my knees intact."

"I'm serious."

"I'm serious too. They rely on people like me to mess up and I messed up. I also know I can't do anything else. I'm a gambler."

"You could do other things."

"We all could do other things. I like walking into a room and people knowing that I do something out of the ordinary. I like being treated nicely when I walk into a casino. Is your room okay, Mr. Rose? Can we get you something to drink, Mr. Rose? Would you like some cologne, Mr. Rose? That's a beautiful looking car, Mr. Rose."

"It's not your car."

"Look. It's what I do. I've lived a long time making money this way. I never had to be some poor loser working my ass off for nothing. I'd rather lose it all than do that. You ever look closely at these people? The dealers. They're bored out of their fucking skulls. The pit bosses. They might as well be in an office counting money. The cocktail waitresses. They hate being subservient. And for my money, they're still better off than office workers. Why do you think I tip so well? It's my way of saying keep on going if that's all you can do. I know they hate their jobs and when they get a good tip it makes their burden a little easier."

"What about your burden?"

"Usually I don't have any burdens. I'm a free man."

"You pretend you're free."

"You sound like your dad."

"Maybe that's not such a bad thing."

"I'm going to win."

"You might win."

"I'll win. I always get the money somehow. All I need is a real streak."

"There are other jobs besides working in a cubicle. You don't have to hate what you do."

"And what career are you going to pursue? Without a gold medal you're not going to get your pretty face on a Wheaties box."

"I'll figure something out."

"I hope you do."

"Thanks."

"I mean it. You're a good kid. A good man."

"Not that good."

"No one's that good."

"Maybe we could do something together."

"Let's do this together first."

We walked on. I was looking at the pavement. Gary bumped into my arm. I looked at him and he was looking straight ahead like he had looked in the car. He was under more pressure than any worker I knew and getting fired was nothing next to this. I didn't know what I wanted but it wasn't this. There was a giant pyramid on our right with a blue and gold sphinx in front and palm trees strung with tacky Christmas lights. Las Vegas in all its glory.

"What's that one?" I said.

"The Luxor. Can you guess the motif?"

"Give me a minute."

We turned and walked back past the MGM, past New York, New York.

"What about this Denny's?" Gary said.

"As long as it's not a buffet."

We went into Denny's, stood in front of the PLEASE WAIT TO BE SEATED sign, followed a hostess past the booths to a table where Gary would have more room. There were a lot of families in the restaurant. Gary looked over the menu and started to spin the ketchup bottle.

She was beautiful, even in her awful uniform, pad at the ready, asking us what we'd like to order as if she cared. Her name tag read HI MY NAME IS and underneath in pen TIA. Gary ordered a cheeseburger deluxe, a grilled cheese with bacon deluxe, two Cokes. I ordered a tuna sandwich on whole wheat. I waited just so I could hear her voice ask what I'd like to drink. I said water would be fine.

"Do the deluxes come with coffee or Tia?" Gary said.

"Neither. They don't even come with the two Cokes you ordered. Beverages are a separate charge."

"No offense. Just making small talk."

"You're a very clever man."

"I like this girl. Service without a smile. Happy with her job."

"Tell me when you're done so I can place your order."

"Do you know what happened to the last waitress who tried to crucify me? My cousin here had to take care of her. He just about ended her restaurant career."

"Is that right?"

She looked at me. She had great eyes and I wasn't even an eye man. Blue eyes with bursts of gray in them. Moody eyes but clear at the same time. I looked at her and she kept her eyes on mine and I narrowed my eyes the way I did when I was in a bar and saw the girl I wanted. She looked away and back at Gary.

"Merry Christmas," she said.

I cleared my throat. I wanted it to come out just right.

"Actually, I stoned her with after-dinner mints. Do you have mints here?"

Tia smiled.

"Only toothpicks."

She walked away. She had great posture. Great balance. A tall 110-pounder from behind, long legs, her brown hair cut short to show off her neck. She placed the check where the cook could see it and went over to another table.

"The mints got her," Gary said.

"I hope so."

"I could use a woman myself."

"I'd be happy just to look at her for a while."

"I thought you didn't get attached."

Gary spun the ketchup bottle. It rolled without falling, stopped.

"Have you ever had a serious relationship?" I said.

"Women aren't exactly knocking down the doors to get a piece of me."

"If I were a woman I would."

"Stop. I'm starting to blush."

"You have charm. You make people laugh. You're the most memorable person I know."

"No time," Gary said. "I was seeing one girl once. We got pretty close, but she ended up marrying a guy from the neighborhood. A real asshole. I went after the guy when I saw him in the local McDonald's, but he ran away. I'm not cut out for a serious relationship. I'm close to my dogs. They're close to me. But they don't miss me and I don't miss them either."

Tia walked past our table with someone else's order, three plates stacked up her arm. Her nails were cut short and painted dark red. I could tell that she was trying not to look at me. I didn't flex my arms for her or square up my shoulders. I just watched her eyes.

"She really is beautiful," I said.

"She sure isn't happy."

"She's a worker."

"I get the point. I'll leave her a good tip if she eases up on me."

Tia walked back, past our table. Gary spun the ketchup bottle. Tia brought the Cokes and my water. I said Thank you. She said You're welcome. She dropped a straw down for Gary.

"One straw for two Cokes?" Gary said.

"Do you drink them at the same time?"

"I thought my cousin and I would share."

"That's very sweet."

"I'm just busting your chops. My cousin's in love with you."

Tia looked at me. Blue with gray bursts. I kept my eyes narrow but I wasn't playing a part anymore.

"Does your cousin do all the talking for you?"

"No. I told him I thought you were beautiful. I do. I think you're beautiful. I think your eyes are beautiful and I'm not even an eye man. That's what I was thinking. That's what I'm telling you. I'm talking for myself now. How was that?"

"That was very nice," she said.

"Thank you."

"Where are you two cousins from?"

"New York," I said.

"The Big Apple. I've never been."

"I've never been to Las Vegas."

"You're here now."

Tia held my eye and I felt it and I made her feel it. I nodded just a little, just for her. She held my eye some more and then walked away.

"We have a full day of gambling," Gary said. "If you want to take her in the back for a quickie I'm sure you could, but just a quickie. You're here to count cards for me. All day. All night."

"Yes sir, Mr. Rose."

"Did you know that matadors have sex before they get in the bullring? That way they won't get distracted by anyone in the crowd. They shoot their load so they can give the bull their full attention. Then again, boxers aren't supposed to fuck before they fight. What about wrestlers?"

"My coaches never said anything about it."

"Either way. As long as you keep a perfect card count. That's why you're here."

"Anybody could have counted cards for you. Your dogs could practically count cards for you."

Gary didn't say anything.

"I'm with you," I said.

"They come after people that owe a lot less."

"I know."

"A lot less."

"We're safe in Denny's."

Gary took the wrapper off and put the straw in the Coke.

"She's not," he said.

Gary smiled. It was a smile just for me. It was a great smile but not for selling burgers on TV commercials. It had pain in it and fear and reassurance and it was a gentle smile all at the same time.

Tia came with the food. She told us to enjoy our meal and walked away. I wasn't that hungry anymore. I wasn't sure if I'd been hungry when I ordered. I ate half the tuna sandwich. Gary finished his two meals, asked if I was done, ate the rest of my sandwich. He signaled for the check. Tia brought it over.

"Compliments to the chef," Gary said.

"Believe me, he's no chef. He's hardly a cook."

"What's in a name?" I said.

Tia looked at me. I looked at her. She cleared the three plates, told us to have a good day, walked away. I watched her walk. I counted her steps to the back, through the swinging door, a peek at a man in uniform whites leaning over a sink spraying water. I nodded for myself. It was something I did before I walked to the mat, a quick shake of hands, the full match ahead of me, seven long minutes of struggle. We had a full day ahead of us and maybe another full day and another. It depended on the cards. It depended on the luck. Gary left a twenty-dollar bill on the table and a five-dollar chip, one of the chips he'd won our first meal with. One of the lucky ones. He paid the bill at the cash register. I went outside. It was hot. I looked at the strip and at the lion's head in the distance.

"You think she plays?" Gary said.

"I doubt it."

We started to walk back to Bally's. Gary bumped into my arm once, a second time. He was breathing heavy.

"I doubt many of the residents play," I said.

"What do you think she'll do with the chip?"

"Maybe she'll just cash it in."

"That's no fun."

"It was one of your lucky chips."

"I've got some left."

Gary wiped his sleeve against his forehead.

"She liked you," he said.

"She doesn't know me."

"When she looks at the chip she'll know you're playing at Bally's."

"That's a start."

19

I PRESSED MY FINGER hard into Gary's back. It wasn't for a plus four count. The count was plus nine and Gary started to turn his head to ask me what was up. The blue sunglasses were not tinted the way I'd pictured them. The glasses were clear through with black plastic rims. He was standing by the velvet rope that separated players from workers. Gary nodded his head and went back to the cards. He wasn't going anywhere. The dealer had a four card showing and Gary split the eights in front of him, putting two more black chips into the circle to cover the bet. He won both hands. Gary's nod had told me all I needed to know. It was for Blue. It was for me. The count was still plus nine and I pressed Gary's back three times. Blue became a peripheral man, the glasses a peripheral color, but they were there, he was there. Gary won the next three hands before the count shifted and returned to zero.

Two people left the table and Blue slid into the seat next to Gary's. The glasses made sense. Plastic didn't bend in a fight the way wire did. I wondered if he even needed glasses. He was a strong looking man with big arms cut like an athlete's in a short sleeved polo, not beefy arms but defined. His face was intelligent from the side. I couldn't see his eyes as he cashed in one hundred bucks and put the minimum twenty-five-dollar green chip in the betting circle. I heard a cocktail waitress behind us ask anyone if they wanted a drink and Gary ordered a Coke, calm voiced and cool like he had all the time in the world. Blue matched him, asked for a bottled water. The game had gone from blackjack to poker. The dealer started to shuffle, separating and reseparating the cards.

"Gary Rose. How are the tables treating you?"

"This table was treating me well. I thought you only operated in New York."

"I go where the wind takes me and the wind was blowing west. Your roommate told me you took a little drive. How were the sights?"

"Great. We stopped at the Grand Canyon and went whitewater rafting. We visited Old Faithful in Yellowstone. We're on our way to Disneyland."

"Your roommate didn't call you, did he?"

"My ex-roommate."

Blue had strong hands, palms on the table, tapping to some beat he had in his head. The knuckles on his index and middle fingers were flattened. He didn't wear any rings, nothing to reinforce his punches.

"Don't be hard on the poor bastard," Blue said. "He was scared. Everybody gets scared once in a while, right? He's very fond of you. He just wasn't fond of the blowtorch."

He laughed like it was a big joke, reassuring the people at the table, making the dealer smile, putting his arm around

Gary's fat shoulders, his forearm too close to my chin, announcing that they went way back, still worked in the same business, they were in for the convention and wasn't the weather great compared to the snow we were having back east. The guy on the other side of Blue said it didn't feel like Christmas in the desert and Blue agreed to that, said no place but New England really felt like Christmas, pegged the guy from his accent or from something. The guy said he was from Concord, New Hampshire, and wasn't that the truth. Blue's back was to me. I could have taken him down.

The dealer slid the yellow card to Gary. He'd been at the table the longest. Gary picked it up and placed it in the center of the deck. The dealer cut the cards, fit the cards into the shoe, burned the first card, and started to deal. Blue drew an ace.

"Good cut," he said.

They played side by side without talking while I kept the count. I shifted my weight back and forth, my old habit, getting ready before the match began. I looked at the back of Blue's neck and the way his hair was cut in back, a line straight across, a small mole just below the collar which was pulled down across his strong back from tilting his head forward to watch the cards. I looked at the dealer doing his job. Maybe he'd tell his family when he got home about his day at work, about the talk of blowtorches, a fat man, a man with blue sunglasses, or maybe he'd seen it all, heard it all, just another day at work before he went home. I thought of Tia a few streets away serving burgers, fries, shakes with her brown Denny's uniform on looking sexy even in that but hating it. I pictured her taking it off as soon as she got home, getting into the shower, her long body under the water, moving her painted fingers over her skin, soap turning to lather, washing her hair, putting her head under the water and staying there to wash the day off like washing garage dirt and exhaust fumes off the way I had done, washing the match off the way I had done.

The shoe was done. The dealer started to shuffle. Blue put his hand on Gary's shoulder. I shifted my weight.

"Let's get some lunch," Blue said.

"Lunch sounds great," Gary said.

Blue stood up. He was a little taller than me in cowboy boots and about three weight classes higher, close to two hundred pounds. Gary stood up, slower than Blue.

"Who's your friend?" Blue said.

"Some guy I met here."

"How come you didn't massage my back?" Blue said. "I like a good massage."

"It takes awhile to gain my trust," I said.

"Fair enough. Strong connections don't just happen overnight, right? It takes time for muscle to meld with bone, or for cartilage to mesh with joints. I guess we'll never be friends."

Blue cracked up and a single dimple cut into his left cheek.

"Damn," I said, exaggerating the word.

Blue got a kick out of that and laughed harder, genuinely. Gary smiled at me. Nothing showing. I wanted to squeeze Gary's hand hard to show him he could take it.

The carver was happy to see Gary. He piled pastrami on rye, corned beef on rye, asked Gary if he wanted some fresh potato salad and Gary said Great. Blue asked for a turkey sandwich. I asked for the same. I watched Gary piling fish sticks onto a second plate. We sat down and the waiter brought two Cokes for Gary and one for me. Blue ordered a bottled water.

"I've become a big health nut in my old age," Blue said. "I

drink gallons of water a day to flush out my body. It's good for the skin."

"You wouldn't want to see my body flushed out," Gary said.

"Lay off the fatty meats for a while. Drink plenty of water to fill up on zero calories. I'm in better shape now than when I was the kid's age."

Still the kid. The kid.

"I've heard a lot of stories about you," Gary said.

"I've heard some stories about you too," Blue said.

"Our small world. Did you really hang that guy off the roof at Yankee Stadium?"

"Yes I did. The guy shit his pants so much the grounds crew could have fertilized the entire outfield. For that split second I have a feeling that guy hated baseball more than he loved it."

"You never know. There are a lot of die-hard Yankee fans."

"Not that die-hard. What about you? I heard you won the Coney Island hot dog eating contest two years in a row. I heard you made enough money on side bets to retire for life."

"I did that right out of college. Eating and gambling were my two major strengths. How could I lose?"

"You can always lose."

"Yes you can. That's why we're having this power lunch."

Gary finished his pastrami sandwich and started his corned beef. He hadn't told me that story. I wondered how many hot dogs he'd eaten, how quickly, and if there was a plaque in Coney Island commemorating the young Gary's victory.

"What about you?" Blue said to me. "Are you famous for anything?"

"Not me."

"You're a mystery, right? That's a good thing to hold on to. I'm so mysterious I don't have a last name. Blue. Madonna. Prince. Casanova. Babe. As in the Babe, Babe Ruth. I'm a big baseball fan."

"Ruth is a last name," I said.

"So it is, kid." He turned to Gary. "How'd you do on the World Series this year?"

"I won about ten grand," Gary said.

"I used to love baseball, but I'm too busy to get to many games these days. That's the price you pay for having a solid reputation. Everything has a price, right? They send me out west, they send me to Europe. I even had to go to Japan last year to take care of some business."

Blue straightened his hand, made a high pitched *hiiii yaaaa* sound, karate chopped the table. He started cracking up. People seated at the other tables stopped feeding to turn around.

"It's important to keep a sense of humor about things, right?"

"I'm having a lot of fun," Gary said.

"There you go. My therapist told me I feel no remorse for the consequences of my actions which makes me perfect for the job."

"That would make you a good gambler," Gary said.

"Why is that?"

Gary pulled the plate of fish sticks closer to him, picked one up with his fingers, put it in his mouth, chewed, swallowed.

"If you think about the consequences, you can go in with a losing attitude and then you're definitely going to lose."

"So you had a bad attitude."

"No. I had bad luck."

"Of course."

Blue drank some water.

"My old man was a gambler," he said. "That's where all the problems started."

"Are you sure?" I said. "You can trace things back farther than that."

"I probably could. My old man's old man was a dick, but I never met the guy so I couldn't tell you firsthand. My old man was a dick too so maybe his assessment of his old man was wrong. Then again, maybe it wasn't. It takes one to know one, right? My old man lost a lot of money and as a kid growing up, eating scraps of shit everyday to support his habit, I learned to hate him. How's that for a talk show subject?"

"It's probably been done. You do what you do for revenge. Easy pop psychology."

"Give me some credit, kid. I hope I'm a little more complicated than that."

"I hope so."

I watched his eyes. He didn't give a shit. Sometimes I pushed my opponents' heads harder than I was supposed to, got them riled up so they would hate me and once they hated me they lost their skills. I knew about loss of control. I watched his eyes behind the blue lenses.

"I like this kid."

Blue lifted his leg and put it on the table.

"You like my boots? These are some very expensive shit kickers. Snakeskin."

I didn't say anything. He didn't care. Blue looked at his boots, rubbed his hand over the scales, and reached a finger under the inside of the boot like he was feeling the texture for the first time. Gary looked at me between fish sticks. He was no longer sizing me up. He liked how I was handling Blue. I liked how Gary had nodded his head at the blackjack table.

"Gary Rose," Blue said. "How are those fish sticks?"

"Delicious," Gary said. "I think it's whiting."

He put a fish stick in his mouth.

"Maybe halibut."

He put another fish stick in his mouth.

"Whiting. It's definitely whiting."

"I appreciate your taking me to lunch. Most of my so-called clients are weasels like my pop psychology father. It makes my life easier because they're used to being bullied, but I get tired of them sometimes. You remember those school yard bullies, right kid? You're usually better off just taking a beating without fighting back."

"Whatever," I said.

"I once broke a bully's nose," Gary said. "When I was a kid, the playground bully used to pick on me. He called me a pig, a fat hog, a porker. He had a new name for me every day. He was a real creative kid. One day I got sick of it and punched him in the nose. I got suspended from school for a week which was fine with me. I snuck out of the house everyday to Baskin Robbins for ice cream."

"I broke a guy's nose once," Blue said. "My old man's."

I watched his eyes. He didn't give a shit about his father.

"I'm getting some dessert," Gary said.

"No desserts for me, thanks," Blue said.

Gary walked to the buffet line. From the table I watched his wide back, his body moving more side to side than forward, his small hands swinging.

"He's certainly as big as they said he'd be."

"He's a big man."

"Where do you know him from?" Blue said.

"Around. We're friends."

"There you go. Keep it vague, right? Vague and mysterious. You're a smart kid."

Blue fondled his boot.

"It's good to have friends," Blue said. "I had one good friend once. We were in the minor leagues together and every time we played an away game we would go out afterward, pick up women and paint the town. Both of us were outfielders. Then he got moved up to Triple A and we sort of lost touch."

"I guess you weren't such good friends."

"You've got something there, kid. All we had in common was baseball. He ended up hurting his knee. He wasn't good enough at the plate to be a designated hitter so that was it for him too. He was a great fielder though. He would chase balls down that seemed untouchable and he always looked like he thought he'd make the catch. That's how you have to chase balls down, right? He was so close to getting the big call and now all he probably has is a bunch of trophies in his office to remind him of the days when he could have made it to the majors. The great American pastime gave me a good ass fucking too. It took three years out of my life."

"Sports will do that to you."

"There you go. Did you play ball?"

"Play ball? No. Team sports weren't for me."

"Why is that? I hear some pop psychology philosophy in your voice."

"When you have people to rely on it's not the same level of competition."

"That would depend on the situation."

"If you're not alone, the responsibility isn't all yours. It's just like blaming your old man for your lot in life."

"I don't blame him. I do what I do."

"You're all grown up then," I said.

Blue's eyes were clear behind the blue lenses. He leaned back, put his hands behind his neck and I recognized how his arms automatically flexed and relaxed. He wasn't putting on a show for me. He'd been physical all his life. Not like the guys who puffed their chests when they walked down the street, flexed their muscles so long that when it came time to really use them they were tight. Those were the easiest to spot and the easiest to finish.

"I like team sports," Blue said. "Thanks to baseball I learned to swing a bat. I could hit a ball a country mile. I was a hitter, which is a very individual part of the sport. It's just you and the pitcher, right? Teamwork and individuality all rolled into one, which is why it's the great American pastime. The selfish good working toward the common good. The fathers of the Constitution would have loved the game of baseball with all of its American implications. Wide-open spaces in the out-field. It-ain't-over-till-it's-over opportunities. Endless possibilities. It's what our country was built on, right?"

"It's what the casinos were built on."

"There you go. All of gambling is built on that premise. It keeps the suckers coming back for more. Like baseball. It's possible to score a million runs before you get that last out. It's not probable, but it's possible, right? There's no time limit on a baseball game. An inning can last forever if the third out is never made. You have to be a real idiot to think that way, but it is possible."

"Until you come along."

"Right. I don't come along until the possibilities are pretty much over."

"Pretty much. Not completely."

"Pretty much completely."

Blue smiled.

"I like that," he said. "Pretty much completely. I'm good."

"Why don't you give Gary some time? He's been winning. He's been making back the money."

"Why are you so interested in Gary?"

"He's my friend."

"So you said, but that goes against all of your ideas about individual sports. It's Gary against the people I work for. Now it's Gary against me so why are you interfering? He's a big boy, right? He's a very big boy. I never saw a man eat twenty-three fish sticks in a row. I was counting. Twenty-three fish sticks on top of two giant sandwiches and now he's loading up on dessert. I'm about ready to vomit just watching him. Look at that."

Gary had created one of his giant sundaes and was carrying it across the room.

"Maybe you have a weak stomach," I said.

"My stomach is fine. How's that bump on your head?"

"It's a bump."

"Did somebody kick your ass?"

"Let's talk about Gary. Let him make back the money."

"He had his chance."

"Give him some time."

"You're not telling me something. Why do you care about him so much?"

"I like him. He's a good guy."

"Now there's where your point about team sports starts to

unravel. You like him. You're connected by like. You're a team. Does that make you weak?"

"It really bothers you that baseball is for pussies."

"It bothers me that you're such a confused kid. I bet you're a college grad."

Gary put the sundae on the table and sat down.

"Did you go to college?" Blue asked Gary.

"Where do you think I learned to eat like this?"

"I dropped out of college to play ball," Blue said. "My sophomoric sophomore year. Still, a few things did sink in. Psychology. Philosophy. Do you know what a syllogism is?"

"It's a proof," Gary said. "If, but, therefore."

"There you go."

Blue turned to me.

"With what you've given me, kid, I can prove that team sports are as hard as individual sports."

Gary looked up from his sundae.

"It can't be done," Gary said.

"Hear me out."

"Baseballs are round," Gary said, knocking out the syllogism like he was writing it on the blackboard. "But horse shit is also round. Therefore baseball players suck."

I laughed extra loud for Blue's sake. Blue's eyes were slits behind his sunglasses.

"Have a sense of humor," Gary said.

"I've got a sense of humor," Blue said. "That wasn't a syllogism. Hear me out."

"Are you sure you can do this on your own?" I said. "Maybe you need your teammates around."

Blue took his boot off the table and leaned forward.

"A roommate is not a teammate," Blue said. "Gary Rose's

roommate is scared of blowtorches. Therefore, I have found Gary Rose."

Blue's laugh wasn't convincing. Gary went back to spooning ice cream. I shifted my weight in the chair.

"Now your friend here, he's a better friend," Blue said, smiling at Gary and then at me, his eyes more than a little off behind the blue sunglasses. "He's worried about you so he wants to make a deal. He's trying to keep you from suffering for the consequences of your actions by proposing a solution to your problem which involves time and money and needing more time for money which is always the dilemma and which bores the fuck out of me. So in a way you are stronger as individuals by sticking up for the team just like I was when I played ball, right? Like the army says, You're only as strong as your weakest man. Which one of you is weaker?"

"Maybe you're the weakest," I said.

Blue kept smiling.

"Very funny kid. You're a regular comedian."

Blue leaned forward some more.

"Which one?" Blue said. "Is it the fat fuck or the fucking kid?"

I was out of the chair before Blue could move. I put a half nelson on him, pushed his head into the table. He struggled and I felt his strength and I shifted my feet and held his head down. I felt the weight on me. Four hundred pounds and more. I tried to hold my balance while I pressed Blue's head but Gary's weight was too much and I struggled against it, the panic starting to come in, the weight of losing completely touching my shoulders, my shoulders sinking from the weight, all of the weight, and I heard Gary's voice in my ear saying Wait, wait, wait. I pushed Blue's head into the table and Gary

said Wait and I eased my hands off Blue. Blue sat up. He adjusted his blue glasses that were unbroken, still on.

"Gary Rose," Blue said. "A weasel like all the others. You
don't think I know why you stopped the kid? You're afraid for
yourself. If I get hurt, someone will really make you pay. And
kid, you pull a stunt like that again, I'll split your fucking head
open like a soggy baseball."

Gary was holding me around. I breathed to stay calm. I
had to worry about Gary and not just me.

"Let us play a little longer," Gary said.

"Us? Did you say us?"

"Let me play a little longer."

"How much longer? Time and money. Money and time."

We were back to poker. Gary had to show his hand first.

"Give me until Sunday," Gary said.

"Sunday day? Sunday night? I have to be back on Sunday.
It's Christmas Eve on Sunday and even I take off for that."

Gary knew how the count fluctuated and then evened out.
He knew how blackjack flowed. We'd been big winners the first
night. Medium winners the next day. The winnings had mostly
slowed. He knew how long he might need.

"By the end of Saturday night," Gary said.

"That means I have to catch the redeye out of here. With
the time difference it won't be the merriest Christmas."

"No one knows you found me yet. I'll pay you two hundred a day for the four days. Make it an even thousand."

"That won't cover a good-looking hooker to tuck me in at
night."

"Two thousand."

"How much do you have in your pocket?"

"What I have in my pocket doesn't concern you."

Blue turned to me.

"See that, kid? I'm trying to be friendly and look what I get. You better remember that, kid. It's tough to change a man's nature. There's a syllogism in there somewhere, but fuck this logic shit, right? Are you going to make a serious offer or not? I'm a professional and a professional upholds his reputation."

I watched Gary spoon the melted ice cream into his mouth and swallow. Gary needed both knees. He needed as much support as he could get. He also needed money. I was starting to feel a little nervous for my cousin.

"I'll give you three thousand," Gary said.

"Four thousand."

Gary dipped his finger into the plate, came up with a drop of brown liquid, all the flavors melted together. He put his finger into his mouth, swallowed.

"You're in the driver's seat. Four thousand."

"Sold to the big man," Blue said, his fist coming down on the table like a gavel, his voice an auctioneer's.

Gary took the money from his left pocket, counted out forty crisp hundred-dollar bills, handed them to Blue. Blue took the money and filled his wallet. It was a brown snakeskin wallet a shade darker than his boots.

"Wait," Blue said.

He handed the money back to Gary.

"Put it in my hand like we're shaking hands and you're my fat uncle or something giving me a Christmas present. That shit always made me laugh."

Gary took a moment to fold the bills in his small palm. He leaned over the table, put one hand on Blue's shoulder, put his other hand into Blue's hand, became the uncle, looking at Blue like he was the kid, like he looked at me when I was a kid. If a casting director had observed closely he would have seen more than a four-hundred-pound man. Gary lowered his voice.

"Here you go, son. Don't spend it all in one place."

Blue slapped his hand down on the table, doubled over laughing, the plastic bottle of spring water falling to the floor.

"I love it. I love it. Didn't that just kill you when you were a kid? It's probably real fresh in the kid's memory. They'd give you fifty cents or a buck and tell you not to spend it all in one place, right? I love it."

Gary smiled.

"I'll book that Sunday redeye back to the city," Blue said.

Blue's dimple disappeared. He leaned over the table and looked straight at Gary. I shifted my weight.

"I'll meet you in your room at a minute past midnight on Sunday and I won't even charge you for that minute. I don't care if you win or not, but if you don't win I'm going to make you pay in a big way so that my friends, so that my connections, so that the men who pay my wages are happy, so that you'll know better for next time, so that you'll have more motivation to come up with the money this time and next time and the time after that if you live that long."

Like a method actor I kept my mouth shut because the whole scene called for that. It was like a fucking movie only it wasn't.

"See you on Sunday," Gary said.

Blue leaned in a little more, his eyes still on Gary's eyes. He lowered his voice, not like an uncle to a kid.

"He'll pay too. He's in on it now."

"He has nothing to do with this."

"Do you want your money back?"

Gary didn't say anything.

"Do you?"

"No," Gary said and he kept his eyes down.

Blue looked at me.

"I didn't think so," he said.

I breathed. Blue sat back.

"Four grand for four days," Blue said. "An all-expenses-paid Las Vegas vacation. Maybe we can have dinner one night. I'd love to see the damage that the famous Gary Rose does to the night time buffet."

Blue put a ten on the table for the waiter and walked out. His muscular arms looked more pumped than they had been. He'd been angry for a moment. It was in his blood too. I could picture him swinging the bat, driving balls over the left field fence in some minor league stadium, shattering kneecaps with textbook perfection right down the middle, a perfect fracture, a straight line.

20

I REMEMBERED MY DAD'S explanation to my brother about opportunity cost. He said it was like buying a candy bar that turned out to be lousy. It was better to throw it away than to eat it since the money had already been spent and there was no point in suffering. It was just another way of saying cut your losses.

Outside it was Thursday. Inside Gary had started losing some of his big bets, pulling low cards when the count said high cards should come out. I thought that when it was over, when we finally left the tables of Las Vegas, I would try to talk to Gary. I would use a food analogy to make him see. You have a Bally's buffet. It's the most delicious buffet you've ever seen. Juicy prime rib. Golden turkey breasts. Creamy mashed potatoes. Ice cream sundaes with as many sweet maraschinos as you want, pretty please. It's there. It's yours. There is only one problem, a single dilemma built in. If you start to eat, then you have to finish the entire buffet. If you don't finish the buffet, you will never be able to eat again and you will starve to death like your parrot that said Eat me and died not eating. But if you steer clear of the buffet, if you never touch it, you will live a long life full of sensible meals. A salad, a main dish, a scoop of ice cream. You'll never be able to eat more than that, you'll never be able to eat until you're completely content. You will be able to enjoy your meal and the meal will get you to the next meal but you will never be full, totally and gluttonously satisfied. What would you do? I had the food analogy in my head, rehearsed and ready to deliver and redeliver until Gary understood that to eat three square meals a day was a real possibility. Of course Gary would probably turn it around and tell me to curb my behavior too. I didn't know what I'd say to that.

In all the gambling books, Gary said, there was a discussion of that moment of clarity when the cards came up right. In wrestling there were clear moments too. Seeing the free hand, the unbalanced leg, the lapse in concentration in an opponent's eyes, the fear when I started to lift the opponent, the fear when I lifted the chair and brought it down on Evan Kessler's head. That had been the clearest moment of all. It was clear every time I replayed it. I wanted other clear moments. I wanted to sit down with my father and just talk. I wanted moments like that so that the other moments became memories like the childhood story of me clenching my hands and holding my breath. It was so long ago that it was me but not me. But it was still me.

Gary got up from the table and walked slowly past the Bally's registration desk to the shop that sold postcards, film, pens, cigarettes, candy. He bought three Snickers bars and two PayDays. The cashier wished Gary good luck.

"I'm still over eighty grand in the hole," Gary said and

ripped open the first Snickers. "Eighty fucking grand. I'm ready to sit down at the roulette table, put all my winnings on red, let it ride twice and pray."

He crumpled the wrapper in a ball.

"You can't fuck up the count."

"I'm not," I said.

"You can't miss any cards. You have to count perfectly. We have to play perfectly."

"I'm keeping the count."

Gary bit into his second Snickers, a line of chewy caramel dangling off the bitten portion, pulled to a point.

"I slept like shit last night," Gary said. "It's too hot in the room."

He kept the air-conditioning all the way up and each night I pulled the sheet, blanket, and comforter tight around me.

Gary opened the PayDay and walked over to the registration desk, cut in front of a Japanese couple waiting to check in. He started complaining about the air-conditioning. He wanted to know if there was a problem with the vents on the twenty-fourth floor and if there was he wanted another room. Gary said he wasn't some penny-ante bum in for a losing night, he expected some good accommodations, he'd been sitting at the tables all day and night for the past four days and what the fuck was up with the air conditioner. The woman behind the desk called up maintenance to check on the air-conditioning. She shook her head a couple of times for Gary's benefit. She hung up the phone and told Gary that no one had reported any problems. Gary said he was reporting a problem and walked away.

"You weren't hot last night?"

"Not really."

"I'm tired. Let's call it a night."

We took the elevator to the twenty-fourth floor. The room was freezing. Gary undressed to his underwear and got into bed. All the buffets had been taking their toll. His stretch marks looked redder, wider, more weltlike. I put on my sweats and got into bed but behind my closed eyes all I saw were cards. I knew I wasn't going to sleep. I got out of bed, dressed, opened the door on one of Gary's snores, closed the door on the next.

It was warm out. Except for the signs on the strip that wished people happy holidays and advertised special Christmas appearances by some of the biggest Las Vegas stars, it felt like the middle of summer. The casinos were lit up.

I walked to Denny's. When the hostess came over with a stack of menus under her arm, I said I was just here to see Tia. I saw Tia. She was adding up numbers on a check. She looked up and I stayed on her eyes and I felt the dip in the highway and maybe I was fooling myself but I tried to force her to feel the dip too. She tucked her pen behind her ear and walked over to me with graceful balance, one foot in front of the other but easy, calm, she'd been looked at all her life, she had to be, it was a show at first and then no longer a show.

"What are you doing here?" she said.

"I came to see you. Do you get off work soon?"

"Midnight."

"I can wait."

"How do you know I want to see you when I get off?"

"I'm taking a chance. That's what people do in Las Vegas, isn't it?"

"That's what gamblers do in Vegas."

"What do waitresses do?"

"They finish their shifts and go home."

"I thought my cousin told you to ease up on me."

"That would be your cousin who does all the talking for you."

"I'm here alone."

"Very brave."

"Just very tired."

She smiled and I felt myself smile too. Explosions of gray in her blue eyes. I wanted to help her off with her uniform and clean the day away.

"Sit over there in my station. The kitchen just closed, but I can get you some ice cream if you want."

"Water's good."

Tia walked away to bus a table. I sat down and watched her work. She brought me a glass of ice water and a newspaper, told me to read if I got tired of watching her, and went through the swinging doors in back. The same dishwasher was there, dressed in uniform whites, spraying water at dirty dishes, steam rising. His work could qualify for our list of worst jobs. I probably would never see Lou or Berger again. I thought about sending the garage a Wish You Were Here postcard from Las Vegas. I could see Mr. Caparello looking at the card, calling the police, going back to his hovering position at the money drawer. Some connections were just as well cut. I looked over the copy of USA Today. The world went on. The stock market had evened out after a record high, a subject my family would probably discuss. The sports section had an article about the dangers of using aluminum bats in college baseball.

Two waitresses picked up the salt and pepper shakers, the ketchup bottles. Tia sat at a booth sorting the checks and I looked at the back of her neck and her hair. I had been seeing a lot of backs lately. Blue's. Gary's. My back in the hotel room mirrors. If I had been my opponent I would have scored an easy take down. I still looked strong but I wasn't in wrestling shape. My muscles were not cut the same way. Push-ups and pull-ups and sit-ups and a couple of runs a week were nothing to what we did during the season. Some routines were better ended.

Tia went into the restroom. When she came out she wore a summer dress. Her arms and legs were tan. She held a plastic shopping bag with the Denny's uniform folded inside. I stood up. I was aware of everything I was doing, not rehearsed aware, just aware of how I looked. I wanted to look movie star good for her. Not playing a part, not moving this way and that way for the camera. Just moving for her, looking good for her.

"Do I smell like food?"

"You smell fine. Do I smell like gambling?"

"You smell like the chip your cousin left on the table. Come on."

We left Denny's and started to walk the strip in the direction of the MGM casino. The dead eyed lion was lit in the distance.

"Are you winning or losing?"

"We're up. Not enough."

"What's enough?"

"More than we've won."

She kept the plastic bag with the Denny's uniform between us. It swung but not like Gary's arms when he walked. I had my hands in my pockets, looking at her, looking down at the sidewalk, listening to her voice that was low and quiet but easy to hear over the traffic speeding on the strip.

"Maybe it's greed that's keeping you up."

"No. Just cards. I closed my eyes and I was seeing cards. When I opened them I was thinking about you."

"Vegas stirs a young man's blood."

A young man. Better than a kid, I guessed. She was a kid and a woman at the same time. She had that kind of balance. Low voice. Smart eyes. Comfortable walking along the strip with someone she didn't know.

"Las Vegas," I said.

"You said it's your first time."

"It is. I came along for the ride."

"That's a long ride just for a ride."

"It wasn't how I pictured a trip across country would be. We didn't see too much. Interstate 70 straight across."

"You sound like the truckers that come into the restaurant. I always thought that would be a romantic life, but from what they tell me it's not. They insist that every state looks the same from the highway. The only difference is the weather."

"Maybe that's the trouble with highways."

"Maybe you expected too much."

"Maybe I did."

A bus passed us. The noise blocked everything. The windows were tinted so I couldn't see if anyone was inside.

"What about you?" I said. "Are you from here?"

"No. I don't think many people are actually from Vegas. They come to work or to play or to retire."

The plastic bag brushed against my leg.

"I just live here," she said. "Almost a year."

"Where's home?"

"California. A small city called Bishop."

"Bishop, California."

"You've never heard of it. People drive through before or

after they've been to Death Valley. They sell a lot of cold drinks in Bishop and that's about it. "

"Nothing wrong with a cold drink."

"What do you want to do?"

"Walking is good."

"I've been on my feet all day. We can take a drive as long as you're not one of those crazy New Yorkers they warn people about."

"I'm not really a New Yorker. I've only lived there a year and a half."

"Your cousin has an accent."

"He's from New York. You don't have to worry about him either."

"My car is down here."

We took a left and walked to a lot. I looked over the cars trying to guess which one was hers. The cars in the lot were more beat up than the cars on the strip or the cars I had parked. Tia stopped in front of an old Chevy Nova painted red.

She opened the door for me and went around the front. She threw the plastic bag in the backseat, got in, I got in. The seats were worn, not like the fitted leather in Gary's car. She rolled down her window and I rolled down mine.

"What's your name stranger?"

"Dess. Short for Odessa."

"I'm Tia. Nice to meet you."

"Nice to meet you."

Tia turned the key, revved the engine once. She pulled out of the lot, drove on the strip, past the MGM lion, past the Luxor pyramid and then the road opened up. She was a good driver the way I knew she would be. Her hands were easy on the steering wheel and I leaned back and watched the road in front of me. She didn't weave. She didn't crowd, flash her lights, move cars off the road. We weren't really going anywhere and there was no need to rush. The night air felt good on my arm, on my face, in my hair, against my eyes.

"I always take a drive after my shift."

"I don't want to break your streak. I like your car."

"Vegas is the best city to find secondhand cars. I sometimes wonder how many people drive in by car and leave by bus."

"I'll warn my cousin."

"You do that."

Tia was talking over the wind coming through the windows. The wind pressed her hair across her forehead.

"We used to drive from Bishop to Death Valley in the summer to see if we could take it. The heat's unbearable. Cactus can't even grow there, only some scrub brush that barely survives. If you see a live animal you're supposed to report it to the rangers. We'd dare each other to get out of the car and take the heat."

"It sounds like a game I used to play with my grandfather."

"I stayed out for twenty-eight minutes one time. That night we watched the weather and they said it was one hundred twenty-three degrees. It felt like there was an unbearable weight on my back. It was almost too much to take."

I knew how that was.

"Las Vegas must be brutal in the summer," I said.

"It's not so bad. There's always an air-conditioned room to duck into. Or a Denny's to work in. Even when the weather's good people aren't exactly spending their days outside."

"They have other agendas."

"They have the same agenda. They want to make money. Like you two."

I looked in the side mirror and watched the Las Vegas

lights dim, the strip become a strip, defined in distance. It felt good to be away. It was a clear night. The stars increased and I could fit my right fist into the sliver of waning moon. A left fist meant the moon was waxing. That was the trick.

"I'm not like my cousin that way."

"I forgot. You only came along for the ride."

"That's all."

I wanted to feel the speed from the driver's seat, my foot against the gas, the body of the red Nova turning the way I wanted it to turn. I had been the wrestler with the best record but the coach had never asked me to be team captain. He knew I would decline. Before my matches I never watched the other wrestlers. I'd prepare myself to face my own opponent, shifting my weight back and forth, rolling my neck, shaking my head to test that my headgear was tight. I didn't need a team and then they'd kicked me off. At the garage when things were slow, I'd sometimes stand out on the street and think about where I went wrong. The blood rushes had been handed down to me but I wasn't a kid anymore.

"There's a good place to look at the sky near here. You can hardly see the glow of Vegas."

"Like Central Park."

"What's that like?"

"It's a park in the middle of the city. When I get sick of the noise and the people and the miles of streets and sidewalks and skyscrapers, I go to Central Park and walk into the woods. From some parts I can't see a single building."

"Escape."

"It was an escape. Where I grew up I could go into my backyard and practically get the same feeling. There was plenty of country there. I guess I didn't fully appreciate it."

I felt very tired all of a sudden. It had been a long day but she was next to me and I wanted to be with her, to be awake. I leaned my head out the window and took the air full force. She drove on. There was hardly any traffic. She took a left onto an unpaved road, rolled her window up and I did the same. The desert dust made a gritty sound against the glass. The beams from the two headlights merged into one and died in the darkness somewhere out there. I thought of the movies and I was sure that Gary thought of them too. Movies about gangsters driven into the desert never to be found again. Gary was too big. Too hard to carry. Blue wouldn't do that anyway. He needed to collect the money. That was what was important. The thoughts were stupid. I was tired.

"Is it like Central Park now?"

Her voice was low again. With the windows closed, she didn't have to talk over the wind.

"In a way it is," I said.

Tia pulled off the road, stopped, and turned off the lights. We got out of the car and sat on the hood of her Nova that was hot from the engine. Her legs were bare in her summer dress but it was probably nothing to Death Valley heat. The desert air smelled clean and it was the clearest sky with thousands of stars and the constellations highlighted like at a planetarium. The crescent moon looked sharp enough to cut the fist that told it was waning.

"Out here you can almost forget everything."

"Almost."

"Almost," she said.

The engine ticked, winding down, and then the ticking noise stopped.

"Is that why you come here?"

"Sometimes. It beats the view from my place and I got tired of wandering around the casinos. I used to do that when I first moved here."

"Air-conditioned places to duck into."

"With a lot of bells," she said.

"You didn't move here to gamble?"

"Did you move to New York to see the Empire State Building?"

"I thought New York would put some distance on things."

"But now you need Central Park."

"You're right."

"I came to Vegas to get away," Tia said. "I didn't want to be one of those kids that complained about how boring life was and then ended up making a boring life of my own in the same place. The day I finished high school I packed some clothes and came here."

"I'm here because of Gary. We didn't see him that often growing up, but he was always our favorite cousin. He's a professional gambler."

"That's all he does?"

"That's it. He's the real thing. A full-time gambler."

"I'm a full-time waitress."

"I parked cars."

"I guess we're all reaching for the stars."

I lifted my hand, took a swipe at the sky, rested my empty hand on the hood, close to her thigh.

"He must have won along the way, but now he's in trouble."

"Most gamblers are in trouble. Look around."

"Not like he is."

"It's that bad?"

"It's bad."

It was quiet in the desert. No traffic like in New York. No crickets like at home. I felt her hand on mine and I took her hand and held it, all my focus on her hand, warm, her thumb moving over my palm.

"He has to make a certain amount of money in a certain amount of time. That's how bad it is. Where I parked cars, there was a punch clock right behind me. At first I didn't hear it, but after a while I could. After driving across country, I feel like all I remember is that punch clock. I just lost my job."

"What does one have to do to lose a car parking job? Did you miss a space?"

"I asked for some time off. My boss refused to give it to me. I wrote up a letter of resignation and taped it to the punch clock."

"Very symbolic."

There was nothing symbolic about Caparello's bloody face. It had just been a bloody face.

"I'm trying to think of a dramatic exit from Denny's," Tia said. "Not that anyone would care."

"My dad once worked as a busboy and when the manager fired him in the middle of the shift my dad dropped the pile of dishes he was carrying."

"That's an idea."

"I used to think of unloading the cash register one night, stealing a car from the lot and driving into the sunset to start fresh somewhere."

"Like you started fresh in New York?"

"Probably."

"Maybe you would have ended up in Vegas."

It was quiet. Her hand was warm. Her thumb moved slowly

over my palm and back again. The stars filled the sky. It was the perfect setting but it was real and I wanted to draw it out, wait for the right moment. A movie star kiss but only for her. So she would remember me the next time she came here and I was wherever I was.

"When I first moved to Vegas, I did come for the money. I got a job as a cocktail waitress at Caesars. I thought the job might lead to showgirl work or something. When I got here I saw that it wasn't like what I expected. I don't know what I expected. Las Vegas seemed like a place to go. It wasn't in California. It sure as shit wasn't Bishop."

"How did you end up at Denny's?"

"Quite a fall, isn't it? Caesars to Denny's. I got sick of wearing the costume, getting grabbed at. I didn't think it would bother me so much, but after a while it did. At Denny's it's mostly families. I'm making enough money to pass some time."

"That's the kind of money I made. Enough for a beer and a subway ride to Central Park."

"Your cousin wants more than that."

"He wants much more than that. He needs much more than that. What will you do when you finish killing time?"

"I'm still killing it. What are you going to do?"

"I don't know."

"Become a professional gambler?"

"Not me."

I tried not to think about Gary. He was asleep in Bally's resting for another day at the tables. Resting to make it back by Sunday. I tried to concentrate on the stars, the quiet, the warm hood of the car, Tia's hand. I moved her hand into me like she was my opponent and moved her body into me and I kissed her and she kissed back and the kiss was long and hard and I wanted it to be perfect for her and I wanted it to be perfect for me, not counting cards perfect, not playing the hand perfect, not even Hollywood perfect. I wanted it to be one of those moments when time stopped.

21

HER APARTMENT HAD BEEN on the top floor of a three-floor walk-up with a small balcony off the bedroom, a breeze coming through the curtains that I had felt on my back when I rested and then didn't feel until I rested again. She had felt strong under my weight, her legs hard against me, her hands around my arms, her eyes on mine, perfect.

I expected to hear Gary's heavy breathing or a steady snore. The blankets were off the bed. The curtains were open. The lights of Las Vegas were muted from the sky starting to lighten.

I went down. His wide back was hunched over a blackjack table, his shadow on the felt. It was just Gary and the dealer and the black hundred-dollar chips. I put my hand on his back but he didn't look up. We had two days left and he was using every minute of it. I waited for the shoe to run out.

"How long have you been sitting here?"

"I couldn't sleep."

"You were sleeping when I left."

"I couldn't sleep after that. Like the song says, I've grown accustomed to your face. Not having you next to me completely broke my pattern."

"We haven't had a pattern since we left New York."

Gary rubbed his bloodshot eyes. He looked like shit. The lines around his eyes were visible in the casino light, cut into the fat that usually smoothed his face.

"I'm waiting for my streak," Gary said. "Unfortunately, the house's employee is keeping things honest. You're sure you don't want to work something out?"

The dealer smiled while he shuffled the cards with manicured fingers.

"How was she?"

"How do you know where I went?"

"I know everything. I don't mean how was she like how was she. My mind's not always in the gutter. Do you like her?"

"Like you would say, she's great."

"Good. Great. She's definitely as moody as you. Does she still have that chip I gave her or did she put it on her shoulder with the other one?"

"She didn't play it yet."

"Smart girl."

Gary put his hands on the edge of the table and lifted himself up.

"Hold my place," Gary said. "I'll be back in a few minutes. And rethink that offer I made you."

The dealer put a marker in the betting circle to hold Gary's place.

I followed Gary past the blackjack tables and the craps tables. The stick man rested the stick against his lips as he watched the dice roll like telling the room Keep quiet. Here comes Gary Rose. Watch him closely. He has his work cut out.

"I don't want to go into tomorrow like I'm going into today," Gary said. "We've got to stay at the tables until we make a dent. A dent in the dent."

"What's the dent now?"

"The same. About eighty."

"Were you counting?"

"If you don't count you'll lose."

I saw a quarter in the tray of a slot machine. I left the forgotten payoff where it was. It would be back in the slot machine soon enough.

"My concentration is not what it used to be," Gary said. "I used to be able to go for days and days."

We went into the bathroom. Bugsy Siegel's friend wasn't there. An old black man with a closely trimmed mustache sat on a stool reading the paper. I heard him put the paper down behind me. I washed my face in cold water and the attendant handed me a paper towel and I thanked him. I waited for Gary to finish. The attendant adjusted a bottle of cologne on the counter, looked at his watch.

"All right," the attendant said. "Two hours and thirty-two minutes."

"Almost home," I said.

Counting time like that was never a good sign. Gary washed his face, took a bottle of spray cologne and hit himself under each arm. He told the attendant it was going to be a long day. The attendant handed him a paper towel. Gary left twenty bucks in the basket and told the attendant that now it was under two and a half hours. The attendant wished us good luck.

Gary bought three Snickers bars, bit into the first.

"Are you awake?" he said.

"I can count."

"Ace, two, ace, three, ace, four, three, four, five, six, jack, queen, king."

"Like old times. Plus one."

"Three days. Two drivers. You only hear about people driving across country in three days. We did it. We made it in three days. A couple hundred miles short of the California coast."

"That's all?"

"That's all. A day trip."

"We could do it standing on our hands."

"Sure. Kings of the road."

"Two kings. Minus two. I was born to count."

"Your dad would be happy to hear that."

"Real happy."

"I mean the counting part. He'd be cursing me if he knew I took you here."

Gary crumpled the three candy wrappers into a ball and took a ten-foot shot into a Bally's wastebasket.

"Time," Gary said.

We walked to the blackjack table and Gary sat down. I stood behind him. The streak didn't come in the tenth shoe or the twentieth. I forced myself to count but she wasn't all out of me. I forced myself to concentrate. The cards came out. A matador fucked before a fight. A boxer did not. There was the scene from *Raging Bull* Gary had played for me, while we were driving, I wasn't even sure where, Kansas maybe, maybe Colorado, when Jake LaMotta had been beaten and he looked at the victorious Sugar Ray Robinson and said You never got me down, Ray. Gary had taken a sip of the soda he was drinking and let it dribble down his chin like it was blood and he made his eyes almost dead and he delivered the line. Gary said

DeNiro had gained fifty pounds to play Jake LaMotta. Gary said he would have tried to lose his own weight for that part. It was that great a part, he said. They could have filmed him first as the old LaMotta and then he would have fasted to play the young LaMotta and he said they both had small hands so it would have been easy once the weight came off. He had smiled one of his smiles, a sadder smile, a smile that was part of giving up, growing older, resolve, the angle of his upturned mouth saying certain things come to pass and others don't.

The dealer was all business and didn't show off with fancy hand work or bullshit talk. He revealed his down card fast to take away the mystery.

The lights stayed the same. The air temperature stayed the same. Dealers and pit bosses were changed. One crew going off. One crew coming on. The casino filled up while I counted, pressed, rubbed. The space between back and seat grew wider and then Gary would catch himself and sit back.

We took a lunch break. Gary downed the first Coke in one long drink, rubbed his eyes before he picked up his heaping pastrami sandwich. I wasn't hungry.

"How do I look?" Gary said.

"You look okay."

"That's not what the mirror in the bathroom told me."

"You look tired. So do I."

"No time to rest. Did you see that fucker playing next to me?"

"He sticks too much."

"He's a fucking moron. A submoron. He's fucking the cards up."

"You think it matters?"

"His stupidity was fucking up my concentration."

Gary drank his second Coke.

"We should have slept last night," he said.

"What do you want me to do?"

"Nothing."

"You want me to apologize for running over to Denny's?"

"We're here to play blackjack."

I smashed my hand on the table.

"Play blackjack? We're here to play blackjack? We're working blackjack. We've been working our asses off since we got here."

"I thought you were stoical like Grandpa."

"I guess they don't make men like they used to."

"I guess not," Gary said.

"I wasn't the one crying out when my hand got squeezed."

"And that makes you a man?"

"It makes me the winner."

"Those were Grandpa's rules."

"I like his rules."

"It was a stupid game."

"But blackjack isn't? What are your rules? The more money you lose, the more of a man you are?"

I looked Gary down. I looked across the room. Busboys were clearing plates, wiping tables. Gary finished the rest of his sandwich.

"All it takes is a real streak," Gary said. "One real streak and I'll pay that bastard off and tell him to go fuck himself."

"I'd like to do more than that."

"So would I. I can't."

"What if you only pay half of what you owe? Or two-thirds? Is there some kind of cut off?"

"They cut off your thumb. I don't know. They want their money. It's a business."

"Could you buy some more time with a partial payment?"

"This isn't economics."

"Blue took your deal."

"Blue took my money. Blue's a psychotic. He knows he can get away with a few days off so that's what he's doing while he spends four grand of my money. You can see in his eyes that Blue enjoys his work."

"There's something to be said for that."

"Sure. I have all the respect for him in the world, especially with a baseball bat in his hand. If I don't come up with the money he'll enjoy taking a few swings on me. I've seen guys after he got through with them. They never walk right again. It's hard to notice sometimes, years later, but if you look closely it's there. A little hitch in the step, a little off."

"Maybe not enough."

"How's that?"

"You're still playing. You still put yourself at risk. What the fuck were you thinking knowing what you know?"

"We all do things that may not be the best for us."

"Maybe."

"Not maybe. All of us do. All of us."

We were eye to eye.

"Even Grandpa," Gary said.

"Grandpa did what he did for the family."

"Your dad never told you why Grandpa came to this country?"

"He came for the same reasons everyone else came. Freedom and opportunity."

"Sure," Gary said. "Lady Liberty was welcoming him with open legs. That's not why he came."

"Why did he come?"

"My dad told me the story."

"What story?" I said.

"He told it to me after I wiped out his life savings. A guy like Blue visited our house looking for me and my dad went to the bank and took out all his money. I was in the Caribbean hiding out for a few days. I even made a few bucks at the casinos. When I came home there was a message on my machine. My dad was scared and angry. I called him and he told me to come over right away. He sat me down and told me what had happened and he told me he had no more to give. He had taken all his savings to bail me out. He told me to tell whatever scumbag it was I had to tell that there was no more money on his end. Then he slapped me in the face and called me a sick boy. He said I was a sick boy. You think I'm a sick boy?"

I didn't say anything.

"I walked out of the house. I didn't talk to him for a couple of months. Then my mom invited me to dinner and we pretended everything was all right. We never touched the subject again. I know that's what he's thinking when he looks at me. That I'm a sick boy. Not even a sick man."

Gary looked at his plate. He picked up a piece of meat that had fallen from his sandwich and ate it.

"My dad told me a story about Grandpa right before he called me a sick boy. Grandpa put his father in the hospital."

"What are you talking about?"

"He beat his father so badly they had to put him in the hospital."

"That's a lie."

"It's the truth. Grandpa's father was a small-time government clerk. When Grandpa was a kid he got in a lot of fights and not just wrestling fights. Some of the parents of the kids he beat up also worked in the government. Even back then, Odessa was a gangster city and Grandpa got in so much trouble that people assumed he was part of that world."

"He wasn't."

"Were you there?"

"He was a hard worker."

"He worked in New York."

"He supported his family."

"It doesn't matter. I'm telling you what happened in Odessa. Grandpa's father never got promoted because the people in high places, higher places than a small-time clerk, held some serious grudges. Grandpa's father decided that if his son went into the military then maybe his past actions would be forgiven and a government promotion would be possible. So he told Grandpa to join the army. Grandpa refused. All that for-the-family crap was just crap. At least for the family he came from."

"He had his own life."

"We all have our own lives. That's the point. But when his father insisted he join the army, Grandpa lost his temper. He beat up his father. He beat his father so badly his mother had to call the neighbors to restrain him. And then he beat some of them too and then he ran. He'd been in trouble with the law and he'd beaten his father and he knew if he was caught they'd lock him up. That's when he came to New York."

Gary picked up his pickle, bit off half of it.

"We all have our weaknesses," he said. "I can judge you too."

"Judge me for what?"

"You're judging me for gambling. I can judge you too. The story you told me about losing your scholarship. What you did in that restaurant. You're just like Grandpa that way. I am too, but not like you. You change. I see the way you look sometimes."

"How do I look?"

"Don't tell me that's the first fight you've been in since you got kicked off the wrestling team. Your boss wasn't the first one you beat up since then. Don't be high and mighty."

"I'm not being high and mighty."

"Understand how hard it is for me to break it."

He was right. I beat them. Until they were broken. Until they were out. Then I ran. I was never caught. Afterward I walked along the Hudson River to slow the blood rush, the Statue of Liberty in the distance, the torch lit up.

"Who told you that story about Grandpa?"

"My dad."

"Who told him?"

"Grandma. She was from the same part of Odessa. They met in New York, but she knew of the Roses in Odessa."

"So why did she marry him?"

"For protection. I don't know."

"My dad never told me that story."

"He didn't want to ruin your hero for you. He was being nice."

"I don't believe you."

"Don't."

"He could have told me."

"It was the worst story."

The pickpocket story had been my favorite. Grandpa had shown restraint. He walked the pickpocket to the precinct and turned him in.

"After he paid off what I owed, my dad told me that story,"

Gary said. "When Grandpa's father got out of the hospital he disowned his son. They never saw each other again. After my father bailed me out, he disowned me. He said he would never do it again. If something bad happened to me, he would just accept it like Grandpa's father had accepted not seeing his son. He had done as much as he was willing to do. I was on my own."

Gary worked himself out of the seat. I watched him move across the dining room to get his dessert. It was a sad walk or maybe it just looked that way.

Gary came back and sat down. He ate his sundae. We walked back to the tables. I automatically squared my feet for balance but it didn't matter.

We worked.

It became like at night when I closed my eyes and all I could see were the cards coming out. I forced myself to concentrate, to not close my eyes, but I still saw the picture. It was a new picture, the colors too vivid. Grandpa beating his father. I felt weak. Physically weak.

The next shoe started and the next and the next and the next. Outside day turned to night. Inside it stayed the same. The cards came. I counted.

My hand was on his back and he was leaning over the chips and I felt a hand on my back. I didn't turn around. I had to keep the count. The dealer flipped his down card, pulled an eight to a twenty-one, took everybody's chips.

I turned around. She was there, her eyes clear, a full shift worked and not a line of red. Her Denny's uniform was in the plastic bag.

"Is there a free spot at this table, young man?"

Tia held up the red chip that Gary had given her.

"How's it going?" she said.

"Fine. How are you?"

"I'm done until Monday."

"Hold on."

I turned around. I kept count. The shoe came to an end.

"I see you brought some high stakes money," Gary said.

"Big time," Tia said.

"Stay away from this table. I'm getting killed. What time is it?"

"A little after midnight."

"You want to take a break?" Gary said.

"Whatever you want," I said.

"We can take a quick break."

Gary picked up the remaining black chips and handed them to me. They fit in one hand.

"You hungry?" Gary said.

"Not really," Tia said.

"There's no such thing as not really when it comes to food. I am definitively and absolutely hungry. How's about some dessert? My treat."

"I like pie."

"I know a place that serves great pie. All you can eat."

We walked across the casino to the Bally's buffet. She took my hand on the escalator. Gary's wide back blocked the view in front of us. Behind us the panels of escalator going down flattened and disappeared.

"Are you okay?"

"I'm fine. Did you make it through the shift?"

"I slept a little before work. What about you?"

"I've been up."

"I thought we could take a drive tonight."

"I can't. Tomorrow's the last day."

"The last day for what?"

"I don't know. He owes some money."

We followed Gary to the buffet line. Tia put a scoop of chocolate ice cream on her pie. I took an apple from the untouched fruit display. It wasn't the kind of thing people paid for at a buffet. We waited for Gary to return from the slicing station and found a table.

"You ever play at Bally's?" Gary said.

"I don't go to the casinos anymore," Tia said.

"What do you do in Vegas if not gamble?"

"Live a regular life."

"What's that?"

Gary smiled. He dipped a hunk of meat into the au jus and brought it to his mouth.

"I used to get these junkets," Gary said. "I'd bring a bunch of friends to Vegas for a long weekend and we'd always eat here at Bally's. My friends don't take long weekends anymore. Dess is the last of a dying breed."

"Is that right?"

"Did you know that Dess was a great wrestler?"

"He didn't tell me that," Tia said.

"He is. Full scholarship, the works. Don't tell me you didn't see some of his wrestling skills."

"Shut up," I said.

Tia pressed her fork through the pie until it hit the plate.

"So Tia," Gary said. "What are your plans for this weekend? We're booked."

"Don't worry. I won't cut into your quality time."

"I'm just telling you. How's the pie? Better than Denny's?"

"Denny's has pretty good pie."

"I'll have to try it. I never had their pie. How's the apple?"

"Great," I said.

Gary finished his prime rib in silence. Tia pulled her fork through the melted ice cream, watched the marks fade. I felt it in my throat. For her. For Gary. I had to call home and tell everyone that I would be late. I would say the garage got busy near the holidays. I would say I had to work. I could hear my grandfather's voice but it sounded different to me and I swallowed.

"Why don't you two go up to the room and hang out for a while," Gary said. "I'm going to finish this delicious prime rib, maybe have some mediocre Bally's pie. Take a break, Dess. Be a matador. Meet me in front of the elevators in an hour. What time is it? You don't wear a watch either?"

"My shift ends at midnight whether I have a watch on or not," Tia said.

"So does mine," Gary said.

There was a couple drinking coffee at the next table. Gary asked them the time and the man and woman both looked at their watches. The woman got it out first. Five to one. The man said the same thing a beat after her. They'd been together long enough to talk the same. Gary thanked them, said those sounded like pretty good odds and the couple laughed.

"Meet me at two," Gary said.

"Two."

"You can join him, Tia."

"Won't I be interrupting your game?" she said

"As long as you don't distract Dess you can do whatever you want. It's a free country. There should be all kinds of people watching me."

We went up to the room. Room service had made the beds

but hadn't touched Gary's clothes, wide swatches of material piled along the carpeted floor. Tia put down her bag with her uniform. I called the operator and put in a wake-up call for five to two. I was raw and I was sick but I couldn't wait to be with her. I pressed into her, held her arms against the bed so her face would be under mine, so I could look at her mouth and see the sounds as they came out, so I could look at her forehead and see her hair start to wet, see the sweat form and run down her skin, so I could look at her eyes and see the pupils and the blue and the explosions of gray, so I could fuck her for her and fuck her for me and make the time stop, needing her, needing to rip her even more, to be ripped even more, needing to rip through it all and make it stop, time stop, stop to not remember, stop to not think, stop to make it just her and just me and just us, perfect like that and we fucked and fucked and fucked and I tasted my own sweat and tasted her sweat and we fucked until the phone rang and through the phone ringing and then the ringing stopped and I looked at her and told her Now, looking at her, making the now one of those moments, making her know it was one of those moments, so perfect the memory couldn't make it better, and I said Now and she said Now, the Nows overlapping, eyes to eyes, connected, clear, and it was just the moment and she said Now, her voice lower, quiet.

We dressed. I had been wearing the same pants for days. I put on fresh underwear and my garage uniform, washed and pressed.

"Is that your new look?"

"I'm auditioning for the part of a guy who parks cars for a living. What do you think?"

"I think you can pull it off."

"Put on your Denny's outfit and we can pretend we're going to work together."

"There's nothing to pretend for you."

"You're right."

"I know about the matadors."

"Gary was just talking."

"You didn't say it. I'm not blaming you. So that's your uniform."

"Service with a smile."

"You smile a lot for Gary. At least you did in the restaurant."

"Sometimes it's a real smile. Sometimes I just smile to reassure him. He can tell when. We both have our parts to play."

"You're the wrestler."

"I wrestled. Not anymore."

I sat on the bed and laced up my work boots.

"Why did you choose that sport?"

"My grandfather wrestled."

I pulled the laces tight.

"It can be a beautiful sport when it's done right," I said. "Did you ever see a match?"

"I haven't. Our high school had a team, but I never watched them. Sometimes when I'm flipping channels I see those idiots on TV jumping on top of each other."

"That's not wrestling. Not real wrestling."

"It's not even real entertainment."

"My college coach was sort of a Renaissance man. The first day of practice every year he would sit all of the wrestlers down and talk to us about the history of wrestling. Then he'd show us some slides of wrestlers depicted in art. He wanted to impress upon us that the sport had a history and that we were carrying on a tradition. He said our sport was that holy. Then he'd shut off the slide projector and read to us from Homer in Greek. He told us we should all study Greek to learn discipline, that with a knowledge of Greek we could read the stories about the ancient wrestlers who were noble and brave. Then he'd translate the great man on man battle he'd read from Homer. He told us if we did it right, if we wrestled like the old wrestlers, we'd be moving in a way worthy of being sculpted or painted, worthy of being written about, worthy of poetry, beautiful like that if we did it right."

"Did you do it right?"

"Sometimes."

"What about your grandfather?"

"I never saw him wrestle."

I pressed my work boots into the carpet.

"You're not here for the art of it. You're in too much of a rush."

"My cousin is in a rush."

"You're here with him. I've seen college kids come into town for a good time and lose all their tuition money. I've seen couples cut their honeymoons short after an hour at the tables. I've seen men carried out of the casinos screaming and I've seen other men crying in the street."

"It's not just the casino. I'd walk away if it was just the casino."

"It's that bad."

"I told you it was bad."

"And your cousin won't let you walk away."

"Before we got here he gave me an out. He was ready to buy me a plane ticket back to New York. I can't leave him. He's my cousin and he's in trouble."

"Would he help you if you were in trouble?"

"I hope he would."

"You don't know."

"There's a lot I don't know. I'd like to think he would help me if I was in a bind. I'd like to think he'd help me since I'm his cousin. I don't know. I'm all he has left. There's no one else he could have turned to."

"Plus you're a wrestler worthy of being sculpted."

"Plus that. There's nothing wrong with knowing how to defend yourself."

"You're not defending yourself."

I looked at my work boots. The steel toes were scuffed.

"I have to go down."

"I know you do."

She picked up the plastic bag with her uniform in it.

"Are you going?" I said.

"I don't want to get in the way. You could be there all night."

"We could. It's up to Gary. I don't know how much he's going to play or how much he's going to bet."

"Or how much he's going to lose."

"I don't know that either."

"That bruise above your eye. Did you get that wrestling right?"

"No. I didn't."

She touched where I'd been hit and smoothed it with her thumb. I looked past her. The clock on the night table said it was time. I stood up.

"Try not to blow all your garage money."

"It's all Gary's money."

"Good."

"Don't worry. I'm done with school. I don't have a mortgage to lose. I'm not even on my honeymoon."

"Vegas is the worst place for a honeymoon."

"But the best place to find secondhand cars."

"The best."

"Come down with me. He won't mind as long as I keep the count."

"I'll stay with you for a while."

Tia put the plastic bag on the bed. I took her head in my hand and kissed her and let go and we left the room and went down.

Gary was walking back and forth in front of the elevators.

"It's now or never," Gary said.

"Positive attitude," I said.

He started to sing it. *It's now or never.* He had a nice voice when he sang and even though he wasn't belting it out his voice filled the marble area in front of the elevators. Tia looked comfortable looking at him, listening to him. She wasn't embarrassed the way most people would be. Gary ended the song singing just to her. She clapped when he was done and Gary bowed gracefully.

Gary chose a table, took the black chips he'd been playing with from his pocket, put them on the table and sat down. He waited for the shoe to end, looked at me, nodded, looked back at the table. The dealer fit the cards into the shoe. Gary placed a black chip into the betting circle. We were lined up. Gary. Me. Tia. On the other side of the chip was the casino.

We worked.

The streak did not come.

Outside it was Saturday morning.

It took a long time for Gary to get himself out of the seat.

He was exhausted. He cashed in the few black chips he'd won, put the bills into his deep pocket.

"We still have some time," Gary said. "When the real streak comes I'll have enough money to back it up."

"What if we leave?"

"And go where?"

"I don't know. Just leave Las Vegas."

"It's not that easy. It's like Blue said. There are other Blues. We'll rest up. We still have a shot. I can always bet it all on red."

"That's what they want you to do."

"Let's get some sleep."

Tia touched my arm.

"Get some sleep," she said.

"You can stay with us," Gary said. "Whatever you want."

"What do you want to do?" I said.

"I'll stay," she said.

"Are you sure?"

"Sure."

We took the elevator up. Gary let Tia use the bathroom first and then me. I looked at my eyes in the mirror. I made a muscle. I hadn't run in a week, had hardly walked. I had stood. I automatically shifted my weight and faked a shoot at myself, arms out, going for my legs. It didn't matter. The garage uniform looked smaller than I remembered it.

Gary asked Tia if the cooks at Denny's ever messed with the food. Tia said only when the customers were a pain and she asked them to. Gary went to the bathroom. We undressed and got into bed. It was freezing in the room but I didn't want to wear anything. Tia felt warm against me. Gary came out of the bathroom and shut the lights. There was some daylight coming through the curtains and I watched him put his pants under his pillow. I didn't blame him. She wasn't family. He picked up the phone and put in a wake-up call for noon. His breath was labored from getting undressed. He told the operator to write it down twice, to put in two calls. He said he had a plane to catch and couldn't afford to be late. It was a funny way of putting it.

"Good night," he said.

"Good night," Tia said.

"Good night," I said.

"Good night, John Boy," Gary said. "You ever see *The Waltons?*"

"I saw some reruns," Tia said. "Do they still make families like that?"

"Somewhere they must. Good night, Mary Ellen."

"Good night."

"Twelve hours," Gary said. "It's like an old-time movie with this guy coming for me. The whole point of Las Vegas was to legitimize these tough guys. When Bugsy Siegel got killed it wasn't in some seedy back alley. He built Vegas. He made them all gentlemen. When they took him out it was in Beverly Hills."

"No one's taking anyone out," I said.

"Hey, Dess?"

"What?"

"Cut the roughhousing."

Gary started laughing.

"Remember that? Your dad used to tell you that when you and your brother were wrestling around the living room. I used to love watching you two."

"I remember."

"Cut the roughhousing. A lot of roughhousing with the Roses."

"Is that right?" Tia said.

"All the Roses," Gary said. "A lot of roughhousing in our house."

I closed my eyes. "A lot."

Gary's breaths became heavy. It didn't take him long to start snoring. Tia moved against me, her hand in my hand, her thumb moving over my palm. I wanted her again but I felt myself going out as hard as I'd gone out the first time I'd been in this bed, after the trip across country, after the lights of Las Vegas brought us in, after we'd won some money that first night, easy money it had seemed to me, easy and fast, all those stories Gary had told us as kids practically true.

22

GARY'S FACE RIGHT UP to mine. Hair wet. Dressed. Ready to face the day like he was going to work on a Monday morning. His hand shaking my shoulder. I looked past Gary. Las Vegas light.

"You up?"

"They rang already?"

"We have to play."

He was whispering. Her arm was around me. I lifted her hand and moved away from her sleeping body. I sat up in bed.

"I need you today," Gary said.

"I'm here."

Gary stepped away from me. Thighs. Crotch. Gut. Chest. Neck. All bigger than life.

"Do some push-ups or something. Take a shower. Meet me downstairs in half an hour."

It was a struggle to do fifty push-ups and I waited for my breath to come back and it was a struggle to do fifty more. I showered and put on my garage uniform and my work boots with the steel toes. I put my hand through her hair. She opened her eyes. I told her to stay in bed, that we'd be downstairs, that she should sleep. I kissed her forehead and pulled the blanket tight around her.

I leaned against the side of the elevator and closed my eyes to the numbers going down. I hadn't slept right in days. Our college coach told us that sleep was essential for every athlete and that rest meant strength, quickness and mental alacrity. The tired I felt in the elevator was like being sick. I felt dizzy and weak. I put my hands in front of me. I wasn't steady and I needed to be steady.

Gary was red-eyed, pacing, his small hands swinging. He handed me a piece of bread for energy. I bit into it but I wasn't hungry.

"Last call," Gary said.

"Have you seen him?"

"He'll show up. You can bet on that."

"I can take him."

Gary looked at me.

"If you don't jump on my back I can take him," I said.

"We're going to win. I bought a watch so we'll know exactly where we stand. Here. It doesn't fit around my wrist."

I put it around my wrist. It had a white face, black numbers, a second hand that stopped on the second, then moved.

"You ready?" Gary said.

"Will you remember this?"

"Remember what?"

"This. The way you feel right now. A tie around your neck is nothing compared to this."

It wasn't my grandfather's voice in my head anymore. It was my father's.

232

"Did you ever have a tie around your neck?"

"No."

"I didn't think so. I've never even had a watch around my wrist. I don't care what I'll remember or won't remember right now. Right now I have to win some serious money. Are you with me right now?"

"What do you think?"

"I think it's time."

The digital numbers behind the wrestling mat. A punch clock ticking off the minutes. A cheap watch with a stuttering second hand. I followed Gary's wide back. He took a seat two seats away from a man in a cowboy hat. I lined up behind Gary. I looked around the casino but the only blue was a string of Christmas lights draped over the rotating car above the slots. Gary reached into his deep pocket and placed the money on the table. The dealer called Check change and the pit boss came over to double-check the counting of bills, the stacking of chips. The dealer slid the chips to Gary. Gary put two black chips in the circle and the last day began.

Gary bet two hundred dollars a hand. When he lost, he repeated the bet. When he won, he doubled the bet. When he won again, he doubled that. When he won a third time, he doubled again. Then he went back to two hundred. He won four times in a row a few times. He won three times in a row more times than that but then lost on the fourth bet.

I felt Tia's hand on my back. The shoe ran out and I looked at her and a new shoe started. Gary won more than he lost but there were no streaks like he had told me about. He asked me the time and I told him it was almost eleven. He asked what I meant by almost. I said three to eleven, telling time perfectly. Gary took a candy bar from his pocket and opened it. A cocktail waitress holding a tray of drinks told Gary he wasn't allowed to eat at the table. Gary gave her a twenty but she didn't thank him. Gary asked if she had a problem. She said she was just doing her job and those were the house rules. Gary told her to shut her mouth, that she was breaking his concentration, that he'd eat wherever the fuck he wanted to eat. The waitress walked away. Gary leaned back and I felt the weight of his back against my hand which was one way to steady the shakes.

We worked. I focused on the cards. The count went to plus four. I pressed my finger into his back. He started playing his system again. Bet two hundred. Won. Bet four hundred. Won. Bet eight hundred. Won. Bet sixteen hundred. Won. His hand hesitated. He pulled the chips away from the circle. Bet two hundred. Won. I saw his jaw tighten. He had been feeling for a hunch. He would have won. If only.

We worked. I was so tired I was in a kind of zone, a place where athletes can do no wrong. Pitch no-hitters. Pass through defenders. Shoot three-pointers. See the pin before it happens. If only.

We worked. Gary asked me the time. We went to the buffet. He didn't get any dessert and he forgot to leave the waiter a tip. On the escalator back to the casino Tia asked me how bad it was. I told her it was bad. She said Gary looked terrible. I told her he had stamina. She asked how long I thought we would be staying in Vegas and the escalator flattened out and I said I didn't know.

Gary found a table. I closed my eyes. The shuffle. I opened my eyes. The cards came and I counted. One after another. After another.

I heard his voice behind me, behind Tia.

"Have you joined the group?"

"Do I know you?" she said.

"Not yet. I just want to get in line. Gary Rose is a popular man."

Some people at the table turned around but Gary stayed on the cards and I stayed on the count. We had to play perfectly. I felt Tia's hand against my back. Blue waited for the game to run out and then stood next to me, looked me over, his eyes calm and rested behind the blue sunglasses. He wore a sport jacket with one button buttoned to conceal whatever he packed to do his work. I checked to see if there was a bulge. A Louisville Slugger. An Adirondack. Maybe he used an aluminum bat. I didn't see anything.

"Cuts," Blue said.

He smiled. The dimple cut his cheek. He leaned into Gary and I shifted my weight.

"How's it going, Gary Rose? Have you put the buffets out of business yet?"

"What time is it?"

"Five fourteen," I said.

"I still have seven hours."

"Six and change," Blue said. "That's always the way with you weasels. Down to the wire. I shouldn't complain, right? If there wasn't a wire I'd be out of a job."

"Lucky you," I said.

"Hey there, kid."

Blue put his arm around Gary's shoulder and smiled at the rest of the table. He leaned in closer to Gary.

"I'm just checking in," Blue said. "You have quite a little following. Who's the beautiful girl?"

"One of my apostles. Give me some room."

"Some room? You don't think you take up enough room?"

"I need to concentrate."

"If it wasn't for my good graces you'd be in a wheelchair right now, you fat fuck."

I was watching Blue's head. I could push it down, throw him off balance, get hold of a leg. He stood up straight and looked me in the eye. He moved closer and put his mouth near my ear.

"Not this time, kid. You'll only make it worse for Gary Rose."

Blue stood back and smiled at the rest of the table, shook his head like Can you believe my buddies are getting sore just because the cards aren't coming out right.

"I love this big guy," Blue said for their benefit, put his hand on Gary's shoulder, left it there for Gary, to let Gary know he could keep it there.

I shifted my weight on the casino floor and the feeling moved away from the pin but not all away.

"We're here for the medical convention," Blue said to the table. "Supply side. My big friend here is the best designer of wheelchairs in the business. I hope all of you walk straight the rest of your lives, but should something happen you'd be smart to consider our product instead of the competition's. Even he can sit comfortably in one."

The dealer dealt. I counted. Pressed Gary once.

"Still the spectator," Blue said.

I didn't say anything. I kept the count.

"You're in on this too," he said.

I rubbed my free hand over Gary's back but not for a minus sign.

"Is that one of your syllogisms, Blue?"

"It's not a syllogism, kid. It just is."

"Sunny in here, Blue?"

"The two of you are hurting my eyes. It's a good thing the girl is around."

"Good thing. Do you just have bad taste when it comes to glasses or are you going blind?"

"My eyes are fine. For instance, I can see the day is almost up. I can see Mr. Gary Rose. I can see you. Nice uniform, by the way. When I'm done with you, you can change the tires on my car."

"Whatever," I said.

"I'll be staying with you the rest of the day."

"It's a free country. Just give us some room."

"Us. Team sports. Do you really want to use that word and connect yourself to him?"

"I do. Give us some room."

Blue laughed too loud, then stopped laughing.

"You force me to draw such logical conclusions."

If I had been in a bar, if I had seen my eyes in the mirror, if I was alone, if Tia wasn't next to me, if I wasn't here for Gary, I would have taken him down. The dealer dealt. The shoe ended. Gary stood up.

"You're not leaving are you?" Blue said. "Or is it time for your third lunch?"

"I'm not going anywhere," Gary said.

"I could have told you that. You still have money to play with?"

"Plenty of money."

"Pay me the plenty you owe and I'll give you two all the room you need."

Gary's bloodshot eyes stayed on Blue.

"I didn't think so," Blue said. "Down to the fucking wire like my pop psychology old man. You disgust me, Gary Rose. Play on. A deal's a deal, right? One minute into Sunday. I'm just keeping an eye on you so I don't have to hunt you down at the last minute. The airports get busy around the holidays and I've got a flight to catch."

Gary stood there. Blue stood there. Face to face. A fun-house reflection. The fat mirror. They were connected by money owed. If only he could put his hand in his pocket, take out the money, move his small hand to the mirror as Blue reflected that motion, moved his hand to the mirror, took the money. If only.

Gary turned and started walking. I followed him. Tia followed me. Blue followed us. It was a hot desert day outside the casino and the sun hurt my eyes. My body was tired. The sun made the mica in the sidewalk glitter and created waves of heat over the pavement in the distance, farther down the strip. Blue was probably happy to take a walk to relieve his boredom. He'd probably stayed inside his air-conditioned hotel room catching up on sleep and swinging his bat, practice makes perfect.

The lion in front of the MGM took the sunlight full in the face, didn't turn, didn't flinch. We walked into the air-conditioning. In front Dorothy stood on the yellow brick road with her friends and Toto her little dog too. The Wicked Witch of the West straddled her broom waiting to swoop in. Behind them was the Emerald Forest. The kids would forget about the heat and the boredom and look at the four unlikely friends and the scary witch and the too green forest not dense enough to hide in and then Daddy would excuse himself and buy some chips. We walked around the display and into the playing area that was brighter than Bally's with carpeting full of colorful swirls. There were plenty of blackjack tables. Gary sat down at a hundred-dollar-minimum table and I stood behind Gary. Tia stood behind me. Blue was around somewhere. I didn't waste my energy looking for him. His job was to be around. Gary's job was to play but there was nothing playful about it. People played ball. People played parts. People didn't play gambling. Not real gamblers waiting for real streaks. I didn't play wrestling. The dealer was shuffling the cards with the MGM logo but it was all the same. Bally's. Caesars. The Luxor. MGM. A blackjack table was a blackjack table. Gary turned around.

"I've won some good money here before. Maybe we need a change of scenery. The MGM Grand is where they hold all the big fights."

"I saw the posters."

"Don't let that sick fuck distract you."

"He's not."

"Keep the faith," Gary said. "Positive attitude. We can win."

"Keep the faith," I said, repeating his words, like *sure*, like *great*, like *hit*, like *stick*, like *up card*, like *down card*, like *cut card*, a whole new vocabulary since I'd stepped into his Jaguar, left the garage where I didn't have to use many words, just got in and out of cars, pocketed tips, said quiet thank-yous, stood around, the only sounds street sounds and car sounds, a gunned engine, the ripple of a pulled parking brake, the time clock punching minutes. If he kept the faith, if he kept saying he could win, then he could keep playing. If I kept saying Grandpa had done everything for the family then maybe I'd believe it too but I already knew I didn't.

The dealer fit the cards into the shoe and Gary bet two black chips.

Hours went by. He would ask me the time and I would tell him the time. Gary hunched lower and lower, the days of gambling and the days of driving pressing his back. Between shoes Gary looked around. His shirt was soaked through. Dealers were changed and changed again, a procession of manicures, clapping their hands before they left the table and opening their hands for all to see. No chips here. Nothing taken. Gary lost four hands in a row, won one hand, lost five hands in a row, slammed his fist on the table.

He stood up. He started walking. We followed him. All the tables were full. The ringing didn't stop. A siren went off somewhere, MGM's way of letting everyone know that jackpots could be won. Gary asked me the time. He looked like he was about to go down. He found a seat at another table. We worked through the shoes. Won some. Lost some. He stood up, walked around the tables, looked over the dealers, tried to feel a streak about to happen. He sat at one table, moved on, sat at another. He pulled to twenty. The dealer pulled to twenty-one. He pulled to twenty again. The dealer beat him with another twenty-one and Gary slammed his fist on the table. His back was bent. He worked himself out of the seat. He picked up the seat, moved it aside so he could get away from the table, set the seat down. He asked me the time. I told him it was almost ten and caught myself. I was also tired. I looked at the second hand, stuttering, shaky, and I told him it was four minutes to ten. He cashed in his chips.

"You see him anywhere?" Gary said.

"No."

"Let's go back to Bally's. We put in our time there. It's time for our streak."

Along the Las Vegas strip Gary walked more quickly than

I'd ever seen him walk, more forward, less side to side, his small hands swinging. There was no point in making small talk. I stayed a few feet behind Gary. Tia's plastic shopping bag with her Denny's uniform touched my leg. I saw myself getting into the Nova, the driver's seat, Tia in the passenger seat, Gary in the back, able to stretch his large body out and rest, the three of us driving west into the sunset and leaving it all behind, the lights and noise and people and just driving to the water like that was our destination, just a drive from New York to California, coast to coast, ocean to ocean, something to do, killing time for the fun of it without implications. I watched his foot slip off the curb at the crosswalk. Gary fell.

I ran to him. He had a cut on his forehead. I spread my feet and lifted him to a sitting position. He dusted off his hands and checked to see if they were skinned. Tia reached into her bag, took a napkin from the pocket of her uniform, pressed it against Gary's head, wiped at the cut, looked at it.

"It's not deep," she said.

"Thanks. Help me up, Dess."

I took one arm and Tia took the other and we stood Gary up. He looked more embarrassed than hurt. He was exhausted. Blue walked by, looked at Gary, shook his head and the dimple started to cut his cheek.

"Via Dolor Vegas. No street like it in America."

He walked on.

"Forget him," Gary said.

Gary pressed the napkin against his head and tried to make a joke out of it. He asked Tia if she was always prepared to set a table at a moment's notice and if she kept anything else in the bag besides napkins, silverware maybe, a dessert tray. We walked. I looked down the strip at each casino trying to outdo

the next. The more lights, the more action inside. The more action, the more money. Bally's was actually the quietest looking casino. It was a tall building that could pass for an office,
squared and plain and mostly glass like the buildings on the
Avenue of the Americas.

We went inside. It was all too familiar. I could be blind
and still make it to the blackjack tables. Gary went into the
bathroom to wash the cut on his forehead. I waited outside
with Tia.

"He's beat up," I said.

"So are you."

I didn't say anything.

"Vegas," Tia said and there was no faith in her voice.

"Las Vegas. The city where everything is possible. What a
fucking joke."

"Remember that."

I looked at her. Blue eyes with explosions of gray.

"I remember."

"Good."

We stood there. I was aware of people passing by, of casino
noise, of cool air, but I felt alone with her.

"I have to stay with him."

"That man with the sunglasses is dangerous. I can see it in
his eyes behind those glasses."

"We can be dangerous too."

"You're not like he is."

"I've done some things."

"I don't care what you've done. You're not like him."

"If only."

"If only what?"

"If only I was different I wouldn't be here. I wouldn't have been the one Gary asked to come along. But I was the one. He chose me."

A steady bell went off mixed with screams of joy.

"Somebody won," Tia said.

Gary came out of the bathroom. There were two bandages across his forehead. He smelled of cologne sprayed under his arms.

"Now or never," Gary said.

He found an end seat at the farthest table and we fell into line. Gary placed his hundred-dollar bills on the table and received the chips. He asked the time. I told him. The count went to plus eight. Gary bet a thousand. Won. Bet another thousand. Won again. Bet two thousand. Won. Bet two thousand. Lost. The count evened out but Gary kept the two-thousand-dollar bets going. He rubbed at his forehead, checked his hand for blood. He asked the time. It was eleven-thirty. Exactly. He started to bet four thousand dollars a hand. Four red-and-white chips. A lighter red than the five-dollar reds. He pulled to nineteens and twenties. He busted on fifteen, pulled an eight when the dealer had a ten showing. He doubled down on eleven, eight thousand dollars in the circle. He lost. He asked the time. I told him. Fourteen minutes to twelve. I heard Blue laugh behind me, drawn out and too loud. I felt the weight of Gary and the weight of my past. I felt the weight on me, felt the impending pin, felt the panic and I shifted my weight and it wasn't just me and I forced myself to take Blue's laugh.

Gary sat up straight. He told the dealer he might want to play over the ten-thousand-dollar table limit. The dealer looked at the pit boss and the pit boss picked up the phone. The other players at the table waited patiently. It was worth it, someone was going to bet big, over the limit big, the kind of bet that made for an impressive story after the question was asked and answered. How did you do? A story about a fat man who bet it all. The pit boss hung up the phone and nodded his head.

Gary stood. He pulled all the bills out of his pocket, placed them on the table, put the red-and-white chips and the remaining black chips onto the bills. Check change. The dealer counted out the money, stacked and restacked the chips. The pit boss watched. The dealer took six chips from the stack farthest to his right, the ones worth five thousand dollars, and slid them to Gary. I wondered if they had a different weight. Gary worked himself into the seat and placed two gray chips in the circle, a ten-thousand-dollar bet. The dealer dealt. Gary stuck at eighteen. The dealer flipped his bottom card. He had twenty. He pulled away Gary's chips and fit them into the farthest stack with a silver dollar on top. Gary bet ten thousand dollars again. He pulled to twenty-one. The dealer took the chips from the holder and stacked them against Gary's chips. Gary bet ten thousand. The dealer busted and stacked two more gray chips against Gary's chips. Gary asked the time. I told him. He asked for the watch. I took it off my wrist and put it on the felt in front of him, the green bringing out the watch like a velvet backdrop in a jewelry store display case, highlighting the stuttering second hand. Gary bet twenty thousand. He got a ten and then an ace. Blackjack. The dealer slid over thirty thousand dollars. Six gray chips. Gary bet twenty thousand on the next hand. He stuck on nineteen. The dealer had twenty.

The second hand stuttered and started. It was almost midnight. Two minutes. People crowded around the table to see the action. I listened to the clicking sound as Gary stacked and restacked the gray chips in his small hands. He owed twice what he had in front of him. There weren't many cards left in the shoe and the count was even. I put both my hands on Gary's back and Gary turned to me. A look just for me.

He slid all ten chips into the circle. All those miles, all those days, down to a stack of gray chips. Gary tipped the dealer the four black chips. He didn't place it as part of the bet, the tip contingent on winning. The dealer looked at the pit boss. The pit boss nodded. The dealer wished Gary good luck and dropped the black chips into the slot.

"Batter up," Blue said.

People turned around and then looked back to Gary.

The dealer dealt the cards. First cards for the players. Gary was the last to receive. A ten. The dealer kept his first card down, dealt the second cards. Gary got a six. The dealer dealt himself his up card. A seven. The count was zero. I stood there, my finger not moving against Gary's back. The other players made their decisions. I counted the cards coming out. The count stayed the same. I stood there. Gary had a sixteen. The dealer had a seven showing. The hand that separated the men from the boys Gary had said in the car. It was a hard play to make. Very hard when the stakes were high. The stakes were high.

Gary hesitated. I had been with him long enough to know that he wasn't really weighing the options. He had already made his decision and he hesitated because it was one of those moments for him, the romance of gambling, the stuff that kept two kids up past their bedtime so they could hear one more story, pleading with their parents Just one more. People surrounded the table, three deep, watching and waiting. Gary had his audience and he was the leading man. I watched the second hand stutter and start. One card. The dealer's finger rested softly upon its straight back, ready to pull it from the shoe.

Gary relaxed into the moment and I stood still and watched him. He lifted his small hand, so cool, like he had all the time in the world and pointed his index finger until it touched the felt. Like he'd rehearsed it a hundred times in front of the mirror. The dealer took the card from the shoe, turned it over, and placed it on Gary's sixteen. It was a two-eyed jack. A red jack. Of hearts. The prince. The son of the king. The one to carry on the tradition but as a card he never would, always the prince, sandwiched in like that, just a card, a red card, worth ten, too much.

Gary stood. The crowd opened and a few people who knew blackjack applauded. He'd taken a chance that a lesser player would not have taken, he'd played tough, he'd hit on sixteen with big money riding, the kind of money they told stories about.

Gary walked to the elevator. Blue was behind him.

"You should go now," I said to Tia.

"I'm not going," she said.

We walked into the elevator. I kept myself from looking at Blue. I needed to focus. I needed to think.

I shifted my weight. I thought about some kind of deal. I could find some money somewhere. I could trade my garage uniform in for a valet's outfit, park cars until I made the money back, tips better in the desert, they had to be better, Gary could do something else but I knew he couldn't and he knew he couldn't and the elevator stopped at the twenty-fourth floor and we got out, Gary walking, forward, side to side, forward, my blood rushing. Gary stopped in front of the room.

"We're not doing this," I said.

"Yes we are," Blue said.

"No."

"Don't be stupid, kid."

"No."

"You'll make it worse for him than it already is."

"No."

"Wait," Gary said. His voice was tired and scared. "Stay outside. I don't want you here now. I've made up my mind. It has nothing to do with you. You hear that, Blue. It has nothing to do with him."

"Whatever. That was the kid's word, right?"

"Give me your word," Gary said.

"Give me your money."

"He was just along for the ride," Gary said. "Leave him out of it."

"Go inside," Blue said.

"Leave him out."

"I'll tell you what, Gary Rose. I'll leave him out if you admit you're a fat fucking loser. Say it. Say you're a fat fucking loser who eats like a pig."

"I'm a loser."

"Say it," Blue said.

"No," I said.

I shifted my weight.

"Stop," Gary said.

Loud. Gary never spoke loud like that. He was looking at me, eye to eye. It was for Gary. I had to control it.

"Say it," Blue said.

"I'm a fat fucking loser who eats like a pig."

"Make me believe you, Gary Rose."

"I am a fat fucking loser who eats like a pig."

"There you go. Yes you are. Now get inside."

Gary took the card key from his shirt pocket and slid it into the door. His frame filled the door and then Blue went through the door and closed it. The coach said that when it was done right it was beautiful. It hadn't been beautiful. Not on the mat in my last match. Not in New York. Not in the diner. It was ugly. It would be ugly in the room.

Tia slid down against the wall. I just stood there. I heard a dull sound but no cry of pain. Grandpa had taught us the Hand Game but I no longer knew if keeping it in was the best way. I wanted to cry out, a cry past the panic, a cry past the blood rush, a cry for him and my family. I wanted to cry past the black outline of a wrestling mat. I was ready to leave the circle, take a U-turn, take a straight line like the road across America, home.

I stood there. I waited. I heard a crash inside the room. It did not fit what I had pictured. I put my room card into the door and charged in. Gary on top of Blue. Right leg hanging off to side. Awkward angle. Broken knee. Blue underneath. Legs kicking out. Snakeskin boots. Sliding against carpet. Blue tried to move but Gary stayed on top of him. Gary's hand was in Blue's mouth. His small hand all the way in, his arm shoved down past his fat wrist. He was saying Eat me, eat me, eat me, shoving his hand deeper and deeper into Blue's throat. I saw Blue's hand against Gary's side and I saw the knife in his hand and I went for his arm. I turned his arm and heard a high-pitched sound. There was no room in his throat to get the scream out all the way. I turned his arm some more until I heard it break and the high-pitched sound became higher. I took the handle of the knife and pulled it out of Gary. Gary didn't scream. Blood leaked from Gary's side and Gary shoved his hand deeper and deeper into Blue's throat. Blue's legs kicked out and one of his legs kicked at Gary and I moved to Blue's leg and listened to Blue's high-pitched sound while I broke the leg kicking Gary. I looked at Blue's mouth. His mouth was stretched open and his lips were tight lines of pink. I could see his bottom teeth biting down on Gary's arm, scraping, puncturing, blood. Gary said Eat me, fed Blue his hand and arm, all those fat jokes backed up in Blue's throat. Gary was bleeding. Blue was still biting. His eyes were white, the irises and pupils in the back of his head. Gary stayed on him. Four hundred pounds. The high-pitched sound had reached a higher pitch. Blue's good leg kicked again and Gary shoved his arm deeper into Blue's throat. I moved over Gary's back and put a hold on Blue's head. I looked into his white eyes and he was still biting my cousin's arm and it was in me and I took his head and turned it. Blue's body stopped moving, pressed down by Gary, his leg broken, his arm broken, no way for him to resist and I turned his head some more until I heard his neck break. It was a different sound from other bones I'd broken. It was loud and defined and final. The high-pitched sound stopped. The leg that had been kicking shivered and stopped. My hands were still on his head and I took my hands away. Gary said Eat me, eat me, eat me but his voice was more of a whisper. He was out of breath. His back was heaving.

I pulled Gary's arm out of Blue's mouth. It was bloody and chewed. Tia was next to me, her face pale. She helped me lift Gary and we moved him to the bed and sat him down. His leg stayed off at an angle. The pipe Blue had used to break Gary's knee was on the floor. It was short enough to fit in a sport jacket and hard enough to break bone. The knife was on the floor, blood on metal. Gary held his side with his good hand. His shirt was covered in blood.

Tia unbuttoned his shirt and opened it, wiped at the cut with a towel. It wasn't the kind of cut a napkin could stop. Gary clenched his jaw in pain.

"You need to get to the hospital," Tia said.

"Dess. He was going to break your knees. On the way out."

Tia told me to get another towel from the bathroom. I got a towel and gave it to her. She wiped at the cut and for a moment his stomach was clean, white with stretch marks, then the cut in his side started to leak and she pressed the towel against it. She told me to get another towel. There was one face towel left. She used it to wrap Gary's hand.

"He was going to break your knees. He said it like it was already done."

"I wasn't supposed to let this happen."

"You didn't."

"I was supposed to protect you."

"I told you to stay outside."

"He was supposed to break something and that's all. I could have taken him down before all of this. I could have just taken him down and we could have left."

"I was tired," Gary said. "I'm tired."

Gary smiled for me and I had to smile back. I couldn't help myself.

"We need to get you to a hospital," Tia said.

"He broke my knee," Gary said.

I picked up the phone.

"Hang up," he said.

"You're hurt."

"I don't want you two here. I don't want anyone to know you were here."

"Do you want to make the call?"

"I want you to drive me," Gary said.

"Where's the hospital?"

"I'll tell you how to get there."

"I'm calling an ambulance."

"No you're not," Gary said. Like he wasn't bleeding. Like his knee wasn't broken. Like he was stopping someone from ordering room service when a whole buffet waited downstairs.

"Get me down to the car."

"You're bleeding."

"It's not that deep. I've got plenty of layers to get through." Gary smiled, then coughed.

"He had a knife in his boot. He thought I'd sit my fat ass down when he told me about you. Not you."

Gary coughed. He was sweating.

"I didn't make a sound. You didn't hear me make a sound, did you?"

"No," I said.

"We killed him."

Tia was kneeling at his feet and pressing the towel against Gary's side. I started to make the call. He still had quick reflexes. With his good hand he knocked the phone off the night table.

"Either you drive me there or I'll drive myself."

"You can't drive yourself."

"I can if I have to."

There was no talking to Gary.

"Will you drive me?" he said.

"I'll drive you."

"Button me up."

Tia pressed the towel against the cut, pulled his shirt together and buttoned it. Gary pressed his hand against his shirt to hold the towel in place. He told me to take the shoeshine cloth from the bathroom. I asked him why and he said to get it. I went and got it and put it in my pocket. I picked Blue's glasses off the floor and put them in my pocket. I looked at Gary's wide back. From behind he looked as if he were just sitting on the bed taking a break.

"I was alone in the room if anyone asks," Gary said to Tia. "Understand?"

"I understand," she said.

"Understand?" Gary said to me.

"Yes."

"Great. Get your stuff together."

I picked up my clothes and put them in my bag like packing for a fucking vacation.

"Let's go," he said.

I took Gary under one arm, Tia took him under the other and we lifted him. His leg touched the ground. Gary breathed through the pain, nodded his head. There was blood on the bed, the knife, the pipe, the hotel reading material that had been knocked to the floor, a room service menu, a Welcome to Las Vegas shopping guide, a pamphlet on casino gaming. Blue was dead on the floor. His eyes were still white. I didn't force the irises down to see what color they really were. What was once his mouth looked like an overripe tomato, too long in the sun, burst on the vine. Ripped lips. Torn tongue. Hemorrhaged gums. Loose teeth, bits of Gary stuck between them. His head was off to the side. His neck was broken. It was ugly. We got Gary out the door.

The casino was still so crowded, the sounds so loud, the lights so flashy, that a fat man with a knife wound and a broken knee being helped across the floor wasn't that striking a sight.

People looked at Gary's face, at his girth, but they didn't seem to notice that anything was wrong. It was late. Maybe he'd had one too many at the tables.

It was hot outside. I helped Gary lean against a wall. I went to valet parking and got the Jaguar. I put my bag in the trunk. I got in the driver's seat, pushed down the hand brake and put the car in drive.

Tia was talking to Gary and he was smiling for her. Blood was leaking through his shirt. There was nothing I could do. I put the car in park, pulled the hand brake, got out of the car, walked around the front and opened the passenger side door and we walked Gary forward and eased him into the seat. He breathed through the pain. He kept his good hand against the cut in his side. I lifted his one leg in and then the other, the leg with the broken knee. I closed the door.

Tia sat on one side of the driver's seat and I squeezed in next to her.

"Let Tia get her car," Gary said.

"We don't have time."

"She's parked close by."

"How do you know?"

"She told me. She'll get her car. Then we can follow her to the hospital."

It was hard to steer but I pulled onto the strip and then off at Tia's lot. Tia ran to her car, threw the plastic bag with her uniform onto the backseat, revved the engine once, pulled in front of me and I started to follow her. She weaved through the traffic until she hit a clear patch of road.

"Pass her," Gary said.

"I'm not passing her."

"Pass her."

He coughed.

"Pass her. I want to take a drive. I just want to drive."

"We're going to the hospital."

"We will. Just drive."

"We'll drive after they sew you up."

"It's still my car. You're still my younger cousin. I said drive."

Gary's eyes were tired.

"You're wasting time," he said. "Go on."

I pulled into the left lane and pressed my foot on the gas. I turned to see Tia looking at us and then we were past her.

"Jaguar is the best city car," Gary said.

"I'll take that Jaguar," I said.

Gary held the towel against his side with his left hand, the hand that wasn't half eaten. His jaw was clenched. His hair was wet from sweat. He was breathing hard and looking at the road.

"Reach into my pocket."

"Which pocket?"

"The deep one."

Gary shivered. I reached into his pocket. I felt the crispness of new money and I pulled out a small stack of bills. There was no blood on them. Not really.

"That's for you."

"I don't want your money."

"It's two grand. It's enough to hold you over. I thought we'd win. I really did. I thought we'd win, pay him off, have some money of our own to play with. It wouldn't have mattered on the last bet anyway. I thought we'd get on a streak of our own."

"Sure."

"You never thought we'd do it."

"I didn't know."

Gary shivered.

"It would have been a great time if we'd won," Gary said.

"I liked just driving."

"Then drive."

"I am."

"Drive faster."

"I think we should go to the hospital now."

"Fold them up."

I folded the bills in half as best as I could.

"Hey, champ. Don't spend it all in one place."

I wasn't the champ but the way he said it almost made me believe it was true. He was good. I put the money in my pocket.

"Faster," Gary said.

"I'm going fast."

"Go on," Gary said.

I pressed my foot down. We were well past the strip. There were no hospitals in sight. It was desert and night sky and the road straight ahead.

"Wipe the wheel down with that shoeshine cloth. Then get out of Vegas. Your friend promised me she'd drive you to California. Buy yourself a plane ticket and go home. Say hi to your folks and your brother for me."

Gary shivered.

"Faster," he said.

I pressed my foot down.

"That's right," Gary said.

"Faster," I said.

"Faster. Press it all the way."

"Faster."

"Keep going."

"You can't drive forever."

"I never worried about forever. Faster."

"Faster."

The speed took it all away. We were just driving. It was one of those moments and I relaxed into the speed. The rush was outside of me now. The car was rushing, was doing the work, was moving forward and with my hands on the wheel I relaxed into it.

"Faster," I said.

"Great," Gary said.

I held the wheel and we moved. It was us and the road and the speed and we were flying out of Las Vegas back to the darkness of desert sky and Gary shivered and started coughing. I looked at him and I knew he was trying to keep his eyes open. I slowed the car and he didn't say anything. I slowed the car some more. He shivered.

"I'm not even hungry."

"I'm taking you to a hospital."

"You'll wipe down the wheel and she'll drive you to California."

He was breathing fast. He shivered and his eyes went scared and then the shiver passed and his eyes were calm again. I thought about telling him to imagine sundaes the way he'd told my brother and me when we'd pissed in our pants and had to finish those cold grilled cheese sandwiches but I didn't.

"Pull over," he said.

"I'm turning around."

"Pull over. I don't want them finding me in the passenger seat. Do what I say. Pull over."

"You can't drive."

"Pull over."

I slowed the car and pulled onto the breakdown lane. I put the car in park and turned off the ignition. The headlights lit some of the desert.

"Help me out."

I pulled the hand brake and went around to the other side of the car. I opened the door and helped Gary move his body, bad leg first, good leg second. He breathed short breaths through the pain. The towel around his chewed up hand had started to come undone. His fingers had turned purple. Some blood rubbed off on my uniform and made the blue dark. Gary held the towel in place against the cut in his stomach. Blood soaked through the cloth. I struggled to lift him out of the car and I walked him forward. I was exhausted. I half leaned half sat him down on the hood of the Jaguar. The car sank under his weight. Gary held himself up with his good hand. His jaw was clenched. His eyes were sleepy.

"What do you think?" he said.

"What?"

"You have to admit, it's pretty beautiful around here. All this space."

Gary wasn't in a rush anymore. On the trip I never thought he looked at the scenery. I felt it in my throat.

"Three days," Gary said. "We made it across country in three days."

"Almost."

"California's just a day trip away."

I went to lift Gary but he put his good hand on my shoulder to stop me.

"You ever been to California?" he said.

"Never."

"Your family never went there?"

"We never did."

"I've never been there either. I told you. I was all packed and ready to go."

"You'll go another time."

"Sure," Gary said.

He was breathing fast.

"People just talk about driving across country in three days. We did it."

"Yes we did."

"That's something."

"That is something."

Gary smiled.

"Just driving."

"Fast," I said.

"Fast."

He fell gracefully for a four hundred pound man. His weight cushioned the fall and he collapsed one part at a time against the trunk. His lower back, his back, his shoulders, his neck, his head, his arms fell open, his eyes closed.

I stood there. I looked at his face. There was no one around and there was still some time to do what he'd told me. Wipe down the wheel, get to the airport. Buy a ticket home. I just wanted to sit at the dinner table with my family and make small talk for a while. I put my hand in the pocket of my garage uniform and pushed the money all the way down. I opened the car door and took the camera off the dashboard.

There was plenty of film left. I should have taken some more pictures of Gary during the trip. His different smiles. The best just for me.

I heard a car slow and pull onto the breakdown lane. The car door opened and closed and I looked at her and nodded my head and looked away.

23

THE SIGN WELCOMED US to California. We stayed on Interstate 15, which was the route Gary and I had picked up all those days ago. I tried counting back and stopped myself.

I remembered the joke my dad often told. A man goes to a doctor for a routine checkup. The doctor looks him over and says he has good news and bad news. The bad news is that the man will be dead in a week. The good news is that since he knows he's going to die, he can finally do the one thing he always wanted to do. The doctor asks the man if there's one thing he always wanted to do in his life and the man says that yes, as a matter of fact he always wanted to have a piece of Bavarian cream pie. The real thing. From Bavaria. The doctor tells him that now is his chance. The man goes home, packs a bag, says good-bye to his wife and kids and heads out. He takes a plane to Europe. He takes a train to Bavaria. He gets off at the capital of Bavaria and takes a bus to the small mountain town where they make Bavarian cream pie. He gets off the bus and starts to walk. All the time he's getting weaker and weaker but he keeps walking and walking and finally he reaches the mountain he's been looking for. On top of the mountain is this little bakery that makes the best Bavarian cream pie in the world. The man starts climbing the mountain. He's getting weaker by the minute, his time is running out, but he still keeps climbing, up and up and up. Finally, he makes it to the top of the mountain and crawls into the bakery. He pulls himself up to the counter, out of breath, and tells the woman behind the counter that he'd like a piece of Bavarian cream pie. The woman shakes her head. I'm sorry, sir, she says, but that won't be possible. What do you mean it won't be possible, the man says. I left my family, I traveled thousands of miles, I'm on my last breath and I came all this way just to try a piece of your famous Bavarian cream pie. I understand, sir, the woman behind the counter says, but there's one big problem. It's Tuesday. And on Tuesdays we don't bake Bavarian cream pie. The man takes a final breath, looks at the woman behind the counter and says, Okay, just give me a slice of apple.

When I was a kid I'd always hoped the slice of apple pie tasted delicious for the dying man. I didn't want the man going all that way for nothing.

Tia's Nova didn't handle like a Jaguar but there were no cars on the road and I didn't have to weave. I didn't have to get to the airport at a specific time. I'd buy a ticket for whatever flight was leaving. The signs for Los Angeles started to increase and so did the signs for the towns that had sprung out from L.A., eastward since there was no room going west. The sun would be out soon. Christmas Eve day.

"How are you holding up?" she said.

"I'm awake."

"I can take over if you want."

"I'll let you know."

I put my hand on her leg and she took my hand and moved her thumb over it.

"You're not going home for the holidays?" I said.

"I might. I didn't make any promises. I could drive up to Bishop and surprise everyone."

"My family expected me home days ago."

"They must be worried."

"They're used to worrying about me."

Dawn started in the rearview mirror. It was always getting lighter behind us. It was the opposite of coming to America for my grandfather. Promises ahead, not behind. In some ways that was easier. Even if he hadn't come purely. Maybe no one came purely.

"I killed him."

"He was trying to kill your cousin."

"But I killed him."

I looked in the rearview mirror. The few clouds were outlined in hard edges. I looked at the road and waited and looked back in the rearview mirror, remembering how the light had been and comparing it to how the light was to see if I could tell the difference.

"When I was in school I picked up a copy of *The Iliad* because our coach always read from it. Most of the great battles ended in death. What I did wasn't great at all. I killed him and I don't feel anything. It's like someone else did it. Only it was me."

"It's not like you went after an innocent victim."

I didn't say anything.

The sun started to rise. A top slice before the road turned and the sun was out of view and when I saw it again it was all the way up. I adjusted the side mirror so I wouldn't get the glare.

"Good morning," she said.

I looked at her and she smiled and I looked back at the road.

"We could drive to New York. It's a great city."

"I'm sure it is."

"It's so big you can get lost there."

"I'm already a little lost. That's why I moved to Vegas."

Tia's thumb stopped moving across my hand and then started again.

"I don't think my car would make it," she said. "It's not ready for such a long trip."

I pretended I was driving east and Tia was next to me. It would be night and the highway would be quiet and it would be just us in the car. I would look over at her, see that she was sleeping, that she was okay, put my hand through her hair to let her know I was with her even as she slept. It was a nice day-dream. She wasn't ready to take a drive. Taking a drive was a place between killing time and moving ahead. The destination did not matter, driving across and not to, but if the time was not right it would end with lines like the movie line Gary told me many miles ago from *Easy Rider*. *We blew it.* For me the drive had come at the perfect time. He had come at the perfect time. I had been ready, uniform and all.

It was light but there still weren't many cars on the high-way. We passed a lone bus. It looked like a city bus, smaller than the giant charters that shuttled people in and out of Las Vegas.

"We should stop and ask directions to the airport," Tia said.

"Gary never needed a map. He could sense where things were."

"Did he teach you?"

"Not that."

There was an exit sign for a gas station. I pulled off the highway and onto smaller roads. A pickup truck and a car were parked in the lot but there was no one at any of the pumps. The attached convenience store was lit up and I could see a man standing behind the cash register and another man facing the soda cooler. I got out of the car, unscrewed the gas cap, put in the nozzle, pressed it down. Nothing came out. I rubbed my eyes. I looked at the pump and read that I had to pay first. I walked into the store and handed the cashier a twenty.

"What number?" he said.

"Whatever that pump is."

"What number? There are three pumps there."

"And one car."

"I don't care how many cars are there. I need to know the pump number."

"Regular unleaded. Whatever pump that is."

"That's pump number two for future reference. Count it. Pump number two."

"Give me the twenty."

"I'll give you your change after you fill up."

I grabbed his hand.

I stopped.

"If you knew me you wouldn't do this," I said.

I looked at the man. I was talking to him. I was talking to me. My eyes had hundreds of matches behind them and too many ugly fights and now my eyes had more. I had killed a man. I looked at the man with my eyes and he didn't say anything. I let go. I tilted my head to the left. I tilted my head to the right. Balance.

I walked out of the store. The sun was out. Tia sat in the car watching me. I put the nozzle back in the pump. I put the twenty back in my pocket. I felt the glasses. I put the sunglasses on. Plastic frames. Blue lenses. I looked past the lot and past the road and past everything and up at the sky that looked too blue in the blue colored rose colored glasses. I took the glasses off and threw them as far as I could and watched them skid to a stop on the pavement.

I got back in the car.

"They're out of gas," I said.

"It's Sunday."

"We'll find another place down the road."

"We're almost there anyway."

"Almost. Let's drive."